THE GATE HOUSE

KATHLEEN HEADY

A Virtual Tales Book

The Gate House

Edited by Jake George (www.sagewordservices.com)

A Virtual Tales Book
PO Box 822674
Vancouver, WA 98682 USA

www.VirtualTales.com

ISBN 1-935460-00-5

First Edition: June 2009

Printed in the United States of America

9 7 8 1 9 3 5 4 6 0 0 0 8

This book is dedicated to my dad,
Herbert Heady,
who took me to England for the first time, and
taught me to appreciate the big, wide world.

ONE

Nara Blake punched her pillow for the fifth time, kicked off her twisted blankets, and sat up in bed. She had to stop this—this feeling of helplessness. She was not the type of person to continue pining for what she couldn't have.

The windows in her upstairs bedroom were still dark, but she was wide awake, with the familiar sense of dread and loneliness that had kept her awake so many nights since she and her father, Jack Blake, had moved to England. She shivered in the chilly bedroom. It was only September; she had not expected to feel so cold so soon.

Nara pulled the blankets around her body and allowed herself the luxury of missing the warm tropical nights in St. Clare—and Davis. She hugged herself and thought of the way his strong arms felt wrapped around her body the night before she left St. Clare, his warm breath as he whispered in her ear, the tingling in every fiber of her body as his lips brushed her face, her throat. They were warm and safe, with the sounds of the tropical night and the waves of the Caribbean lulling them to sleep; they planned to marry. They talked endlessly about what they would do when he finished his pediatric residency and established his clinic on the island. Nara would be working with her father, managing his import business, preparing to take over the company sometime in the future when he retired. Eventually they would build a house on the island and have children.

Then everything changed.

The nagging cough that had plagued her father for months turned out to be lung cancer. The doctors in St. Clare recommended treatment in London; it was superior to what they could provide in their small Caribbean hospital. Jack's sister Sue had just purchased a bed and breakfast in Springfield, Lincolnshire, about an hour from the hospital in north London. Sue had been a nurse and would be able to provide proper care for her brother—if Nara would help run the bed and breakfast.

Nara was devastated when her father told her the plans he had made for both of them—not only because she was being torn away from the man she loved, but she had no interest in changing sheets and cleaning bathrooms for tourists, or "guests," as Sue insisted she call them. The hearty English breakfasts she learned to cook for the guests—a fry-up of eggs, sausage, beans, mushrooms and tomatoes —turned her stomach, and she longed for the fresh papaya and pineapple she had enjoyed on St. Clare.

Nara had begged her father to let her stay in St. Clare to oversee the import company, but he was adamant. He had a capable manager, Michael, who had worked for the company for ten years and knew every aspect of the business, and Jack trusted him implicitly. Besides, her father wanted Nara near him in what could be his last few months of life, and she couldn't deny him that. They had always been close. She had the rest of her life to spend with Davis; she could give a few months, or even a year, to her father.

But now, after a month in England, e-mails from Davis had grown more and more infrequent. He was busy; she knew that. The pediatric residency in the small hospital demanded his time. She had tried to call him soon after her arrival in Springfield, but he always seemed to be out. She left messages at the hospital, but he had not returned her calls. Now, in the darkness and quiet of the Lincolnshire night, Nara could admit to herself that her sense of foreboding was real. Obviously, the relationship had meant more to her than it had to Davis.

She was here in Lincolnshire, buying woolen sweaters to bundle up against the rainy fall days that would soon turn into the cold days of winter. Nara had never experienced winter—she had attended college in Miami—and if the cold chill of September was any indication of what was to come, she was not going to enjoy it. Especially when the man she loved was a world away.

Even as she thought about letting go of Davis, at least for now, tears slid unbidden down her face. Wiping them away impatiently with the back of her hand, she slipped out of bed, wriggling her toes to find her fuzzy blue slippers. *Imagine—fuzzy slippers in September,* she thought crossly as she pulled her robe from the tangled bed covers and tied it around her. The robe was too large for her, although it was the smallest the store carried. Nara's slight build made her look far younger than her 22 years. She pushed her wavy black hair back from her face and thought again that it needed a trim. She definitely looked more mature with a good hair cut and makeup, but it seemed too much bother when the main part of her day was spent doing housework, caring for her dad, and occasionally shopping in the town market.

Nara quietly opened her bedroom door and stepped out into the hall, which was illuminated by one of Aunt Sue's ever-present night lights. This one was in the shape of a diminutive Victorian milk maid with a pail in her hand. There was no sound from her father's room; he was sleeping for once. Perhaps the new medicines were working.

Nara tiptoed carefully down the carpeted stairway, her thoughts on a cup of tea. She would get a pad of paper and a pencil and make a list of things she needed to do to get her life back on track. She had to face the fact that she was going to be here for a while, and by the time she got back to St. Clare, Davis might not be part of her life. She had picked herself up and worked through the pain before; she could do it again.

When she reached the ground floor hallway, Nara gasped. A dim light shone in the den just off the guest sitting room, and it seemed to move slowly back and forth just inside the doorway. The house was old; it had been a railroad gate house in the 19th century, and of course there were stories of railway workers who had been killed on the tracks and were now stuck here forever as ghosts, unable to go home.

Nara was enough of an island girl that she half believed all the ghost stories that were told to frighten children. In fact, the nanny who raised her after her mother's death always comforted Nara when she came home in tears, scared to death of the stories the older children told of the "child-eaters" and the old woman with the skull face hidden beneath her scarf. She would wrap her arms around the little girl and hold her close. Nara would listen to the woman's heart beating beneath her ample bosom and know she was safe from unseen things. But she had also watched her nanny kiss the amulet she wore around her neck when a hurricane hit the island, or someone had been found murdered. She hung little crosses in the rooms of their house and touched them when she was afraid, when she thought little Nara wasn't looking.

Nara heard a scraping noise in the den and walked quickly over to the doorway, causing the old wooden boards under her feet to creak. Immediately the light went out, and she heard a soft curse from outside the window. A cold draught of night air coming out from under the door told her the window was open. *Someone is trying to break in,* she thought. Heart pounding, she switched on the overhead light and opened the door. The room was empty. She glanced at the darkened window and realized that whoever was outside would be able to see her standing there in her robe. Switching off the light, she retreated to the kitchen. She picked up the phone and with shaking fingers dialed the police.

"Someone just tried to break into our house." Her voice sounded unnaturally loud in the sleeping house.

"All right, miss. What is your address?" The tired voice on the other end of the line answered, followed by a muffled, "It's another break-in," to someone else at the police station.

Nara recited the information and the dispatch officer promised to have someone there in a few minutes. She mulled over what he meant by "another break-in." Hands trembling, she filled the kettle for tea. She would have to wake Aunt Sue immediately, but the whole house would be awake once the police arrived anyway. The small battery clock on the kitchen counter showed

4:00 a.m. These tourists—or rather guests—would have a story to tell when they arrived home.

Nara climbed back up the stairs and knocked on Sue's bedroom door. Without waiting for an answer, she opened the door a crack. "Aunt Sue? Aunt Sue? Someone just tried to break into the house. I called the police and they're on their way."

Aunt Sue leapt out of bed quickly, then sat down again on the edge of the bed. She rubbed her hand across her stomach as it growled with hunger. "That's impossible, Nara. There are no break-ins in Springfield. Why would anyone want to break in here? Maybe you left the window open and forgot about it."

Nara gave an exasperated sigh. *This is a waste of time.* Like her father, Nara liked to cut to the heart of the matter. What was, was—then you dealt with it.

"I went downstairs to the den and there was someone outside with a light, opening the window." She was still keeping her voice to a whisper, but it seemed to her as loud as Big Ben.

Sue looked at her bedside clock. "What are you doing in the den at 4:00 in the morning?"

Nara was becoming more and more exasperated with her aunt. Sometimes she had a difficult time understanding how this stubborn woman could be her father's sister. She shifted back and forth in her slippered feet; whether from impatience, anxiety or the cold, she wasn't sure. "I went downstairs to make myself a cup of tea because I couldn't sleep. I saw the light and went into the den. Now get up! The police will be here any minute."

Nara turned and left the room, closing the door behind her. She stood shivering in the hall, astonished at the way she had just spoken to her aunt, whom she had only met a few times in her life and in whose house she was living. A moment later Sue emerged from the bedroom, wrapped in a maroon silk robe that Nara had never seen before.

"There couldn't possibly have been break-in, Nara." Her voice betrayed both her sleepiness and her exasperation with her niece. "There must be a simple explanation. It was probably someone wandering home after too many hours at the pub and stumbling into the wrong house."

"The pubs closed hours ago, Sue."

The older woman sighed and followed her niece downstairs to wait for the police.

Downstairs Nara and Sue met the two constables at the door. "I'm sure it's nothing," Sue said. "Nara heard a noise and overreacted."

"That's not what happened, Aunt Sue."

The sergeant, smiled at the contradictory reactions of the two women. "Why don't we come in and take down some information?" he asked.

"Then can I get you some tea?" Sue asked, pulling the belt of her robe more tightly around her waist. Nara suppressed a smile at Sue's obvious discomfort in the robe whose fabric clung to her generous curves.

"No, thank you," the sergeant replied as he stepped inside, followed by his colleague.

Nara showed the two of them to seats in the lounge and sat down herself on a wooden straight-backed chair. Sue looked around and then chose a similar chair for herself.

The sergeant asked the questions, which Nara answered clearly and succinctly. He ignored Sue's protests that it couldn't have been a burglary.

When they finished their questions, the junior of the two officers went out to inspect the ground outside the window, while the sergeant examined the den. When they met back at the door, the junior officer announced that there were clear signs of forced entry. Nara had caught the intruders just as they had pried open the window. "A few minutes later and he would have been in the room," he added.

Both Sue and Nara were silent as the reality of what might have happened sunk in.

The sergeant closed his notebook with a snap and replaced his pen in his pocket. "We're taking this seriously. You have a lot of antiques here, Sue." He looked around at the shelves full of delicate porcelain with elaborate designs, nineteenth century photographs, and Victorian-style lamps, some with fringed shades, others with colorful glass shades in the style of Tiffany. "There was another burglary in town tonight." He cleared his throat before continuing. "Someone broke into the church and stole that seventeenth century tapestry that hangs in the small chapel and a pair of gold candlesticks. They are probably the two most valuable pieces in the church. Obviously knew what they were looking for. And they removed a stained glass window and took that along with them. The vicar is beside himself. Who around here would break into a church? And they can barely keep up the building, old as it is, and now to worry about security." He sighed and looked around the room again. "Strange that they would come here on the same night—assuming it was the same people."

Nara felt cold, as if a sudden draft had gone through the room. She had admired the vast collection of antiques and bric-a-brac that decorated every room in the house. She had picked up the treasures, examined the marks on the bases, and stroked some appreciatively. But she hadn't had time to learn anything about them. Now the little animal figurines and china cups and saucers took on a sinister look. These trinkets couldn't be worth enough that someone would try to burglarize the house? Or perhaps, were they looking for something else?

By the time the police had finished their inspection of the crime scene, the sky had lightened to pink along the horizon. Nara put on a pot of coffee and started chopping fruit for breakfast. It was better to keep busy. Sue nibbled on a piece of dry toast, then set the table for their guests. Nora sat silent with her own thoughts of the night's events.

The first of the guests came down for breakfast, asking questions about the medieval church in the neighboring town of Donington, which was mentioned in the *Domesday Book of William the Conqueror.* Sue told them the church contained stained glass windows from the 15th Century. Their interest, however, was in the stained glass window in honor of Matthew Flinders, a Lincolnshire native who, in his ship the *Investigator,* was the first man to circumnavigate Australia and had sailed with Captain Cook. Sue answered their questions cheerfully while Nara started bacon and sausage sizzling in a pan.

She was going to Lincoln today to register for business classes at the college, and although she still couldn't see herself running a company, she was excited about the classes. It would give her an opportunity to meet new people, make new friends her age. She was eager to do something—be someone—but she wasn't sure what or who. She moved the bacon and sausage to a covered plate to keep it warm and started frying eggs. While they cooked she popped two more slices of bread in the toaster. How someone could eat all this food for breakfast was beyond her.

When the eggs were done as the guests had requested, soft but not runny, she moved them to two plates and arranged the meat, along with the fried mushrooms, tomatoes and beans and carried them in to the dining room, automatically putting a smile on her face. "I'll be back in a moment with your toast. Is there anything else I can get you?"

The couple tucked into their breakfast with satisfaction. "No. Nothing at all. This looks wonderful."

Jack Blake lay in his bed upstairs, free for the moment from the coughing spells that wracked his chest all too frequently these days. He felt well and surprisingly comfortable, lying there in the dim room. The street light cast a glow across the foot of his bed, reminding him of the moon in St. Clare. But he wasn't in St. Clare. He was in Lincolnshire, England, in his sister's home, and it had been his idea to come here. The chemotherapy treatments were going well, and he was not as sick as he had been warned he might be. True, he had lost his hair, but he rather liked himself bald. There was a certain sexiness about a bald head; *just think of Yul Brynner,* he thought. Yul Brynner had died of lung cancer, too. Not a good line of thinking to pursue. *Sean Connery, then. Or Michael Jordan.* Jack was not an old man; he was just 52 years old. He would get through this, and he and Nara would go back to the Caribbean where they belonged.

Jack listened to his sister and his daughter tiptoeing around the house. He had heard them much earlier, he remembered now. At one time he would have been out of bed like a shot, taking over, managing the emergency, whatever it was. Tonight he had been content to just lie in his bed and listen. They would tell him in the morning, or they might not. He had just about drifted back to sleep when the room was filled with the glare of headlights, and he heard the sound of a car in the gravel car park. *Must be a late guest arriving*, he thought, as he drifted back to sleep.

The smell of coffee and bacon woke him up soon after, and Jack sat up and stretched. He felt well today. Maybe he wasn't going to die after all, at least not yet. And damn it, he wanted to live. He wanted to see Nara married, with children—his grandchildren. And he really didn't care if she took over the business or not. He had a capable shipping manager in St. Clare. Maybe he could give him a nice raise in salary—a part ownership, and Nara could do what she wanted in life. She deserved it. He would tell her today to forget the business classes and do what she wanted, whatever it was. Jack headed for the shower with a spring in his step.

TWO

On the other side of Springfield, Alex Collier was getting ready for work. He sipped a mug of hot coffee as he dressed, listening to the morning news on the BBC. He was actually more concerned about the local news this morning than events in London, or even the U.S. Presidential contest, or the on-going strife in the Middle East. Harry Nichols, the chief of police in Springfield, had rung him early that morning—awakened him actually, to tell him that there had been another attempted burglary in town.

The tapestry and the stained glass window stolen from the church had been a tragic loss, but it was difficult to imagine what burglars might have been after in the small guest house along the old rail line. The owner, Sue Blanchard, had only bought the place six months ago. Most of the furnishings and antiques had been purchased along with the house from the previous owner's estate. Alex had looked over the items when the place had been up for sale and didn't remember anything noteworthy—mostly the kind of stuff you could find in any antique shop. Over-priced to be sure, but not of any real value to a collector.

Of course, there might not even be a connection. It might not be the same burglars. It would be better to concentrate on the church. Alex finished dressing and rang his supervisor at the Victoria and Albert Museum in London. Alex's job title was curator of British antiquities, but much of his time was spent performing undercover work in cooperation with the police. He wanted to go to the church and see what had been stolen and how, as well as get photos of the crime scene if possible.

There had been an increasing number of burglaries of artifacts excavated from historic sites, in Lincolnshire and elsewhere in England. Alex's residence in Springfield allowed him an easy commute to London, as well as to Lincoln and other towns in the area. It angered him that private collectors with unlimited funds would pay for stolen artifacts so they could horde them in private collections, while the people of Britain and the world at large, were deprived of the pleasure of seeing them.

Alex swallowed the rest of his tea and turned off the radio. No time for breakfast—again. He would grab a scone later in the morning, or maybe a bagel, one of those chewy concoctions from America that were increasingly available. Alex glanced around the kitchen before he left—a habit he had picked up from his ex-wife. She always checked to make sure the gas was off and the kettle unplugged.

They had bought the house together shortly after their marriage, but he had always loved the beautiful Georgian building with a view of the River Witham and the small town of Springfield more than she had, so after six months commuting together to their jobs in the city, she convinced him to purchase a flat in Pimlico that they could use during the week.

She worked at Harrod's as a buyer in the bridal department, and wasn't keen on giving up her social activities in town for the quiet of Lincolnshire. Increasingly, she stayed in the flat even on the weekends, leaving Alex to make the trip back to Springfield alone most weekends. Occasionally he stayed with her in London, but he often felt like a fifth wheel around Laura and her high fashion friends. Divorce seemed inevitable at that point, and few of their friends were surprised. Alex's twin brother David had even commented, "I wondered about you two from the beginning. You didn't seem to have much in common. But you never listened to me when we were kids, even though I am six minutes older."

Alex had to admit David was right, but he had managed to put his failed marriage behind him and only thought of Laura occasionally, like when he checked the gas on his way out the door. They had equitably agreed that she would keep the flat in Pimlico, and he would keep the house in Springfield. In truth, they had both realized that neither of them wanted it the other way around they discovered later.

It was raining this morning or Alex would have walked the short distance to the church. He enjoyed the river walk and often jogged there in the evenings. He enjoyed greeting the families, pushing prams or riding bicycles, as well as the other solitary joggers and dog walkers. He was a familiar face in town, although no one knew him well. They had, of course, noticed when his wife was no longer in residence, but no one had spoken directly to him about it. That wasn't their way.

The church had been built in 1284, but there was evidence that the site had been a place of worship since 1051. The church tower had been added around 1360 and the spire about 100 years later. Alex had been here several times before, examining the grave stones in the floor, the gold and silver candlesticks, and the paintings. The rood screen, which divided the nave from the chancel, had been reconstructed in the 1800s using parts of the old 15th Century screen. Tapestries and paintings lined the walls of the small side chapel, known as the "Lady Chapel" in honor of the Virgin Mary.

Alex always felt a sense of awe in these churches. Although he did not now attend church as he had as a child, there was something special about these ancient buildings, where believers had come to pray and lift up their hearts for so many centuries. He enjoyed chatting with the vicar, as well as the two elderly women who ran the church store, selling religious items, postcards and souvenirs for the occasional tourist.

As he pulled his car into the small car park next to the church, Alex was horrified to see the gaping hole where the stained glass window had been removed. It stood like a yawning mouth with the darkness of the church within and orange police tape marked off the area just outside the window. He walked around to the entrance on the other side, relieved to see that no other windows had suffered damage. He lowered his umbrella in the small entry way, between the bulletin boards covered with announcements of the schedule of weekly masses, children's activities, and social engagements for the parish. A laminated sign explained that churches in England were home to bats as well as human beings and explained the place of bats in the ecosystem. The sign made Alex smile—if only bats were his biggest problem! At least the bats minded their own business and didn't try to steal anything.

Alex pushed open the heavy wooden door and stepped carefully down several ancient stone steps into the cool nave of the church. The church was in darkness except for the small shop where Mrs. Dorkins and Mrs. Westmoreland sat quietly talking. They looked up at the sound of his footsteps, and Mrs. Westmoreland hurried to meet him, her eyes red from weeping.

"Mr. Collier, I'm so glad to see you. You have heard about the tragedy that happened here last night? We are just beside ourselves! Jane and I both offered to spend the night here so the building wouldn't be deserted at night, but the vicar and the police both said no. I suppose it was just our initial reaction. But you will want to know what happened, so the museum can be informed. Come. We'll show you."

Just then the door creaked open and Vicar Andrews entered the church. His ancient, careworn face looked even more so this morning, and the bags under his eyes showed lack of sleep.

"Ah, Mr. Collier. What a sad occasion this is. I feel as if a part of me has died. Who would break into a holy place and steal valuables? And our window. I knew that window was loose and needed repairing, but it appears they just lifted it out to get into the church and then took the window with them. And what can they do with such a thing? Who would buy it?"

Alex shook the man's hand. "Unfortunately there are private collectors with more money than they know what to do with, who will eagerly buy such things from unscrupulous dealers. There is a big market for stolen antiquities all over the world."

"You mean the thieves might not even be in England?"

"Eventually, no. Right now they probably are. They'll be careful to keep the artifacts hidden until the investigation appears to have died down."

Mrs. Westmoreland touched Alex's arm tentatively. "You won't let that happen, will you? Let the investigation die down so they take our treasures out of the country?"

Alex looked down at the woman's upturned face. Mrs. Westmoreland's wispy gray hair was held back with a few pins and a cotton dress covered her round body. A worn brown sweater protected her from the chill of the old church, but her bright blue eyes shone with concern and something else. Alex knew she had a husband once, who had died of cancer some years ago. She talked about a daughter occasionally, but she lived on the Continent somewhere and rarely if ever visited. She now looked up to Alex as the savior of what was important to her in these last years of her life.

Alex patted her hand. "I'll do my best. That's my job. The police have a lot of crimes to solve, but the antiquities are my concern."

"Let's look at the damage." Vicar Andrews rescued Alex from Mrs. Westmoreland and guided him up through the nave to the small Lady Chapel to the right of the main sanctuary. The gate to the chapel stood open, as it always did.

"It's really quite straightforward," the vicar said. "They were in and out quickly."

The bare space on the old stone walls gave silent testimony to where the priceless tapestry had hung until last night. "They knew what they were doing. Apparently they brought a ladder with them, or one man boosted the other up and through the window, but more likely a ladder, the police think. Anyway they removed the window, which was loose anyway, as I said, climbed in and helped themselves. They took the gold candlesticks from the altar and the silver plate given in honor of the RAF boys." Vicar Andrews paused to pull his emotions under control before he continued. "They took the tapestry, the one that dates from the 1700s, and the two paintings. We were pretty sure one of them was a Rubens, you know."

"I know," Alex answered sadly. In his years of investigating thefts of antiquities, this one touched him more than he could have imagined.

"Oh, and this makes no sense," the Vicar continued, as he stepped around behind the small altar. "Some of the workmen had been repairing the stone work in here, using the old tools that have been in the church since the last century; err, I mean the 1800s. I keep forgetting we are in a new century now. Anyway, the tools were kept here behind the altar, and now they are gone, too."

"Sounds like the thieves knew what they were looking for and took the tools as a bonus," Alex answered.

"Probably," the Vicar answered and then cleared his throat. "Tell me the truth, Alex. Do you think it was someone who had been in the church, looked around and came back purposely for our things? And why only the Lady Chapel? We have even more valuable chalices and candlesticks in the main sanctuary."

"It's hard to say, Vicar," he answered slowly, but privately Alex was wondering if they planned to come back, once they had shown their buyers what could be had from a small town church in the Midlands.

Alex changed the subject. "When did you notice the theft? Harry from the police called me about 6:00 and told me about it."

"I heard them leave," Vicar Andrews answered. "They hit one of our old grave stones with their car as they drove off. Probably have a pretty good dent in their fender."

"Well, that should give the police a little something to go on," Alex answered, "but if these thieves are as knowledgeable about crime as they are about antiquities, they will get rid of the car quickly."

Alex made a list of the items that had been taken. He had an appointment to look at some items that had been found in the attic of an old house in a nearby town, so he had not planned on going in to London today. But he had photographs of the pieces in his files and would send the report to the museum by post that afternoon. He was shocked and confused by the burglary of the church—not that it was unusual for churches to be broken into for their valuables, but the Springfield church was so humble and the town so small and off the beaten tourist path. It made him wonder if some of the thieves were residents of the town itself.

THREE

Elaine Maxwell pulled a pair of comfortable, yet stylish, tan wool pants and a matching blouse from the closet, along with sturdy walking shoes, to begin her day as a tour guide around the old Roman town. She was dressing and arguing with her husband at the same time, which caused her to lose focus on both activities. She pulled a brown sweater out of the closet. *Too heavy*, she thought. The navy one layered with a wind breaker would be better. The sun was shining now but one never knew. She checked that her umbrella was in the oversized bag she always carried and turned her attention back to the discussion.

"Of course I realize that what you do for the Cathedral is important; I would just appreciate it if you were home to walk the dog once in a while. I have to stay in the tourist office until 5:00, and if there are people there I can't throw them out."

Dennis came into the room, a mug of steaming coffee in his hand. His face was red from the exertion of their argument, and his small blue eyes flashed with anger. "That dog is a menace! He tried to bite me yesterday. You wanted the damn animal as protection, you said. He couldn't protect you from a fly, let alone a burglar."

"If you were home more, I wouldn't worry about burglars." Elaine sighed as the argument wound down the same old path.

Dennis set down his mug on Elaine's dressing table, knowing that the hot mug could possibly leave a mark on the antique wood. Damn it, he knows that will leave a ring and I will have to take care of it before work. Elaine braced herself for what she knew was coming. "How I could find any peace in this house with you—who tricked me into marrying you because you said you were pregnant—I'll never know."

"That was years ago, Dennis," she answered quietly.

"Years ago, and you've tricked me ever since. You weaseled your way into my mother's affections until she would probably have a heart attack if I left you. You've made my life hell." His voice rose with emotion and fury as raised his arm to hit her, but instead knocked the mug of coffee onto the carpet.

He grabbed her by the front of her carefully ironed blouse, and she could feel the stitches rip at the backs of the sleeves.

"Clean it up and get the stain out." He shoved her backward but she was able to catch herself against the side of the bed.

"Bitch," he whispered, then turned and left the room. A moment later the back door slammed.

Elaine pulled out the cleaning supplies, mopped up the spill, and treated the stain. It would come out; she was an expert at removing stains and at smoothing over pain. She changed her blouse and left the house, only 15 minutes behind schedule. As she walked down the high street (Main Street) to the tourist office, she wondered what had sparked Dennis's anger this time. Back before he retired, it was usually some inept student at the university, or an annoying colleague or secretary, who aroused his ire, which he proceeded to take out on his wife.

Now that he was retired, it was difficult to tell. He spent most of his time with various activities in his capacity as member at the Cathedral. Most of the employees and volunteers there were life-long friends, and he never mentioned them as cause for aggravation. She wondered what it was that set him off, but she was also glad that this time, it had only been spilled coffee and a ripped blouse and not an ugly bruise that she would have to try to hide until it had faded.

FOUR

Nara was dressed in trim blue jeans, a crisp white shirt and chunky black shoes she couldn't quite get used to. Her feet still cried for sandals and the beach. She grabbed her umbrella—just in case—and headed for the car. She had just backed around in the gravel car park and was ready to head out onto the road when she saw Aunt Sue waving frantically from the kitchen doorway. Nara rolled down the window so she could hear what her aunt was saying. "The police are coming by about 3:00, Nara. You'll be back by then, won't you?"

"Yes, of course. I'll make sure I am. I'm only going to register, you know."

"I know, but you might meet someone you want to go have tea with."

Nara smiled. "If I do, I'll tell them we will have to do it another day. I'll be here, Aunt Sue."

At last Nara eased into traffic on the road toward Lincoln. Traffic was considerably heavier as she approached the city, the largest in the county, although by no means a large city by national standards. Lincolnshire was essentially an agricultural area. Acres of farmland covered the land called the "fens," land that had been reclaimed from the sea during the nineteenth century, with the help of the Dutch, who were experts at such things. Although now the main crops ran to various types of fruits and vegetables, the area around Springfield was also known for production of flower bulbs. In the spring, sunny daffodils and tulips of every color covered the land surrounding the town.

Now, in September, the land was turning brown. Nara kept her eyes on the road. She was still getting used to all the traffic here. She had, of course, learned to drive in St. Clare, but the island was small and the roads relatively few. The vehicles, too, were relatively few compared to what she saw here, with lorries of all types and sizes carrying goods here and there.

Nara was thankful that the university was on the outskirts of Lincoln, and she did not have to navigate the narrow streets of the old medieval town. Even where they had been widened somewhat to accommodate modern traffic, the streets still wound around to suit the hill that was surmounted by the castle and the cathedral. Nara did not consider herself to be religious, but she was awestruck just looking up at the cathedral. The majesty of the spires, the flying buttresses that had held up those walls for 800 years, never failed to take her breath away. She could not help thinking of the people of long ago who had sacrificed and given of their talents and skills to build this magnificent structure.

When she reached the university she found that parking for registering students was clearly marked, and she had no trouble finding a space. As she walked toward the building a young woman with blonde hair pulled back into a loose ponytail caught up to her. Her coat was open, and her oversized black shoulder bag dangled carelessly from her arm. She looked to be in her mid-twenties, but she had a harried, preoccupied look, not that of a carefree, single college student.

"Are you registering for classes?" When Nara answered yes, the young woman continued in a rush. "I'm Micki. I'm registering too and I'm kind of nervous. It's been ten years since I've been in school, with getting married and having kids and all. I'm taking business classes. How about you?"

Nara extended her hand. "I'm Nara. I'm taking business classes, too." She thought about Aunt Sue's comment that she might find someone to have tea with—although chances were that Sue had a male someone in mind.

"Oh, that's great. Maybe we will be in the same classes." She paused as they passed through the doors with several other students. "I'm sorry. Maybe you don't need company in your classes. That was very presumptuous of me."

"Not at all," Nara answered. "I've only just moved here from St. Clare. I don't know anyone but my dad and my aunt."

"Oh, that's so wonderful. St. Clare?"

They were entering a large room with signs directing new students to various tables for registration.

"Let's meet for lunch, in case we get separated in here," Micki said. She looked at her watch, which had a large face and worn black strap. "It's 11:00 now. This shouldn't take more than an hour and a half. Shall we meet at the door where we just came in at 12:30?"

"Very well." Nara smiled to herself as she headed for the table marked "New Students." Micki might seem flustered and nervous, but there also was a straightforward, efficient side to her. Lunch would be fun.

Back in Springfield, Sue Blanchard efficiently made up the guests rooms, replenishing the tea bags and sugar packets for the tea-making things in each room. She added a few chocolate mints to each tray—her special touch. As she plumped pillows and set out fresh, thick towels, she couldn't help thinking about the events of the previous night. It just didn't make sense that anyone would try to break in here, except maybe as a lark—like some kids out playing pranks. Maybe they just wanted to prove to themselves that they could do it. She would tell Nara and the police when they came this afternoon exactly what she thought. There was no use wasting time on a crime that wasn't really a crime, and the negative publicity could scare away potential guests.

There was nothing in this house but a collection of old pieces of china, some photographs, and some cheap paintings, she thought. There was absolutely nothing of value, and she should know. Hadn't she been an antique collector for years? At least since her marriage had broken up, anyway. She had started picking things up here and there at markets about the time Tim had moved out, and she had certainly never had the money for the really fine pieces. Everything that had been left here from the previous owner was the same type of thing. She hadn't had time to go through all of it, or to have it appraised, but they wouldn't have let it all go with the house if it had been worth anything, would they? More likely the burglars were interested in Nara's computer and stereo. Those would be much more attractive to thieves.

Feeling well pleased with herself and her train of thought, Sue headed down to the kitchen to prepare some lunch for her brother and herself. Jack was sitting out in the back yard now, enjoying the warm fall day. He had been walking around the yard, inspecting the trees and plants, so different from the tropics where he had spent so many years. He looked better today and seemed more energetic. *Maybe the treatments are working*, Sue thought.

As she reached the kitchen, her cell phone rang. She picked it up off the counter and glanced at the number, then quickly answered.

"Sue, can you talk?" a male voice said quietly.

"Just for a minute. I'm about to fix lunch for Jack."

"I've finished my business in Lincoln a little early. Why don't you come meet me at the Grand Hotel? I'm not supposed to be back in Springfield until tomorrow."

Sue explained what had happened last night and that the police were coming at 3:00.

"I think you're right. It was probably a prank. Come after they leave, Sue. I really need to be with you. All I can think of is touching your soft skin."

She quickly gave in, as she always did for Stan. It was so wonderful to be desired, so many years after the humiliating end of her marriage. Despite her graying hair and the additional two and a half stone of weight, Stan was attracted to her more than his slim, elegantly coiffed wife.

"I'll come as soon as the police leave. Nara can make tea for her father." Sue hung up; put down the biscuit she had just grabbed for a snack, then pulled out a bag of carrot sticks from the refrigerator.

FIVE

The registration process at the college took less time than either Nara expected, and 45 minutes later they were out the door and on their way to lunch.

"We'll take my car if you don't mind. I know a place with good sandwiches but there's not much parking. I'll bring you back here afterwards," Micki said.

"Fine. I don't much like driving around here anyway," Nara answered.

"It must be very different from St. Clare. You'll have to tell me all about it." Micki's interest was obvious as she settled herself in the driver's seat of her little Ford Escort.

Nara climbed into the passenger seat, trying to find a place for her feet on a floor filled with small plastic cars and action figures.

"Oh, just toss those in the back seat, or kick them aside if there's room. Those are my son's. I have to have something to keep him occupied."

"How old is your son?"

"He is five; five going on sixteen. Has an eye for the ladies just like his father already." The light in her eyes made it clear that she was the lady in both their eyes. "I also have a daughter who is almost a year old. Quite the lady she is, I tell you."

Micki stopped behind another car at the traffic light at the exit of the campus. She had just begun to accelerate with the green light when a BMW came in suddenly from the left, ran through the red light and narrowly missed being hit by the car in front of Micki's. Both drivers slammed on their brakes. Fortunately, Micki's acceleration had been slow, so she avoided hitting the driver in front of her.

"I caught the bastard's license plate number," Nara shouted.

"Fat lot of good it will do us," Micki replied. "Bloody BMWs think they own the road. Old guy, too. Did you see?"

"I saw."

Traffic was moving again, and the young women continued to lunch, somewhat shaken.

Both women ordered salads with chicken tikka masala, after gazing longingly at the fish and chips. "You certainly don't need to worry about your weight," Micki said to Nara.

"No. I don't." Nara replied rather absentmindedly. "Look." She pointed out the window of the shop. "Isn't that the man who was driving the car that almost hit us?"

"Yes, it is. I would never forget that angry face. I'm just happy my children weren't in the car with me." She reached out and touched Nara's hand. "Not that I would have wanted you to be hurt, but that's the way a mother thinks. You'll know someday."

"Maybe." Nara was still staring at the little man with thinning brown hair who was berating a much younger man, possibly in his mid-twenties, who was dressed like a workman of some kind with a rucksack on his back. The younger man was nodding meekly and saying little, although truth be told the older man wasn't giving him much of a chance.

Nara and Micki finished their salads and decided to splurge on ice cream for dessert. Micki was doing most of the talking—about her children, her husband, the guest house they ran together after his father had become too sick to handle the day to day work. He still helped out occasionally, but he had difficulty with the stairs and was unable to stand for long periods of time.

"I'm boring you," Micki said. "Is he still there?"

"Yes. And he gives me the chills. He's up to something evil, and I just hope our paths don't cross again."

"You don't think he followed us here, do you?"

"I don't know why he would do that." Nara finished the last spoonful of melted ice cream. "Our guest house was almost broken into last night."

Micki's spoon hit the table with a clatter, causing two waitresses to turn, and then quickly go back to their work restocking salt and pepper and sugar on nearby tables.

"You didn't tell me," she gasped. "*Almost* broken into? What does that mean?"

Nara had almost finished her story, to Micki's open-mouthed amazement, when they were interrupted by Nara's cell phone. "Aunt Sue," she said when she looked at the phone's display. Nara smiled at Micki while shrugging showing her aggravation for the interruption.

"Hello. Yes, I'll be home by 3:00. I can take care of the tea. Enjoy your girls' night out. I'm leaving Lincoln right now."

Nara replaced her phone in her purse and pulled out money to pay for lunch. "I need to get back. The police are coming by at 3:00 to ask us a few questions about the break-in, Aunt Sue is in a tither about Dad's tea and now she has decided to go out with the girls tonight."

"I need to get back, too. David will have had enough of the children by now." Micki smiled affectionately as she spoke of her family.

They paid the bill and left. Nara glanced around as they came out, but the angry little man was nowhere to be seen. She drove back to Springfield thinking of Micki and how different their lives were. She also wondered about the man she had seen and why he had disturbed her so.

Dennis Maxwell was hungry and it was beginning to rain—and in Lincoln it was always a cold rain. He had been about to go into the tea shop when Joe finally arrived. As he had glanced through the windows, anticipating a beef sandwich and some strong hot tea, he noticed Nara, whom he recognized from the Gate House in Springfield. She and her father had moved in just about the time he was putting together his plan to break into the place and had complicated things considerably.

Her father was up at all hours of the night, pacing around in his room and looking out the window, and Nara was constantly wandering around too, poking into nooks and crannies both inside and outside the house. He had been in a foul temper because of it for weeks now. Then he saw her sitting there, and Nara had looked directly at him with those big, dark eyes. He wondered if she had seen him around the Gate House, although he had been careful always to dress in workman's clothes when he was in that part of town. He had never actually been on the property, much less spoken to her.

He was always careful to stay on the corner or across the street in the restaurant parking lot, standing beside a lorry, drinking a mug of tea like he was waiting to meet someone for a job. His looks were nondescript, and at this point in his life he was grateful for that. He had the possibility of making millions. The wealthy collectors might change from time to time, with the economic cycles of nations of the world, but they would always be there, the unscrupulous who wanted to possess the treasures of the past, to own them, not to share them with the rest of the world.

"Don't worry. It's all hidden," Joe was saying.

Dennis pulled himself back to the present. "It better be," he growled.

Joe was hopping back and forth from one foot to the other and rubbing his hands together to keep warm. "Shall we have some tea?" He looked longingly to the warmth and the food inside the stop.

"No time today. I've got to go. I'll call you in a few days." Dennis turned abruptly and lost himself in the crowd of shoppers on Lincoln's busy main street. He was still hungry and his hands felt like ice, but he would go home and vent his anger on his wife.

SIX

Sue dressed carefully in trim tan trousers that made her look slimmer and then paired them with a soft silk blouse and sweater. They were expensive and worth every penny. A shopping trip to London every now and then was good for a girl. She looked, she hoped, like she was going out for a nice dinner in a good restaurant. Well, she was. And after that she was going to spend the night in a hotel with her lover. Her *lover.* She smiled at herself in the mirror and whispered the words out loud. "My lover." She felt no guilt. How could she feel guilty about something that had brought so much brightness into her life?

Sue heard Nara's car drive in and looked out the bedroom window in time to watch her bounce across the car park to the kitchen door. She looked excited. That girl always looked excited. Sue smoothed her hair one last time. It was short, but still had a silky texture. Perhaps she would let it grow out a bit.

The house phone rang and she grabbed the bedroom extension. It was the police investigator saying they were on their way. Sue hoped they didn't take too long; she hated to keep Stan waiting.

Sue met her niece in the kitchen, feeling a bit self-conscious. Nara was preparing tea in the kitchen and chatting with her father, who did look extraordinarily well today. He was telling her about a fax he had received that day from the manager of his import company in St. Clare. Nara was listening intently as she measured tea into the pot. The girl refused to use tea bags; she claimed loose tea in a pot tasted better. *She'll learn.*

Nara paused with her hand on the handle of the electric kettle. "You look beautiful, Aunt Sue. Who are you going out with?"

"Just some girl friends that I went to nursing school with—no one you know." *Now why did I say that?* she wondered. Nara had just moved here and knew very few people anyway. It made her sound as if she was hiding something, but the girl was so nosy! Nara was pouring the hot water into the teapot now and listening to something her father was saying.

"He says business is picking up for the higher-end goods. Those new estates on the north end of the island are bringing in people with more disposable income: people who want expensive tiles from Italy and antiques from just about anywhere."

Nara set down the tea kettle and paused to look around the room. "Speaking of antiques, this house is full of them. Is there anything here that is valuable enough that someone would want to steal it? Micki, the woman I had lunch with today, says the little trinkets setting around might be worth more than we think. She had everything in her place appraised when she and her husband took over and found a few paintings that were worth quite a lot."

Their conversation was curtailed when the panda car (Police car) drove into the car park. "Shall I offer them tea?" Nara looked from her father to Sue.

"No," Sue answered quickly; too quickly.

"Yes," her father answered just as quickly. Sue could see the twinkle in his eye. He was baiting her just like he would when they were children. She glared at him as she went to the door, ushering the two men into the lounge.

The problem was solved when Nara offered them tea and they refused. They had just had their tea, they said. The two police officers asked a few questions, mostly the same questions that had already been answered the night before. They left quickly, saying they would be in touch if they found anything out. As they walked out the senior officer turned to Sue and said, "You might consider an alarm system. Things aren't the way they used to be here in Springfield, with all the foreigners coming in."

"Do you have some evidence it was foreigners who broke in?" Nara asked, her face flushing at the man's prejudicial statement.

The man looked at her dark skin, eyes and hair. "No. We don't know who it is." he answered.

As soon as they left, Sue grabbed her purse off the counter quickly, knocking her keys to the floor with a clang. "Now everyone in Springfield will know about the break-in," she fussed. "It will be in the 'Crimes' column in the *Springfield Journal.* That's just the kind of bad publicity that gives people ideas. There's nothing here worth stealing, other than the stereo and the telly, and your computer." She emphasized the word "your" and directed an angry glance at Jack.

"Did you have things appraised when you bought the place?" Jack asked benignly.

"Of course not! It wasn't necessary." Sue's cell phone buzzed in her purse. "I need to go. It's just a pile of junk to amuse tourists. Trust me."

"Does she seem edgy to you?" Nara asked her father as she set out a plate of biscuits she had picked up in Lincoln that day.

"Sue is always edgy," he answered. "That's just her way."

"Maybe, but she seems very defensive about the house and what's in it. I wonder why? And why didn't she answer her cell phone?"

Jack laughed affectionately at his daughter. "Always looking for a mystery, aren't you, Nara? A puzzle to solve." He helped himself to biscuits and added sugar to his tea. "You are actually quite a bit like her, you know. You both have a flare for the dramatic. Always either performing or watching the performance. 'All the world's a stage.' Just don't take Sue too seriously."

Nara poured her own tea and added milk and the teensiest bit of sugar. "Maybe." She scowled, unwillingly to give in .

SEVEN

In his elegant Georgian house by the river, Alex Collier was having tea. He pulled the chocolate brownie out of the paper bakery bag and took a large bite. Great inventions—brownies. Another piece in the deluge of American food one could find on any street corner these days. But he had heard scones were available over there now, too, so he supposed it was all right, sharing each other's cultures—as long as that didn't extend to selling a country's antiquities illegally.

He stared at the screen of his laptop, searching the database for the items that had been stolen from the church. They had all been cataloged by the police, along with photographs. They would be easily recognized when they turned up—if they didn't end up in the hands of some private collector in Hong Kong. He took another bite of the brownie, followed by a sip of tea. He had done about all he could do for one day. He would finish his tea and go for a run. He wrapped up the rest of the brownie for later. If he finished it now it would sit like a rock in his stomach while he ran.

Alex started his run in the direction out of town. He didn't want to see the church again today, after the break-in. He was not a hard-boiled cop, after all. It broke his heart to see these treasures disappear. It was especially difficult in the case of a small country church like this one, or when an item had been in a family for generations, and then turned up missing. It was amazing the lengths some thieves would go to for their own gain. Often family members themselves were involved, either to support a drug or gambling habit, or because they had fallen in with the wrong crowd and wanted to prove themselves.

Alex thought about all this as he ran. It was a great opportunity to work out problems, but he wasn't getting any closer on this one. Then again, he didn't expect to. The thieves who broke into the church were too smart. He wasn't ready to call them professional, but they had certainly done their homework.

The river path took him out of town, where there were fewer pedestrians. He passed the old gate house that had been turned into a bed and breakfast establishment about the time he and Laura had moved here. He pushed the thought of Laura out of his mind; it was not a place he wanted to go today, or any day for that matter. He had made a mistake and it was over. Lots of people made mistakes in marriage. At least his had been corrected. He had not spent miserable years in a marriage and then suddenly awakened to discover that he had passed the best years of his life being unhappy.

Still, he was lonely. He supposed it wasn't so much Laura that he missed, as the warmth of female companionship in his life. He pushed the thoughts away again and concentrated on his running, checking his stride and his time. Ahead of him on the trail he noticed a young woman running. She was petite, with slim, muscular legs and dark brown hair pulled back in a runner's ponytail. Her skin was dark, and he wondered if she was Asian.

Runners wore all kinds of gear, and her tee shirt and navy shorts were not remarkable, but what Alex noticed immediately were her shoes. He thought all runners knew the importance of good running shoes and would spend whatever was necessary for good quality ones. This girl was running in battered sneakers and no socks that he could see. As he overtook her on the path, he slowed down. He started to speak just as she jumped, pulled off the headphones she was wearing and flashed angry brown eyes at him.

Before he could speak, she launched into a tirade. "What are you doing? You scared me to death! You could at least have let me know you were behind me. Who are you anyway, and what do you want? My house was almost broken into last night and I don't need any more scares today, thank you. I came out here for a relaxing run to unwind and then you come up behind me and scare the life out of me. What do you want, anyway?" She paused for breath.

"I just wanted to say something to you about your shoes," he answered.

"My shoes?" She looked down, uncomprehending. "MY SHOES?! You scared the life out of me because of my shoes?"

Alex was taken aback by her violent reaction, when all he intended to do was offer some helpful advice on running shoes—advice that could save her considerable pain in the future.

"I'm sorry," he mumbled.

"Well, you should be." The dark eyes still flashed. "Who are you, anyway?"

"My name's Alex Collier." He held out his hand, which she took grudgingly. Her hand felt small and warm. "I saw your shoes and just wanted to mention that you are going to have problems if you run in those shoes." He looked down at the beat-up shoes, canvas worn thin and heels broken down.

"Why?" Her eyes met his, more bewildered than angry now.

"They don't give you any support. You'll have shin splints, problems with your knees, your heels, not to mention blisters from not wearing socks."

"I've really never done any serious running before."

Alex noticed Nara checking out his running attire—faded tee shirt left over from a marathon two years ago, running shorts, sturdy athletic shoes that looked like he could run to Scotland and back, and, yes, socks. He could just see the wheels spinning in her head as she checked him out and it made him smile that he had that affect on her, or at least hoped he did.

What does she see? Average height, brown hair falling into my brown eyes, a dazzling smile, a physique that shows evidence of plentiful exercise. Skin slightly tan—yes, I present quite the figure of a man.

"I'm sorry. I guess I overreacted." She smiled slightly.

A little unsure of herself, Alex thought as he suddenly realized that he was not as eager to get back to his run as he thought. "There is a shop in town that sells quite good running shoes," he said.

"I wouldn't know what to buy."

"I'd be happy to go with you and help you out."

"I wouldn't want to put you to that much trouble."

"No trouble at all."

"I should let you get back to your running."

"Only if you will promise to meet me tomorrow and buy yourself some decent shoes. And you could tell me your name."

Nara laughed, sending a different kind of sparkle into her dark eyes and into some part of Alex that he thought was dead. "My name is Nara Blake. I live at the Gate House over there." She motioned over her shoulder at the old house behind them.

"Nara," he repeated. "Shall we meet in town tomorrow afternoon? What time would you be free?"

"I'm free after lunch. I usually like to be home for tea with my father."

"Can I buy you lunch?" Alex surprised himself with his impulsiveness.

The little smile again. "That would be nice."

"I'll meet you by the bridge near the town center. That's an easy place to find."

"Are you afraid I'll get lost?"

Alex couldn't tell if the sparkle in her eyes was flirtatious or sarcastic, so decided not to rise to the bait. "Not at all. Shall I see you there about 1:00?"

"All right." Nara pushed her dark hair behind her right ear nervously. "I'll just go walk around the block then. So I don't hurt myself." She didn't move, and her eyes seemed to say, *I'm not going to give you the opportunity to watch me from behind again.*

"I'll see you tomorrow, then." Alex forced himself to turn and continue his run out of town. He didn't dare turn his head to see what Nara did, hoping she stood in the path watching him until the path bent out of sight.

EIGHT

Dennis Maxwell's anger ebbed and flowed throughout the day. It had all started with Elaine, of course, the stupid fool. She had always been a fool. He had been trapped by his mother and Elaine since the two women had met and his mother had decided Elaine was the woman he should marry. But that was all water under the bridge now. He just had to slap Elaine in line every once in a while and watch her take the abuse, which only made him more angry at her. He was sure his mother knew nothing of the situation. Elaine would never dare tell her.

Dennis stepped into The Cave, the tea shop where he was to meet a client. He was about fifteen minutes early, time enough to calm himself before the man arrived. That incident with Joe early in the afternoon hadn't helped his mood either. And then there was the girl from the bed and breakfast whom he had seen in the restaurant. She had stared at him as if she recognized him, too. His stomach clenched as he sat down at a secluded table in the basement room. Only a few tourists were here this late in the day. He fleetingly wondered if Elaine would have one of her pathetic little dinners waiting for him. She frequently did after they had a row in the morning.

A tall, elegant blonde woman walked into the room; Dennis glanced up at her, then back to his notebook. All at once she was standing next to him, and there was nothing for it but to look up at her towering above him in her elegant red suit, long manicured nails to match, blonde hair pulled efficiently back from her face.

"Dennis Maxwell?"

"Yes." He stood up, but she was still a good six inches taller than he was.

"I'm Terry Clark from Hadley's auction house in London." She held out her hand.

It took Dennis a moment to compose himself. *Another dominating woman*, he thought. *Just my luck*. His moment's hesitation gave her the upper hand.

"Do you mind if I sit down?" she said.

"Of course. Please. Would you like some tea?"

"I gave my order at the counter when I came in." She turned her head as the young waitress came in carrying a tray. "Ah. There it is."

"Thank you." She smiled pleasantly at the young girl, who blushed. While the tea steeped, Terry Clark pulled a notebook and expensive looking pen out of her leather bag.

Dennis sipped his tea and tried to decide how best to handle the situation. She wasn't simple like Elaine, but she was sure to have a weak spot. All women did.

"You said you have some items my superiors might be interested in." There was something about the way she pronounced the word "superiors." As if she wanted to emphasize that although she was far superior to a mere retired teacher in the Midlands, the people who had sent her on this business had even more money, knowledge, and connections. For a split second Dennis felt out of his league. But he knew what he had was valuable, and only he knew where the items were hidden after their removal from their former locations. She was still a woman, like Elaine or his mother, even with the makeup and expensive clothes. He briefly imagined her naked, her blonde hair down around her shoulders.

Dennis took a bite of his carrot cake to stall for time. He chewed carefully and swallowed. The cake tasted dry and stuck to the roof of his mouth.

"I have some things and can obtain more."

"What kind of things?" She tapped her pen against her notebook impatiently; she clearly wasn't used to wasting time. Her impatience could be the flaw in her perfection. He would go slowly, keep her waiting.

"I have a tapestry, some gold candlesticks, some silver-plate, and stained glass." He paused for another bite of cake and a sip of tea. Terry Clark's pen scratched on her notebook. This tea was good—not the watery stuff Elaine made. He poured more and added sugar.

Terry looked up, pen poised above the notebook.

"I also have come across a number of items that have been in storage since the death of the owner. He was ready to sell to us when he died, unfortunately." Terry's blue eyes never left his face. "I've not been able to gain access to them, but I believe I shall soon."

"What kinds of things would these be that are in storage?" Terry's voice was calm, but held an edge.

"That's the trouble. You see, I don't know. If a list was made, it was with the man's personal effects. Then the place was sold, lock, stock and barrel, and I haven't been able to gain access."

Terry capped her pen and placed it neatly on the table with her notebook. "So you are saying that these items, which you think I would be interested in, are resting in boxes somewhere, and you can't get to them?" Her eyes bored into his and he was forced to look away. "Find out what is there, and bring me some samples. I don't care how you do it." She replaced her pen and notebook in her bag and snapped it shut. "Otherwise we cannot do business. Your tapestry and candlesticks are worthless, small time. I don't bother with those. I was given information by someone I know as reliable, that you had access to some valuable pieces." She opened her bag again and handed him a business card. "Call me when you have something, and quickly. Buyers don't wait around forever."

She stood, towering above him again. "And wipe the crumbs off your chin." She walked out, and Dennis tentatively put his hand to his chin and wiped off the cake crumbs.

He would have gain to access to the Gate House somehow. That was where the goods were. He would get up early tomorrow morning and work out a plan, then call in the chaps who did his dirty work. He would have to go along when the job was done because he wanted it done right. No slip-ups like last time, when the girl caught the fellow opening the window. It would be done right this time.

Dennis stood up and thought about Elaine. It was time to go home where he could take his anger out on someone.

NINE

Alex was thinking about Nara. He smiled as he thought about those shapely legs running with those awful shoes, and her fiery indignation when he spoke to her. He was looking forward to helping her pick out some good shoes tomorrow.

He had taken a quick shower when he arrived back at his house. There were several messages on his answering machine, but he would deal with those later. He pulled on jeans and a tee shirt, and padded around his kitchen barefoot. He searched the cabinets for something to call dinner. *Damn it.* He should have invited Nara out for dinner tonight, but that seemed a little too abrupt, and he couldn't have used the excuse of buying running shoes.

He settled for some yogurt. Maybe he would fry some eggs later. Laura had always been after him for eating too many eggs. *Too much cholesterol,* she said. Alex ate another spoonful of yogurt while he booted up his laptop. He had the gut feeling that the thefts at the church were part of a bigger picture. The business had been done in too professional a manner to be small time thieves. And then there was the other attempted theft the same night. He needed to at least run that down. He found the phone number for the Springfield Police Station and then remembered to check his messages.

The first was from Laura. Did he still have the photographs she took of the interior of the house when they first decorated it? She wanted to show them to someone in London. And was he thinking of selling the house? She could find a buyer. "Forget it," Alex muttered to himself and went to the next message.

The second message was from his boss in London, wondering what he had found out about the theft at the Springfield church, and did it tie in with the items that had disappeared from the Lincoln Cathedral the previous month? He didn't know; in fact, he had doubted at the time if those items had even been stolen, or just misplaced by some doddering sexton. That often happened and things were found a generation—or even a century later—hidden in some forgotten closet. He would check it out, however. It might be time to pay another visit to Lincoln Cathedral.

Maybe Nara would like to go with me. He wondered if she had seen the cathedral. Didn't she say she had just come from Barbados or somewhere? Alex shook his head to get back on track. He was usually more focused than this.

The third message was from Harry at the Springfield police department, left just an hour ago. Would Alex ring him back as soon as possible? He had discovered something interesting. *Maybe important, maybe not,* Alex thought, as he dialed the number.

Nara arrived back at the Gate House to find her father sitting in the darkening lounge. "Davis called," he said.

Nara said nothing.

"He said he would try to call later. He's been very busy."

"Too busy for an e-mail?"

"That's something you have to decide, Nara dear."

She crossed the room to him where he held out his hand to her in the gloom. She took it and then sat on the arm of his chair, resting her head on his. He was thinner now and did not feel like the strong father she had known and depended on all her life. Her mother had died when she was very small, so it had mostly been just the two of them. Now, here in England, she could feel the balance shifting. She was growing stronger; he was growing weaker. Nara wasn't sure she was comfortable with the change... at least not yet.

"I'm worried about Sue," Jack said suddenly.

"About Aunt Sue?" Nara lifted her head. "Why? I thought you said that was just her way?"

"She seems preoccupied. And where was she going tonight all dressed up?"

"She said she was going out with friends. A girl's night out."

"Sue never had groups of girl friends. She has always been a loner. And recently, since her divorce, she's been lonely. I think that's why she gained so much weight."

"So where do you think she went tonight?" Nara stood up and turned on a small lamp in the room so she could see her father's face.

"I think she's seeing a man and keeping it a secret for some reason."

"Do you think he is married?" A whole new picture of her Aunt Sue was forming in Nara's mind.

"I don't know. But I hate to see her get hurt," he answered.

"Maybe I can find out. You know. Woman to woman." Nara sat down in a chair opposite her father and took off her old shoes. She had to admit they rubbed against her feet in an unpleasant way.

"Be careful. She'll shut you out if you pry too much," he sighed. "But maybe you will have better luck."

Nara looked up. "What happened? Why does she shut people out?"

"Nothing. It was a long time ago." His voice had that tiredness in it, so Nara decided not to pursue it, but it was in her nature to remember and find out. Her family was much more complex than she had imagined, but maybe all families were. It is only as children that families seem simple.

Nara looked down at her old shoes again and decided to tell her father about Alex. "I have a lunch date tomorrow, and then I'm going to buy some new running shoes."

Jack chuckled. "I caught the date part of it. Who's the lucky guy?"

"A guy I met out on the running path. He stopped me to tell me I needed new shoes." Nara held up the old ones she had worn everywhere in St. Clare. "He nearly scared the life out of me when he stopped me."

"And tomorrow he's taking you to lunch and helping you buy shoes." Jack chuckled again and then grew serious. "Just don't get hurt, Nara. I've noticed you mooning around, thinking about Davis. Absence doesn't always make the heart grow fonder."

"I know." Nara stood up, not ready to pursue this conversation. "Are you hungry? I think Aunt Sue left some soup."

"That sounds good. Something light and maybe there's some bread to go with it. Let's explore the kitchen."

TEN

In Lincoln, Elaine was preparing dinner. She was angry with herself as she cut up potatoes and put them in the pot with water. *Dennis has to have his potatoes every night.* No wonder she had gained weight, although the walking she did in her job as tour guide kept her in decent shape. She took two small steaks out of the refrigerator and seasoned them. Every time she had a row with Dennis and he hit her, she somehow felt that it was always her fault—and it made her angry. *If only I was a better wife. If only we had had children. If only I had more money of my own.*

Dennis had retired from his university job with a decent pension and managed to buy an expensive car for himself, but he still only gave her a minimal household allowance. She worked as a tour guide to bring in a bit of her own money, but it wasn't what she was trained for. She had a degree in history and had started doing a Master's in art history when they had married. She had worked a series of part time jobs over the years to supplement their income, but Dennis always went into a rage when she had mentioned finishing her degree, or applying for a full time position. And his mother, whom Elaine idolized, backed her son on that. "You need to be home for the children," she would say.

Even after it was clear that there would be no children, it was always, "Dennis needs you at home." Elaine knew that her mother-in-law was aware of Dennis's rages and supported her in other ways, encouraging Dennis to allow her money for clothes occasionally and to furnish the house attractively, so the years slipped by. Elaine had no other family. She made do with what she had, and sometimes months would go by when her husband would be reasonably pleasant—they even took a trip to Italy once. But lately she had the feeling that life was slipping by, and she was missing out on the best part of it.

She had been born and spent her childhood in London, living in poverty on the East End with her mother, who worked as a waitress when her feet weren't giving her trouble. When they were, she sold her body. Elaine could still remember the men who had been in and out of their shabby flat on Wesley Street. They had moved around a lot, as her mother's whims and finances dictated, but that was the flat she most remembered when she thought about her childhood. Neither Dennis nor his mother liked her to talk about it, and there was no one else to talk to now. She had no close friends. They told her to forget the past and let her know she should be grateful that they had saved her from her sordid beginnings.

She remembered the grime on the windows. The flat was located in a building where the back flats faced the Underground tracks, just at the point where the tracks moved out of the tunnel to travel above ground. Her mother had shown no interest in cleaning the windows. Elaine had tried once, with a rag and some water, but it had only smeared and made a mess that her mother had screamed and slapped her.

Elaine had then taped up some pictures of flowers from a magazine and some of beautiful women wearing long black evening gowns and escorted by handsome, well-groomed men in tuxedos. There had been pictures of decorated cakes and beef roasts—things never seen in Elaine's young life. Her mother had glanced at them when Elaine put them up, but never said anything about them.

Elaine had been a quiet child in school, never talking about her family, since she didn't really have one. Her mother seemed always ready to fly away and disappear. She wasn't a real mother like other children had, or like the ones in the books she read in school. Elaine enjoyed the books. She escaped into them, and that was what saved her. Her teachers liked her, felt sorry for her. She became a stellar student at whatever school she was attending, and she attended every day, getting up and out the door, sometimes with a little food in her stomach, but more often not.

Her teachers usually provided her with something to eat, once they became aware of the situation. And so Elaine had endured. She learned to stay out of the way of her mother's boy friends. She wore her oldest, dirtiest clothes at home, which was easy because most of her clothing was old, and rarely washed. She only combed her hair before she went to school. Once, when she was about eleven, one of the boy friends, a decent enough looking man of about 40, who seemed ancient to Elaine, stroked her face with his hand and commented to Elaine's mother, "She would be pretty enough if she were cleaned up."

Her mother had flown into a rage—at Elaine. "Get out of here, you little slut. What are you doing flirting with my boy friends? Out! Go wherever you go. Go to school! Go to your precious teachers. I might have known this would start. Out!"

She began by throwing Elaine's books at her and then the dirty dishes that were piled on the table. As a bowl of congealed canned soup narrowly missed Elaine's head, she was out the door, fear clenching at her stomach. It wasn't her mother's rage she was afraid of—she had endured enough of those before—it was the look in the man's eyes. Usually the men who visited her mother just ignored the little girl, happy to see her go out the door so they could have time alone with the mother, but this one was different. He looked at her as if he wanted to possess her. And Elaine was terrified.

She went downstairs and out into the cold, shivering and wrapping her arms around herself, since of course she had no coat on. She saw a policeman down at the corner and went the other way. Her mother had taught her to stay away from the police at all costs. A five minute walk took her to the school, where she slipped in an unlocked side door and spent the night sleeping warm but uncomfortably on the floor in a broom closet. She awoke early in the morning when she heard the janitors entering the building, chattering among themselves as they sipped their steaming mugs of tea and talked about the cold.

Elaine rose and quietly left the building the way she had come in. When she let herself into their flat, the man was gone and her mother was sleeping, sprawled diagonally across the bed that mother and daughter shared when there were no guests, still dressed in the mini-skirt and blouse she had been wearing the night before. Elaine changed into a slightly less filthy skirt and blouse, washed her face and combed her hair, and went back to school for her classes.

Something in Elaine had changed that night. She had always been a wary, frightened little girl, but now she was genuinely afraid. She stayed away from the flat more and more at night, avoiding the men who visited her mother and sleeping in the broom closet at school. She never knew that one of the janitors had suspected something and arrived earlier and more quietly than usual one morning and discovered her. He had informed the principal, who told him to continue to leave the door unlocked, and allow the child to sleep there. She was sure it was warmer and safer than the environment she was running away from. Elaine thought it was nothing more than her own good fortune when an old winter jacket or a ragged blanket was left in the closet, or when a few packets of biscuits were stored on a nearby shelf. *Surely one won't be missed.*

During this year Elaine's mother continued to live her own life, with her growing daughter hardly a speck on her horizon. She had stopped waitressing altogether and spent more and more of her days sleeping in the flat, then going out at night, dressed in her mini-skirts and low-cut blouses. Elaine knew what the other children said about her and her mother, but she kept to herself and her books. In truth, Elaine would not have known what to do if she had realized how her mother was slipping into a drug- and sex-induced oblivion. Elaine did what she could to survive, sometimes taking money from her mother's purse while she slept to buy a little food. It was nice in a way because her mother was either sleeping or was out. She never brought men back to the flat anymore. Elaine kept the rooms reasonably clean and orderly, enjoying the sense of order; an enjoyment that she would retain throughout her life.

One night she was straightening her mother's clothing in her closet, thinking maybe there was something old in there that she could wear that was not too flashy, and that her mother would not miss. Back in the corner on the floor

Elaine found a box tied with string. It was old and dusty; obviously it had not been opened for years. Elaine pulled the strings and they loosened at once. When she lifted the cover, she found that the box was filled with papers—documents of all sorts, letters still in their envelopes, some unopened.

Elaine held her breath as she picked up the first paper. It was her birth certificate. She was born December 25, 1950. She knew that. Her mother had told her when she was small how her birth had ruined Christmas for her, that year and all those following.

She was born in the Southwark Hospital at 9:20 a.m. She knew that too. Her mother was Alice Collins, born in Lincoln. She had no idea her mother was from Lincoln; that was something she had never talked about, and Elaine had never thought to ask. With trepidation she read on. In the space next to "father's name," the word "unknown" was filled in. Elaine sighed. She had asked her mother often when she was small who her father was, and her mother's usual answer had been, "You don't have one. You don't need one." And the subject was closed.

The other interesting piece of information was her mother's date of birth—May 5, 1934. She had only been sixteen when Elaine was born. Only four years older than she was now. So she was 28 now. She seemed much older to Elaine.

She looked through the letters, opened and unopened, all postmarked Lincoln. Carefully Elaine removed the fragile paper from one of the opened envelopes, dated October, 1950, just two months before she was born. The handwriting was neat and flowing, easy to read even though the ink was faded. It began:

Dear Daughter,

I wonder if I will ever hear from you again. I have heard from my contacts in London that you and William are no longer together. That may be a good thing. He was not good for you. I have further been told that you are expecting a baby. I know you will do the right thing and allow the child to be adopted by a good family. Any church can help you with that.

Once that is done, you will be welcome to come home and start your life again.

Your father and I love you still.

Mother

Elaine had put down the letter and wondered then, as she wondered still when she allowed herself to remember that moment. Why had her mother kept her? She never showed her the love and affection mothers usually show their children. If she didn't love her, why didn't she put her up for adoption? Was it to spite her own mother?

She would never know. Elaine's mother was found dead that night in an alley not far from their flat where she had apparently passed out from drugs and alcohol. Dead of exposure, the coroner said. Through the letters in the box that Elaine had found, the authorities were able to contact the grandmother in Lincoln, who considered it her Christian duty to take in her granddaughter. It was a difficult adjustment for Elaine, who in spite of being only 12 years old had become quite self-sufficient.

In her grandmother's house, Elaine's every move—every nuance of her voice and facial expression—were scrutinized. Her grandmother was constantly saying, "I don't know what kind of life you led in London," or "I don't know how she raised you," but never waited for an answer before launching into a lecture. Her grandmother was pleased, however, when the teachers at the local school proclaimed Elaine to be an excellent student, although somewhat fearful of speaking out in front of the other students.

She grew into adolescence, but remained a subdued young girl, rarely going out with friends. In fact, she had few friends. She had always kept to herself as a means of protection. She was pretty but rarely smiled, and she was not allowed to wear makeup. She easily won a scholarship to Lincoln University, but continued to live with her grandmother throughout her college years. It was as if she were trudging through life preparing for something, without knowing what or when she would begin to do whatever it was.

After college, she worked at the city museum for several years, researching and presenting programs for tourists and student groups. Her grandmother had died and left her the house, and she had just begun a Master's program in history when she met Dennis. She thought perhaps that this was what she had been preparing for all her life and might actually have a chance at marriage and motherhood—a normal life, after all.

Elaine had just turned 30, and Dennis's mother reminded her of her grandmother, and she fell under her spell immediately. She did as she was told. Dennis was kind in the beginning, and his touch warmed her in a way she had never imagined. No one in her life up to that time had ever touched her with affection or love. She believed that she had found a sense of family at last.

It didn't take long, however, to see the cruelty just beneath the surface. Or perhaps it was the other way around? Was the cruelty the facade he used to hide his vulnerability? It didn't matter; her bruises were real. When he beat her, she accepted it, although intellectually she knew it was wrong and hated herself for putting up with it. She felt simultaneously attracted to and repulsed by him. He could be so kind and gentle when he chose to be. She couldn't say that she loved him anymore, but what options did she have? Occasionally she thought of leaving him, but just never got around to doing it. She was stuck in her life with him.

When Dennis walked in that evening, he was in an unusually foul mood. He glanced at the food she was preparing and apparently found nothing wrong with it. He stomped off to their bedroom and Elaine could hear him on the phone, talking in an angry voice to someone. *Good,* she thought. *Someone else is getting the brunt of his anger tonight; maybe there will be less for me.*

He returned to the kitchen a few moments later and ate his food in silence, stuffing the bites of steak in his mouth, making no comment about the fact that it was done medium rare, just the way he liked it. Elaine had learned that over the years.

When he finished, he stood up, wiped his mouth on a napkin, and took his jacket off the hook by the door.

"I have to go out. I have some business to attend to. I'll be late," he said and was gone.

Elaine smiled to herself at the thought of a quiet evening by herself and reached for the book she had been reading. She arranged it so the pages would stay open with the weight of the salt shaker, while she enjoyed the rest of her meal in peace.

ELEVEN

Nara hoped to spend the evening alone, maybe watching the telly with her father and then going to bed early. She thought she might spend a little time on the computer, looking up some information on the Internet. Her conversation with Micki that afternoon had piqued her interest in antiques, and she was eager to learn more. She looked around the study, the same one where she had surprised the intruder just the night before, and realized that she had no idea what any of the pictures and other *objets d'artes* were worth, if anything.

Were they even the real thing? She had always been interested in art, although she did not feel that she was talented at all. She had even toyed around with the idea of opening a shop to showcase local artists in St. Clare at one time, but then her life had taken a different direction, and here she was in England. It might be worthwhile to try to learn something about the pieces that surrounded her. The textbook for *Introduction to Business* lay on the chair where she had dropped it when she came in. *Time enough for that later,* she thought. The first class wasn't until next Monday.

Before she could sit down at the computer, the phone rang. Nara answered and heard the breathless greeting of a woman with an American accent. "Do you possibly have a room available for tonight? I realize it's short notice. We had a reservation at the Woodbridge Hotel, but apparently they lost it and now they're full, and the owner can't be contacted to straighten it out. They suggested we try you."

Nara sighed. The woman made it sound as if they were a decided second choice. *Oh, well.* They did have a room available.

"Yes, as it happens we have a room. Would that be for two?" Nara reached for paper and a pen to write down the woman's name. "You are just a couple of minutes from us. Keep going on Ripingale Road, cross Waverly Street, and you will see the house on the corner. It's an old stone Gate House. The car park is just past the house."

"Thank you so much," the woman breathed and hung up.

Nara ran upstairs to check the vacant room, calling out to her father as she ran. "We have guests coming. I have to make sure the room is ready."

Nara smoothed the duvet covering the bed, then checked the tea and coffee supplies on the tray on the bureau. The chocolate mints were there as well. She took a stack of clean, fluffy towels out of the linen closet and arranged them attractively at the foot of the bed. The room looked fine. She checked the vase of chrysanthemums on the table in the hallway to be sure they were still fresh. Aunt Sue did not like to put fresh flowers in the bedrooms, because she was concerned about allergies guests might have. Since she grew up in the tropics, Nara loved flowers and sometimes asked the guests if they would like flowers in their room.

As she went back to close the door to the linen closet, Nara suddenly noticed a small key on the shelf she had removed the towels from. It had slipped down into the crack at the side of the shelf and so was partially hidden. She picked it up and looked at it; it was an old key, small and somewhat rusty, and looked as if it might open a box or chest of some kind. Nara put it in her pocket. It might be a good start on her investigation of the antiques in the house, to find out what lock the key fit.

No sooner had she closed the linen closet than the doorbell rang. Nara hurried downstairs to answer it. The woman was just as she had pictured her—a blonde American wearing a lavender pantsuit, her long-suffering husband trailing behind her with several suitcases that he had removed from their rental car.

"Thank you so much for taking us at the last minute. You do accept credit cards, don't you?" She did not wait for a reply. "I can't believe the Woodbridge lost our reservation. And the manager, or the owner, or whoever he was, wasn't even there." She came inside and let her husband go past her with the luggage. "I'm sorry. I'm Stephanie, and this is my husband Steve. We only landed in London two days ago so we are still jet-lagged."

Jet-lagged? Is that a word? Nara thought.

"It's not a problem," Nara answered. "Your room is ready. I've just freshened the linens." She looked at the piles of suitcases in the foyer. "I'll show you to your room then. Would you like a cup of tea to relax?" Nara let the question hang in the air. She wasn't nearly as comfortable with this hostess kind of thing as Aunt Sue was. She wondered how her friend Micki in Lincoln handled late-arriving guests. All Nara wanted to do was go to bed herself.

"Oh, yes!" the woman answered enthusiastically. "English tea! That would be lovely, wouldn't it, Steve?"

Steve muttered something under his breath.

"We love English tea. With crumpets? Isn't that traditional?"

Nara stifled a smile. "I don't happen to have any crumpets. But I think I can provide some biscuits to go with your tea." There would be time enough later to let this annoying woman know that she had only been in England herself for less than two months. She sincerely hoped Aunt Sue would be back early.

She led the couple up the staircase to the back bedroom, the largest of the three they had for rent. The smaller double room was occupied by a couple who were visiting relatives in the area. They generally came in late at night and went out again after breakfast. The third room was a single, currently vacant.

Stephanie gushed over the room—the antique furniture, the chintz wallpaper, the chocolates—while Steve found places for all the suitcases. He had no sooner set them all down than Stephanie began instructing him to move them to different spots. "No, dear. I need that one first thing in the morning. My makeup is in it. And I need that one tonight so I can hang up my clothes for tomorrow. Things wrinkle terribly crammed in suitcases."

"I'll just go down and put the tea on," Nara said in the background, hoping they heard her, and slipped downstairs.

She prepared a tray with a china teapot and matching cups and found some Scottish shortbread in the cupboard. *That should be English enough for Stephanie.* When the water boiled she warmed the pot with a small amount of water, poured it out and added the loose tea, then filled the pot with boiling water.

By the time she had the tea ready and places set at the dining room table, the couple had returned downstairs.

"This is an absolutely lovely place. The antiques must be worth a fortune. I think it was a blessing in disguise that the Woodbridge lost our reservation. We would never have found this place. We must have been led here, don't you think, Steve?" Steve muttered agreement. "I believe in that sort of thing. Don't you?"

Nara realized the woman was talking to her. Quickly she ran possible answers through her mind. Which was the safest? She decided the best was to agree. "Oh, yes. Absolutely."

She turned to the tea. "I'll pour for you." She picked up a silver tea strainer. "I like making tea the traditional way. My aunt teases me about it. She prefers tea bags because they are easier."

The woman smiled. "Your aunt? I thought you looked a little young to be running this place by yourself. Didn't I just say that up in the room, Steve?" Steve nodded as he chewed a biscuit.

Nara bit her lip, struggling to control herself. She just wasn't cut out for this business. Some people didn't deserve being nice to.

Quietly Steve said, "You have no idea how old she is, Steph." He helped himself to another biscuit.

Now they were talking about her as if she weren't even in the room! Trying to control the rising anger in her voice, Nara said, "This is my aunt's bed and breakfast. I live here and help her while I am attending the university in Lincoln. She happens to be out this evening. Any other questions?"

She hoped she didn't sound too rude. Stephanie just stared at her, but Steve answered, "No. Of course not. My wife forgets her manners some times. I apologize."

Stephanie looked as if she were about to say something when the phone rang. It was Sue. Before Nara had a chance to tell her about the new guests, Sue told her that her plans had changed. "My friends and I are having such a good time; we decided to spend the night here. We've had a few drinks, and it wouldn't be wise to drive back, you know. We might get arrested." Sue giggled, very uncharacteristically. "I'm sure you can handle breakfast. You just have the one couple and they aren't too demanding." There was a pause, and Nara was sure she heard a man's voice in the background.

"We have two couples here now. Another couple arrived about an hour ago."

Sue's voice was distracted when she answered. "I'm sure you can handle it. See you in the morning, Nara." Sue rang off.

Nara concentrated on replacing the receiver softly, although all her instinct told her to slam it down. Aunt Sue was not with girl friends; she had a date, and now she was spending the night with him, leaving her here to take care of the guests, cook breakfast, and see to her father. At least she had a date tomorrow with Alex who was going to help her buy new running shoes. She would focus on that, the bright spot on her horizon. She wondered who Sue was with and why it was a secret. She definitely wasn't the type one would picture having an assignation in a hotel with some man. Maybe she was wrong, but all the signs pointed to it—the careful preparations, sexy outfit, the nervousness. Then there was the phone call, and that was a man's voice in the background. She was sure of it. Nara took a deep breath and went back into the dining room where Steve and Stephanie were just getting up from the table.

"We thought we would turn in now," Steve said. Stephanie looked chastised and said nothing. "What time is breakfast?"

"Anytime between 7:00 and 9:00," Nara answered. "Would you like the full English breakfast?"

"Oh, no," Stephanie said. "Toast and fruit will be fine."

Steve looked as if he might say something else, but then repeated, "Toast and fruit are fine."

Dennis Maxwell sat in his car just outside the Cathedral Yard, waiting for Joe, his assistant, to get off his shift as night watchman. He thought of the treasures in the Cathedral, but he didn't dare attempt a burglary there. Not yet. If he were caught he would go to prison, and Dennis was not having a good night. Besides his constant simmering anger at Elaine, and the encounter with the snooty woman at the tea shop, he was angry with Joe for bungling (and bungling badly) the burglaries in Springfield the night before. The first one at the church had yielded very little of any value. The second one, at the Gate House, had been foiled when that nosy young girl had heard something and come to investigate. *Too nosy for her own good, she is.* He could feel the anger rising in his throat; the anger he always felt against women who put themselves in his way.

He knew there were treasures in the Gate House. The former owner had shown him several items that he knew could bring in enough that he could retire for good, if he could only get inside and find them. There had been no estate sale. He had watched the papers carefully after the man had unfortunately died, and that hadn't been his fault, either. The man had simply slipped on the stairs. But then the place had been sold in its entirety to some inane woman who turned it into a bed and breakfast and then invited her whole family to come and live with her.

He tapped his fingers on the steering wheel and thought about lighting a cigarette. He liked to have a cigarette once in a while, but someone might notice the glow and it could call attention to him sitting there in the car. He wondered what he was doing here. All he had ever wanted was the money to sit back and relax, not have to work or worry about where the next car payment was coming from. There always seemed to be bills. He tried to blame Elaine, but the bills, at least, weren't really her fault. He had never allowed her to work, and she didn't spend much of the small amount he allowed her. He didn't really know why he hated Elaine so. Sometimes he felt like killing her, but then he wouldn't be able to hate her anymore.

He tried to blame his mother for the way his life had turned out. She had taught him since birth to feel guilty for whatever he did that displeased her. He still did. That was why he had married Elaine. She had chosen Elaine for him and told him it was time he married. It was time he produced children to carry on the family line. Elaine was subservient and grateful for any crumbs life might toss her way, and in spite of her education, she had never overcome her early brush with poverty. She believed she didn't deserve more than a few crumbs, and that, Dennis thought, was what he really hated about her. She believed that she didn't deserve more than him—and that meant he wasn't much.

Dennis was just about to light a cigarette anyway when there was a tap on the passenger side window. He looked up to see Joe's grinning face, his teeth shining in the moonlight. Dennis unlocked the door and Joe slid into the seat.

"Sorry I'm late," he said. "It took a little longer to lock up. The new night supervisor is picky. Double checks everything. New alarm system is good, too. It would take a professional to break into this place."

"Nobody's planning on breaking into this place." Dennis grumbled.

"Never said they was, boss. Never said they was," said Joe with a knowing smile.

Dennis started up the car and switched on his headlights. No point in being secretive now; he was just picking up his friend after his shift as a night watchman at the Cathedral. The dark shape loomed above them in the night. Dennis had always been in awe of the Cathedral. That was another thing his mother had instilled in him. The Cathedral dominated their lives, as it did the ancient town of Lincoln. The Cathedral sat squarely on the top of the hill, as it had for centuries. You could still see the trowel marks left by the medieval workers above the vaulting beneath the roof. From the balcony at the back of the Cathedral, one could see where the Gothic section had been added on to what was left of the original Norman structure and how the vaulting didn't match up.

When Dennis was just six years old, his father was appointed Dean of the Cathedral, the youngest man ever appointed to that position. Dennis and his mother went to the ceremony in which his father had been installed as Dean in the first major ceremony after the war. They sat proudly in the first row of seats, listening to the prayers, and hearing the inspiring words the father and husband spoke. When it was over, and all the honored guests had enjoyed a small reception in the Bishop's house, the new Dean told his wife that he wanted to spend a few moments alone and that she should go on home and take the boy. Dennis remembered that warm spring air that evening and his excitement as they crossed the cobblestones of the Cathedral Close to the Dean's residence. Dennis's mother told him that his father needed some time alone with God and that he would be along shortly. Dennis wanted to stay with his father, but knew better than to ask. Mother and son went home and she tucked him into bed.

Light was just beginning to illuminate the town and the Cathedral that towered above it, when there was a knock on the door of the new Dean's house. Six year old Dennis heard his mother moving about in the bedroom next to his. He tiptoed to his bedroom door and opened it silently, as he often did when he wanted to hear something not intended for the ears of small boys.

The Bishop himself stood at their front door, flanked by his wife and another man who had been at the ceremony the night before.

"Mrs. Maxwell, may we come in?" he asked.

Wordlessly she opened the door and let them pass. They moved to the small sitting room, and Dennis moved to the top of the staircase so hear could hear what was said. "Mrs. Maxwell. I am afraid there has been an accident. Your husband apparently slipped in the dark on one of our stone steps, worn as they are from centuries of footsteps. He hit his head on the stone flagging, and I am afraid he is dead, Mrs. Maxwell. I'm so sorry."

The Bishop's wife stepped forward and put her arm around Rose Maxwell, as the fear that could no longer be contained in her body emerged in one long frightening moan.

The Bishop's wife helped Rose to lower herself into a chair, while the Bishop himself found a bottle of sherry on the sideboard and poured a small glass for the suffering woman. He poured a second glass and swallowed it quickly. As he set the empty glass and picked up the full one for Mrs. Maxwell, his eyes met those of the small boy standing barefoot on the staircase.

His wife took the glass from her husband's hand and held it to Rose's lips. The younger woman took a sip and then spit it directly into the other woman's face.

"You're lying. You killed him! You know he is a better man than you and so you killed him." She looked at the Bishop as she spoke the words.

He blanched. Even at six years old, Dennis knew that his father was a better man than the Bishop, but he didn't look like a murderer. It was true that he smelled like whiskey whenever he bent his head close to the little boy's, and maybe his mother knew something that he didn't.

The Bishop's wife simply wiped the sherry from her face with a handkerchief and went on soothing Rose. "There now, my dear. This is a great shock. Is there someone we can call? Family members? I will stay until someone else arrives, and you can be sure we will take care of any arrangements for you. Your husband was a very good man."

Rose Maxwell held her head in her shaking hands. Her small son watched her as she lost consciousness and slumped against the Bishop's wife, and he knew his mother for a weak woman.

"Whatcha lookin' at, boss?" Joe asked. He had followed Dennis's gaze up at the buttresses of the Cathedral. "Fomenting a plan for the church ?"

Dennis returned his attention to Joe, who was lighting a cigarette with the car lighter. "What have you done with the goods from the Springfield church?"

"Safely stowed away, boss. Safely stowed away." He took a long drag on his cigarette.

Dennis hated the way Joe habitually repeated things when he answered questions. Why couldn't the man just say something once and be done with it?

"All right," Dennis answered. "Keep it hidden for now. I don't want to try to sell it yet. It's not a big enough heist."

"So what do we do next, boss? Another job planned?"

Dennis stopped at a stop light and turned to consider his companion. "We need to get into the Gate House. That's the treasure trove."

"That's what you keep saying, boss. But that's a touchy one. Very touchy. Police been called once so they're wary. And people seem to be up all times of the night. I've cased the place. Over and over. Upstairs light always seems to be on. Guests coming and going."

"Then figure out a way, damn it." Dennis was losing patience with the man, but he couldn't give him the sack. He knew too much. And he was good at what he did, when he did it.

Joe tossed his cigarette out the window, and the sparks flew behind them as Dennis accelerated from the light.

"I suppose I could pose as an inspector or something. A building inspector looking at the foundation."

"Too risky. They are nervous already. They would probably want to check your credentials, call the town office. Think of something else."

"What about the girl?"

"What girl?"

"The girl that lives there. The pretty one with the dark hair."

"What about her?"

"Use her somehow to get in?"

"If she's young and pretty she's not going to be interested in either of us," Dennis said flatly. He sighed. *Twenty years ago it would have been a great idea.*

"I don't mean that," Joe said. "I mean use her somehow. Pose as a tourist interested in old buildings. Get her to show you around."

"The foot work is your job, Joe."

"Not this time. You're the one with the education. You can play the history buff." Joe started to take out another cigarette, and popped a mint into his mouth instead. "The old lady is always on me for smoking too much." He said shaking his head. " Why don't you take the wife with you for a holiday."

"A holiday in Springfield? You're daft." Dennis exploded.

"Sure. Weekend getaway. Small town. Then you get interested in the place. What to see how it's built. It's perfect."

Dennis slowed the car to a stop in front of Joe's small council house. "Maybe. But it's risky. I don't like being seen. I'm not the front man."

Joe opened the car door. "You want the treasure trove, or whatever you call it, you have to take some risks, that's what I think." Joe glanced at the house. "The kitchen light is on. No sneaking in tonight. Talk to you in the morning boss."

He stepped out of the car and closed the door, leaving Dennis pondering. It was risky, and it would get Elaine involved, which might not be a bad thing. It might be a good foil. He would sleep on it.

TWELVE

Nara slept fitfully that night. Too much had happened the previous day, and Aunt Sue was not home. She hated to admit to herself that she was nervous being in the house tonight, even though two of the guest rooms were occupied. If the house contained something the thieves really wanted, they might rely on surprise. Who would expect them to return the very next night after the first attempted break-in? But it could have been just a random attempt—someone after easy things like a stereo, a coin collection, jewelry. There was no reason to think they were after anything specific. True, the house was full of antiques, but so were lots of houses.

Nara tossed and turned, running the possibilities over in her mind. When she tired of that train of thought, she went back to Aunt Sue. Was she really spending the night with girl friends? It just didn't fit. But nothing fit. Aunt Sue didn't seem the type to have an affair. And why be secretive about it? She was single. Maybe her lover was married. Nara laughed to herself as the ridiculous possibilities bounced in and out of her sleepless brain. She wondered if she should get up and make a cup of tea and remembered that that was how she had discovered the burglars last night.

She turned her thoughts to Alex, the brightest spot in her day and thought of her lunch date the following day—today, actually. It was already past midnight. She really needed to get some sleep or she would look haggard in the morning. And she had to be up to cook breakfast for the guests. She decided to run down quickly to the kitchen and make herself a cup of peppermint tea. That was supposed to be relaxing. And if she had any more sleepless nights, she would bring an electric kettle and tea things up to her room, so she could make her own.

She wrapped her robe around herself and slipped her feet into the fuzzy slippers. She tiptoed soundlessly down the stairs and into the kitchen, where she saw a car passing on the road. It slowed to a crawl when it reached the house and then sped up when it had passed. *It might be a police car,* Nara thought. *I can't tell without my contact lenses.* She put it firmly out of her mind, concentrating on the tea and relaxing. She thought past the drudgery of cooking breakfast and making small talk with guests, to lunch and shopping for running shoes with Alex. She finished her tea in her darkened bedroom, snuggled back down under the covers and was asleep.

Several miles away in her hotel room in Lincoln, Sue Blanchard awoke early as well, earlier than she had expected to. Stan still slept peacefully beside her, the sheet covering him only as far as his chest. She watched his chest rise and fall with his breath, noticing the dark blond hairs scattered across his chest. He was still slim and muscular for a man of nearly fifty. She knew he worked out at the gym regularly. She wanted to reach out and touch the fine hairs and the smooth flesh beneath them, but did not want to wake him.

She still found it difficult to believe that a man as attractive as Stanley Foster could be attracted to someone like her. True, she was several years younger than he was, but her hair was graying, and she had not found time to color it, and she was at least a couple of stone overweight. Maybe she should start going to the gym. She suddenly felt the urge to go to the bathroom and slid quietly out of the bed and walked naked to the bathroom. She giggled to herself as she passed the mirror. She knew she needed to lose weight, but still it was thrilling to walk around a hotel room naked. She used the toilet, came back out into the room, and picked up her watch where she had left it on the dresser. It was 6:00. Nara would be getting up, seeing what her father wanted for breakfast, and then starting things for the guests. She didn't feel guilty leaving Nara with the work. It would be good experience for the girl.

Sue looked toward the bed and realized that Stan had his eyes open and was watching her standing there naked looking at her watch. He chuckled softly. He had thrown back the sheet, so his entire body was visible. He held out his hand to her, and Sue felt desire flood through her, wiping out all thoughts of breakfast, work, and guilt feelings. She slid into the bed next to him, catching her breath and closing her eyes as he ran his hands up across her rib cage, then cupping her breasts.

"You are perfect, Sue," he whispered. "I saw you looking in the mirror, and I don't want you to change a thing about yourself." She ran her hands down his back and he shuddered.

"I could stay here forever," he whispered.

"Then stay," she answered.

He raised his head and looked at her, a bemused expression on his face. "Might be a little inconvenient, don't you think?"

"I mean, you could divorce your wife." The words were out before she could think about them. "Lots of people get divorced. My ex-husband divorced me."

"He was a fool," Stan answered.

"But I would never have found you if I had still been married."

"Sure you would have," he answered, smoothing her short hair with his long fingers. "We live just down the street from each other."

"But I wouldn't have really found you." She struggled to make her meaning clear, even to herself. "If I had been married I would not have spent the night with you."

"Why not?" He grinned as he looked down into her eyes. "Do you have so much reverence for the institution of marriage? It doesn't seem to bother you that I am married."

"No, but that's different." Somehow Sue felt lost. She wished she had never started this conversation.

"How is it different?" He continued to smile at her and play with her hair, while at the same time he began to move his lower body.

"It's different for a woman," she said lamely.

"Ah, that must be it," he mumbled as he diverted her once again with lovemaking.

THIRTEEN

Alex awoke feeling that something exciting and out of the ordinary was going to happen that day, but he couldn't quite remember what it was. Then it came to him. He was meeting a delightful young woman—Nara, was that her name?—for lunch and to help her choose some decent running shoes. He threw back the covers and headed for the shower. He had some calls to make this morning. The items that had been stolen from the Springfield church were of relatively little value as far as antiques were concerned, but it was a devastating loss for a small parish.

In order to preserve their British heritage, these small country churches must be preserved. Even the smallest and most insignificant held historical treasures, even if they were only treasures to the parishioners and townspeople. Alex wasn't much of a churchgoer anymore, but he had been brought up in the Church of England and appreciated its long history, even before Henry VIII, when it had become the Church of England after the break with Rome over his divorce from Katherine of Aragon and subsequent marriage to Anne Boleyn.

Alex thought over all this while he showered; it was what kept him interested in his job—the feeling of helping to preserve history. He detested the thought that some people were so unscrupulous and greedy that they would steal precious historical artifacts for their own personal gain, usually just to pass the artifacts on to someone else, and they would eventually end up in the mansions of the wealthy all over the world.

He dried himself briskly with a towel and dressed in jeans and a sweater. He could do most of his work at home today, maybe with a stop by the police station. He enjoyed these casual days when he didn't have to go in to the city. He started coffee and decided to call the police station just to see if there was any news. He poured the boiling water into the French press, inhaling the coffee aroma as it rose from the pot. He still enjoyed a cup of tea in the afternoon, but there was nothing like a good cup of coffee to get the brain working in the morning. *Thank God you can finally find decent coffee in this country.*

The duty officer answered and put him through immediately to Sgt. Loring. "I have some interesting news, Alex, not that it surprises me."

"Nothing surprises you," Alex answered, chuckling. It amused him the way the officer always claimed his lack of surprise at any development in a case.

"This surprised me less than a lot of things." He paused, seemed to be talking to someone in his office, came back to the phone, and cleared his throat.

"The footprints outside the Gate House and those at the church are the same. Exact match. Size 43 work boots. Cheap, but new. Nice crisp prints so we even have the brand. And small for a man. It's not much, but we know it's the same person. Question is now, will he try again?"

Alex hung up the phone and made himself some toast, while he thought about the latest development. He still didn't think the burglaries were the work of a professional. There was a clumsiness about the attempt at the Gate House especially. He booted up his laptop to check his e-mail. There was a message regarding some documents from the American National Archives that had turned up missing and for British experts to be aware if anything suspicious turned up. Another asking if he would come take a look at some items that had been found in a stall at the Greenwich Market. There was some evidence that they might have come from Lincolnshire.

It looked like he would have to go into the city tomorrow. That was fine. He rather enjoyed the train ride, especially since he didn't have to do it every day. There was nothing he could do about the Springfield burglaries at the moment.

FOURTEEN

Elaine awoke with a headache and with Dennis snoring peacefully beside her. She had not heard him come in the night before, but she knew it had been well after midnight. She assumed he spent his evening out drinking in a pub somewhere. He usually came home smelling of liquor and tobacco smoke, although he didn't smoke. Once he had come in with his shoes and trousers covered with mud, but when she had asked him about it, she had been given a black eye for her trouble. Now she just kept quiet and hoped to get dressed and out of the house before he awoke. It was a lovely sunny day, rare this time of year, and it would be a lovely morning for a tour around the Roman ruins of the town. Tourists were always surprised at the extent of Roman buildings and fortifications in the town, and Elaine loved explaining the history, as it blended in with later buildings.

She was surprised to find a note from Dennis on the kitchen table, telling her to be home early and to pack an overnight bag. They were going away for the night. He had some business in the small town of Springfield, and he thought she might like to come along. Someone had told him about a guest house there that sounded interesting. Elaine was surprised that he would invite her on such an outing, and truthfully didn't relish spending time in close proximity with her husband. But if he had business there...

What business could he have there? Better not to ask any questions and just go along, as she always did. Dennis did these things every once in a while, and if she questioned his motives, he called her unappreciative. She might meet some interesting people and learn some more history of the area.

Elaine finished her coffee and slipped quietly out the door, after scrawling a reply to Dennis's note. She would be home early and ready to go.

Down the hill in Lincoln, Micki Fleming was feeding her children breakfast. She was dressed in her usual morning uniform of jeans, a sweatshirt and floppy slippers. Her dark blonde hair was pulled back in a ponytail. Makeup, even lipstick, would have to wait until later in the day, if at all. Nevertheless, her husband David gazed at her rapturously as he sipped his morning tea. Micki had always been a mystery to him. That was why he had married her.

David had fallen in love with Micki when she had walked into his English class during his last year of school. He was dreading his last year of school, anxious to be out and helping his dad run the guest house. Although truth be told he was more interested in the business end of the guest house, thinking up ways to make more money and keeping the old building in repair, than he was in greeting guests. Both his parents were good at making small talk with their guests and always learned a little bit about them. There were the visitors from America, always friendly, often searching for ancestral roots. There were families from other parts of the UK and Ireland, visiting Lincoln on a holiday. Occasionally there were guests who were in town on business. Mr. and Mr. Fleming spoke to them all, made them feel welcome and served them their eggs just the way they liked them in the morning.

Micki had walked into their English class with the same open smile she gave everyone. She had blue eyes and dark blonde hair that fell straight to her shoulders, with bangs that she pushed to the side with her hand, the only indication that she felt anything other than sure of herself. After she handed her admission slip to the teacher, she sat down next to David, inadvertently knocking his pencil to the floor. It rolled under her chair, and she reached to pick it up. "Sorry," she said with a smile that went right through him.

Micki turned out to be much better in English class than David, and they spent the year doing homework together at one or the other of their kitchen tables. Both sets of parents expected studies to be taken seriously, even if neither of them had plans for university. David had neither the desire nor the will, and Micki's family had no money.

At the end of the year they announced that they wanted to get married. "Wait a year. You are too young," was the advice from both families.

They waited, planning a June wedding. Two weeks before the wedding, Micki found out that she was pregnant and went through the ceremony and reception with a queasy stomach, unable to eat even a bite a wedding cake. Their honeymoon was a weekend in Skegness, a resort not far away on the North Sea, after which the couple came home to share a two room suite on the top floor of the guest house. It was the "Royal Suite," according to David's father, reserved for special guests, although those sorts of people usually stayed at the Grand Hotel, not a humble guest house.

As soon as the morning sickness and sleepiness of early pregnancy had subsided, Micki threw herself wholeheartedly into contributing to the daily work of the guest house. She was a good cook and served the guests with a smile. Occasionally she would make homemade scones or Scottish oatcakes as a treat. For her part, Micki adored David. She had grown up in a solid middle class, loving family. Her brother, two years younger than her, had gone on to university and was now attending law school.

Her parents were both teachers; her father taught history in the local high school and her mother taught kindergarten. They were a few years away from retirement now and looking forward to spending more time exploring antique shops in out of the way hamlets. Their hobby had become more expensive over the years, but that only made it more challenging and fun for them. They would occasionally come home with a real treasure, and after enjoying the items for a while, they often sold them, making a nice profit.

This morning Micki had awakened with her new friend Nara on her mind and had been discussing her with David as she fed the children and sipped her own tea.

"I think she's very brave, driving up here from Springfield for university classes, caring for her father, helping her aunt run their bed and breakfast. She has a lot on her plate. I know I couldn't do it."

David smiled as he took another bit of toast and jam. "Micki you do even more, balancing the running of the guest house, cooking breakfast every morning, caring for our family, and taking university courses. You don't see what you do every day as anything special." He said. "Why don't you invite her over after class one day? She might like to see our guest house."

"You think she would?" Micki paused momentarily. Diana, the baby, reached up a sticky hand and her mother reached down to kiss it.

"I'm sure she would. You two can talk about your classes, and she may get some ideas for her bed and breakfast. After all, our guest house has been in existence for thirty years. We know what works. She might appreciate it."

"Good idea." She walked around the table to give David a hug and a kiss on the cheek. "That's why I love you. You always come up with the best solutions to problems I could never figure out."

They could hear the first guests coming into the dining room for breakfast, and David moved to get up. "No. No. Finish your toast and tea," Micki said, her hands firmly on his shoulders. "I'll take their orders and then you can help me cook."

Micki was out the door her cheerful voice greeting the guests. "Good morning. Did you sleep well? Would you like coffee or tea? And will you have the full English breakfast?"

A moment later she was back in the kitchen, all business. "They would like coffee and just scrambled eggs on toast with bacon."

"I'll start cooking and you bring them coffee." David was at the stove cracking eggs before his wife could disagree.

In London, Terry Clark was already having a bad day. She had customers in the Middle East, several time zones ahead of London, who were anxious to acquire British antiques. There was always that unspoken and often unrecognized admiration for British culture, or the height of England as it once was, however they might disagree with British politics in the present. It was quite incongruous to think of a stained glass window from a small parish church in Lincolnshire in the home of a government official in Uzbekistan, but there it was. Her firm shipped pieces all over the world, and they didn't look too carefully at the means by which they acquired the pieces. They had "subsidiaries" all over the world, too. Usually legitimate import/export firms where a trusted employee shipped stolen goods in and out of the country quickly. One of their best was in St. Clare in the Caribbean.

Terry had arrived back in London later than expected the night before. The meeting with "the little man" in Lincoln had been less than productive. She couldn't help calling him "the little man" to herself. He impressed her as mean-spirited, not too bright, and chauvinistic. But he could be useful. He obviously had the means to obtain some valuable pieces in Lincolnshire. And he knew who she was. If she had known how worthless he was she would have sent someone else, or been more circumspect. She couldn't afford to make an enemy of someone like that, at least not yet.

She had slept later than she should have—the rain always did that, and she was out of coffee. There had been no time to go shopping all week. She had been forced to stop at one of the American style coffee shops that were springing up all over London. Now she sat at her desk, sipping the steaming liquid from the paper cup, and trying to figure out what to tell her boss about her meeting in Lincoln yesterday.

She opened her e-mail and skimmed the messages while she thought about Lincoln. There was a message from Michael Carrington in St. Clare. She opened it; he was one of their best "subsidiaries." The message was brief: I have a customer looking for a stained glass window for the new house he is building here on the island. He wants authentic and old. Do you know of anything? He is willing to pay any price.

Terry knew the type—new money and more of it than they knew what to do with. Likely as not he had made his fortune in off-shore banking, gambling, or the drug trade. The sources were vague enough that the government of a small island nation didn't look into the details too closely, and officials could always be bribed.

The request for a stained glass window solved another problem, too. "The little man" in Lincoln had mentioned a stained glass window that might be available soon. This would justify her trip to Lincoln. Terry took another sip of coffee and then checked her lipstick in her pocket mirror before going in to meet her boss.

Mr. Hadley barely looked up when Terry came into his office. He motioned for her to sit down. He was on the phone, and the person on the other end seemed to be doing all the talking. He mumbled words of agreement now and then and nodded his head vigorously as if the person on the other end could see his total agreement. "All right. Tomorrow then." And he hung up the phone. He jotted a few notes on a small piece of paper which he slipped into his desk drawer, then turned his attention to Terry.

"How was Lincoln?"

"There are possibilities. The contact there is a weasely little man. Not too bright. I'm sure I can handle him. He has a few pieces that may be worth something and there is a possibility of a stained glass window. Michael in St. Clare e-mailed me this morning that he has a client looking for one."

"We have to be careful with the stained glass. They are easily traced."

"I know. I will be. I haven't seen it yet but it's worth looking at." Terry looked out the window for a moment at the crowds on Regent Street. "I have to tell you the guy makes me uneasy." Mr. Hadley looked up sharply. "I mean I can handle him," Terry answered quickly, "but he impresses me as the kind who will make mistakes. As I said, he's not too bright."

Mr. Hadley nodded quickly as if he suddenly clearly understood the situation. "I'll have someone check him out." He picked up the phone and quickly dialed an outside number. "Geoff. I have a job for you." He paused only for a few seconds. "Right." He hung up.

"See what St. Clare wants, and be ready to go back to Lincolnshire." Mr. Hadley turned to his computer, signaling that the meeting was over.

"Yes, sir," Terry replied and quickly left the room.

In Lincoln, Joe awoke feeling good. He had convinced his wife to stay in bed for an extra half hour before she left for her job as a waitress in the tea shop down the hill, The Steep Hill, it was called. An easy walk down, a hard walk up at the end of the day when a body was tired, she always said.

Joe finally roused himself out of bed when he could hear the kettle boiling and showered quickly. Dennis was taking his wife to Springfield today for their supposed getaway and to give him a chance to see inside the Gate House. It was what they needed, an inside look, but it would mean that Dennis would be known to the residents of the house. That made Joe's role even more important, and it had been his idea for Dennis and Elaine to spend the night there. That meant he was an idea man as well as Dennis.

He wasn't in this just to do Dennis's dirty work. It put them on an equal footing. He didn't have to wait for Dennis's instructions; he could take the initiative as well. Joe thought all this over as he drank his morning tea in the kitchen. He was hungry this morning. Thinking made him hungry. Angie never had time to cook him a proper breakfast, so he would go out, maybe down to the shop where she worked, and he wouldn't have to pay full price. He had a couple of errands to run this morning. He needed to make sure the goods from the church were safely stowed in a rarely used storage room at the Cathedral. And one of the day guards owed him a few quid. After that—he had a plan.

He was going to Springfield to do his own surveillance of the Gate House.

Two hours later and with a full stomach, Joe was on his way to Springfield. The day was sunny and clear, unusual for September, with only a slight chill in the air. The countryside was turning brown, and the church steeples in the villages stood out in sharp contrast against the sky. Joe had grown up on the fens, back when a small farmer could make a living. He remembered catching eels with his pa and grandpa. Most of the old farmers were gone now. Joe's pa's farm had been bought by one of the large flower bulb companies. Not that Joe himself had any interest in farming, but it suited him to think that something had been taken away from him, that it was the big company's fault that he had to make his living as a guard at the Cathedral.

The money his father had received had been spent long ago when both Joe's parents were alive. They had ended their days on the dole. When Joe and Dennis made their big haul from the Gate House it would all be put right. Never mind that the owners of the Gate House had nothing to do with the bulb company that had bought his father's farm. They were all the same. There were the people who owned and the people who owned nothing, but had their rights.

Joe did not drive by the Gate House when he came into the town of Springfield. He turned off a short distance before he reached it, down a side road that led across the river and into an area of warehouses and storage buildings for the bulb companies. Joe had an idea. He was going to park the car out of sight, walk through the grassy area near the river, and up to the back of the Gate House. He had a hunch that what he was looking for might be better seen from the back, and he would be less obvious there. He could hide in the tall grass and study the house, take all the time he needed, and in broad daylight. The paths in that area were overgrown with weeds. They were rarely used except by dedicated bird watchers, and they were usually there on weekends, early in the morning. Joe used to go fishing there years ago with his father and had been there alone just a year ago. Some of the land was privately owned, and there was a small area that was set aside as a nature preserve. It would be easy enough to do, and Dennis would be impressed with his cleverness.

Joe parked the car down a narrow lane leading into the fields, pulling it off to the side as far as possible. He locked the car and climbed nimbly over a gate, and then pushed the weeds to one side to reveal the remnants of a path leading toward the river. The Gate House lay just across the river, beyond the old railway bed.

Joe pushed his way determinedly through the tall grass, which swished as he made his way. He stepped carefully to avoid getting his feet tangled in the tall grasses. The swishing of the grass and the gentle fall breeze deadened any other sound, and he did not hear the movement behind him, as the dogs barreled through the grass. They were upon him in an instant. One had jumped on his back and knocked him over, but he had fallen sideways, and the other now had its front paws and the weight of its body on his chest, breathing its foul breath into his face. The dog that had knocked him down, large and black like the one sitting on his chest, circled around, growling.

There was a whistle in the distance, and Joe fleetingly hoped that the owner of the beasts was calling them back and not interested in what or whom they had chased down. The circling dog ran back the direction from which he had come, but the other remained on Joe's chest, growling and baring his yellow teeth. If Joe had been familiar with Sherlock Holmes he would have thought of *The Hound of the Baskervilles*, but such literary references were beyond him in any circumstances.

He heard footsteps approaching; human footsteps and a human voice, and could only think that whoever it was would call off the dogs or at least distract them. The shock was wearing off, and he was beginning to think of what he might say to explain his presence there. He couldn't say he was fishing; he had no fishing equipment with him. He had lost something. That was it. He had lost something by the river when he was here fishing the day before, and had come back to look for it.

Joe was thinking he might say that he had lost his watch, the watch given to him by his father, and was creating a believable story to tell whoever it was that was approaching. He heard a sharp whistle and the dog that was standing on his chest released him and ran to the sound of the whistle. Joe struggled to a sitting position, gasping for breath. The ground was wet and he could feel the muddy water that had seeped into the back of his shirt and pants. It felt cold now that the air could reach it. He wondered briefly if he ought to run while he had the chance, before the man reached him, but he knew he wouldn't make it. He couldn't run fast in this tall grass, and the dogs would be on him in an instant. Better to take his chances.

He was on his feet by the time the other man came through the grass. He was a big man, tall and heavily built, and with a most unpleasant look on his face. "Best come along with me back to the boss to explain what you've been doing here. This is private property."

Joe hesitated, and the man said, "You can come on your own or I can move you along a little bit. That bit is up to you."

Joe had no intention of finding out how the big man would "move him along," so he walked along the path. When they reached the road where Joe had parked his car, the other man motioned that he should continue down the road. A small wooden sign labeled it as Crystal Bulbs, Ltd., Private Property. In a few minutes they drew in sight of a warehouse with a sign above a single door stating "Office." Joe's escort indicated that they should go inside, and Joe complied.

Inside a man in work clothes, only slightly smaller in build, sat working at a computer.

"The dogs found us another trespasser."

The man at the computer looked up, and Joe could see the family resemblance—large dark brown eyes, full mouths, strong jaws. The two were brothers, probably.

"Good work, Gary," the man at the computer replied. "You can go on and feed the dogs now. Take a break yourself." His eyes shifted to Joe for just an instant. "I'll call you if I need you."

"Have a seat," he said to Joe, and Joe sat obediently on a metal folding chair next to the desk. "I would offer you some tea, but the maid's gone out." Joe did not miss the sarcasm in the man's voice.

The man studied Joe for a moment, and then spoke quickly. "What were you doing on my property?"

"I lost my watch here yesterday, when I was fishing. I came back to look for it."

The man continued to study Joe's face, then spoke. "I know where I've seen you. You're the bloke with the paint truck that was parked in the restaurant car park last week. You had engine trouble and one of my men helped you out. Yes," he repeated thoughtfully, "I've seen you around here."

"Now," he pushed his chair out so he sat facing Joe directly. "What were you really doing here?"

"I told you. I lost my watch. Somewhere in the weeds yesterday. It was my father's watch and I felt terrible when I realized it was missing." Joe was sweating and stumbling over his words, but he couldn't seem to stop, even though he knew he wasn't making any sense. "We used to come here fishing together when I was a boy, but he died five years ago. Heart attack. Gone just like that."

The man looked at him steadily, showing no reaction. "So why didn't you come back yesterday, as soon as you realized the watch was missing?"

Joe's eyes showed his panic before he thought of his next lie. "My wife. She wouldn't let me. She wanted me home last night. You know how they are." Joe tried to smile but it felt and looked more like a grimace.

The man stood up and paced to the windows, then turned around to face Joe. "You're a liar." Then he struck Joe's face hard with the palm of his hand. Joe fell onto the floor, writhing in pain. His hands went up to his face and head, giving the man the opportunity to kick him in the stomach with his work boot. As Joe moaned and curled up in a ball, helpless with pain, the man walked to the inner door, opened it and said, "Gary."

Instantly the dogs bounded through the door, and jumped on Joe, sniffing, putting their paws on him. Joe screamed in fear.

The man who had hit and kicked him handed a small revolver to Gary out of Joe's line of sight. "Get rid of him."

Gary picked up Joe as if he were a doll, and then pushed him in front of him through the warehouse door. Joe caught fleeting glimpses of an antique mantel, a stained glass window, and several paintings being unloaded from a lorry. He saw them but his mind didn't absorb what he was seeing. He was consumed with fear, and the dogs kept pace as Gary continued to shove him forward to the other end of the building.

They reached the far door and he had a surge of hope that he might just be released. He might just be able to walk out the door and leave. He heard the sneering voice behind him. "Go ahead. Open the door." He tried but the door seemed to be stuck. He pulled again and never knew that Gary had taken aim with the revolver as the bullet slammed into back of his head.

•

FIFTEEN

Aunt Sue had arrived home around 10:00, uncommunicative and out of sorts. She said she would take care of the morning cleaning and tidying up, and sent Nara off to get ready for her date.

Nara tried on several pairs of pants and several different sweaters before settling on her beige khaki pants and a navy blue turtleneck. *Not too dressy.* They were just going to have lunch and buy shoes. She had only seen the guy in his running clothes, but he seemed the classy type. She brushed her hair, pulling it back in a ponytail with her hands to see the effect. *Should I let my hair grow out or get it cut again?* It would be better to get it cut, or she would look like a teenager again. She brushed it back around her face; no time for a new hairstyle right now. She had thought about walking into town, but that would take time, and she would be windblown and disheveled when she arrived. *Better drive.*

She thought of Davis and wondered if their relationship really was over. Was it fate that she hadn't been home last night when he had called? Did they really have a future? Had they ever?

Nara shook herself out of her reverie. She was here now, in England. It wasn't bad, now that she was getting used to wearing sweaters every day. Her body was adjusting to the climate. She was meeting people. She was having lunch with a handsome, interesting man today, and she had met Micki yesterday. She smiled when she thought of Micki. She seemed so capable and caring, and so in love with her husband. She took on the care of her family and her work with a smile and still had time to take classes and have tea with a new friend.

"I need to quit complaining," Nara said out loud to herself in the mirror. She studied her reflection. She was small and slim, olive skin, big dark eyes, dark hair, full lips. *Not so bad.* She still wasn't used to seeing herself in pants and a heavy sweater. In St. Clare she had always worn sundresses and sandals. It had practically been her uniform. *New climate, new clothes, new life,* she thought. *I might as well get used to it.*

She stopped in to kiss her father goodbye before she left. He said he felt fine, but was going to rest this morning as he had overdone it a little bit the day before puttering around in the garden. Nara pushed her worries about him aside and went downstairs.

Sue was not around. *She must be cleaning the guest rooms,* Nara thought. She heard a cell phone ring somewhere in the house but it stopped after one ring. She grabbed the keys off the shelf by the door and let herself out quietly.

Alex waited for Nara in front of the shoe store on Main Street. It was Tuesday, so the market was in progress. Vendors sold everything from fruits and vegetables to tee shirts, the latest CDs, and a few souvenirs for the tourists. There were even a couple of stalls with some antique household items for sale. Alex looked them over as he waited, but there was nothing of real value. And definitely nothing that was on the "stolen" list. He paced nervously around the market area, keeping his eye on the shoe store for Nara. He felt uncharacteristically self-conscious, as if everyone could tell that he was meeting someone, and that he felt like a school boy when he thought of seeing her running the night before. He could still see those slim, muscular legs, the brown hair swinging, and her feet in those awful shoes.

He had almost finished his second circuit of the market stalls and was beginning to feel conspicuous when he saw her. She was walking briskly up to the front of the shoe store, so Alex walked quickly across the square to meet her, bumping into a couple of women who were chatting as they carried their purchases.

"I'm sorry," he said, looking over at Nara. She was looking over at him now with a smile and a wave. He returned the smile with a wide grin that lit up his face. A few strides brought him to her side. "You're here," he said.

"You're here, too," she answered, and they both laughed.

"There's a nice little restaurant around the corner," Alex said, not taking his eyes off Nara's face.

She smiled. "Let's go. I'm hungry."

"Me, too," he mumbled, although hunger was the farthest thing from his mind at the moment.

A small gray haired woman said, "Excuse me," and Alex realized they were blocking the doorway of the shoe store. Before he could move she said, "Oh, hello," and he recognized her as one of the ladies from the Springfield church.

"I suppose it's too soon to have any news about the thefts from the church? I've been so worried that our precious treasures might be sold out of the country before they are recovered. Do you think there is a chance of that?" All the while she spoke, he noticed that she was glancing at Nara with more than a little interest. There was no doubt that this encounter would be the subject of tea time gossip at the church gift shop. *That investigator was with a pretty young woman in town today...*

"It's too soon," he replied self-consciously. "But we are doing everything we can." *The stock phrase*, he thought. "It's very unlikely that the items will leave the country soon. The thieves usually like to put the goods in storage for a while after a theft. Let things calm down, so the police aren't looking so hard. Right now that theft is my priority." Alex wished he could think of the woman's name. "We have the word out, and if anything that sounds like the items from the Springfield church turns up anywhere in Britain, we will hear about it."

The woman's face relaxed a little and she turned her attention to Nara again. "I don't think we have met," she said, extending her hand. "I'm Nora Dorkins. I work in the church gift shop, and saw your young man there yesterday."

Alex glanced sideways and noticed that Nara's face was flushed. She shook the woman's large, rough hand shyly. "I'm Nara Blake. I live at the Gate House bed and breakfast. My aunt, Sue Blanchard, runs it and I help her out. Our place was almost broken into that same night."

Mrs. Dorkins' eyes widened. "Almost?" she asked eagerly, clearly relishing the opportunity for even more news to spread about. "But they didn't get in?"

"No," Nara replied. "I had come downstairs for a cup of tea and surprised them. They were just opening the window."

Mrs. Dorkins looked up at Alex. "She could have been hurt, you know. I know it isn't your job until antiquities are involved, but the police need to take this very seriously. You don't suppose it could have been the same people?"

"That's very difficult to say at this point," Alex answered, thinking it best to keep this information under wraps for the moment. "But we really must be on our way now—we're running late for lunch."

Mrs. Dorkins said goodbye and dashed off across the river toward the church; a bit too quickly for Alex's liking. But by this time, he was quite hungry. That bagel had been a long time ago.

Alex and Nara walked over to the restaurant with hardly a word and stepped inside. The place was crowded with lunch time customers, but they saw a table for two by the window that was just being cleared.

"Shall we treat ourselves to fish and chips?" he asked. "They are quite good here."

"That's not really the kind of food runners should be eating, is it?" Nara asked teasingly.

"This is a special occasion," he smiled into her eyes.

Nara caught her breath and answered, "I had a salad yesterday, so I guess I can splurge today."

The waitress came and Alex ordered fish and chips for two, then turned his attention back to Nara. "I'm rather surprised you agreed to have lunch with me, after scaring the life out of you yesterday."

"It wasn't your fault. You're right about the shoes. I just felt like running and that was all I had."

"Have you run before?" he asked, as he took the first sip of the tea the waitress had just set in front of him.

"Not seriously, like you."

He laughed. "I hardly call myself a serious runner."

"But you're more serious than I am. I used to run on the beach barefoot, just for the sheer joy of it." Nara stirred sugar into her tea as she talked.

"On the beach! Where?"

"In St. Clare. That's where I grew up. Where I lived until a month ago."

"I thought I detected something different in your accent. It's definitely not Lincolnshire. But Britain has become such a polyglot of nationalities it isn't always easy to say where someone is from. Not that it matters. We are all human beings as far as I'm concerned."

Nara smiled, "And you? Have you always lived in Springfield?"

"Oh, no. I grew up in Sussex. Spent some time in London. I moved here a few years ago with my wife. Ex-wife now."

"And your work has something to do with stolen antiquities?"

So she didn't miss that bit of information that Mrs. Dorkins had dropped into the conversation on the street, he thought. For some reason he had hoped Nara would not pick up on that, so naturally she did. Before he could answer, however, the waitress arrived with their meal. They tucked into the hot fish, and Alex watched with amusement as Nara sprinkled malt vinegar liberally over her chips. That was a taste he had never acquired, although he had grown up with fish and chips.

After swallowing a few mouthfuls, she continued the conversation. "So do you work for the police?"

"No. It would be more accurate to say I work *with* the police. I work for the V&A Museum. I help the police identify and evaluate stolen artifacts. Some are worth more than others, either monetarily or for their historical value. That helps the police put a priority on what they are looking for."

Nara sipped her tea thoughtfully. "And do you only work in Lincolnshire?"

"Primarily, but I have an office in London and occasionally travel to other parts of Britain for an investigation or to help out if a cache of goods is discovered."

"So was the theft at the church a serious one?"

"From an historical standpoint, yes. The most valuable pieces in the church were taken and a stained glass window."

"A stained glass window?" Nara put down her food and looked at him. "They stole a window?"

"Yes, it happens more frequently than you might think. They are very valuable and rare. But also easy to identify if they are found."

"*If* they are found?"

Alex sighed. "Many of the pieces leave the country. They are purchased by wealthy foreign collectors around the world, end up in private collections, and disappear from sight. That's why we have to act quickly if we want to recover the items."

"I knew wealthy people in St. Clare with beautiful antique pieces in their homes and offices. I wonder if they were stolen?" Nara mused.

"It's hard to say," Alex answered. "Many of them are purchased legally. All we can do here is try to stop what we can." He pushed his plate aside and signaled to the waitress for more tea.

"Now you know what I do. What about you? What brought you to Springfield from St. Clare?"

He listened quietly while Nara told him about her father's cancer treatments, keeping his eyes fixed on her face, only sipping tea now and then. When she finished he covered her hand with his and said, "Maybe new running shoes will be just the thing to help you feel better. I started running after my wife left, and there is nothing like exercise to clear the mind."

"Do you miss your wife?" she asked.

That wasn't a question Alex expected. "Occasionally. I think about little things she did. Little habits. But we weren't right for each other. She's happier where she is now, and I'm more satisfied, too."

"But not happier?"

This girl really digs to the heart of the matter, he thought. "I guess happiness is an elusive quality. I prefer satisfaction."

Nara seemed to think about that for a few moments, her eyes soft and distant. "Let's go buy shoes," she said with a smile as she stood up.

SIXTEEN

On a narrow road leading southeast out of Springfield, two cars lumbered along. Gary was driving the dead man's car in the lead, and the body was slumped over in the back seat of the car, out of sight. The dead man's cell phone had been ringing off and on for the last 15 minutes, which Gary found very disconcerting. It was almost as if he expected the man to wake up and answer it. Gary didn't mind transporting stolen goods, but getting rid of dead bodies was not what he had signed on for.

As last they reached a spot where trees lined the river, and a small dirt road led down to its banks. The other car pulled ahead, then motioned to Gary to drive his car off the road. The lane led to a small fishing spot, used by the few eel fishers left in the county. Gary turned off the main road and stopped; his boss was running towards him.

"Quickly now. This road doesn't get much traffic but I'm not taking any chances."

"His cell phone keeps ringing," Gary grumbled.

"Well, get it then. They can be used to track locations."

He started to get out of the car, but his boss stopped him. "No time. I'll get it." He opened the rear door and pulled the phone off Joe's belt loop. "We'll dispose of this somewhere else. The police will find him sooner or later, but later will be better. And there will be nothing to connect him with us." He gave the dead man's vehicle one last scrutiny, making sure that the plates and registration were removed from the car. The police would be able to trace it eventually, but this way it would take a little longer—long enough for "business as usual" to return to Crystal Bulbs, Ltd.

He told Gary to drive the car close to the bank, then the two men pushed the car into the river together. It wasn't very deep there, but deep enough that the roof would lie concealed just below the surface. With the windows rolled down, it sank quickly.

"There. Let's get out of here." The two men returned quickly to the other car and drove away. Two minutes later a lorry drove slowly down the road with a load of fertilizer. The driver passed the fishing spot without so much as a glance.

Dennis was irritated that he couldn't raise Joe on his cell phone. Not that he really needed to talk to him now, but he just wanted to tell him that he and Elaine were almost ready to leave for Springfield; he had reserved a room at the Gate House bed and breakfast. He wanted to be sure Joe wasn't going to be skulking around the place while he was there. He thought the man had enough sense not to do something like that, but Dennis liked to be sure. He was taking no chances and didn't trust anyone but himself. He didn't think Joe was working at the Cathedral today; he supposed he might have left the cell phone at home, or turned it off.

Elaine was ready to go, dressed casually, and with an expectant look on her face. He supposed he would have to play the game. It would be worth it—there was a lot at stake. He needed Elaine to believe that this really was a little vacation. He would go off by himself for a couple of hours later this afternoon, so she would think he had some kind of business there. That would give him a chance to calm his nerves. Besides, they had done things like this before when he had to get away and couldn't risk going by himself. If she was suspicious about anything, she never said a word. She wouldn't risk his anger.

Dennis said little to Elaine on the drive over, and when he did speak it was as though he was making a supreme effort to be amiable, keeping his voice even and resisting the critical comments that usually sprang so easily to his lips.

Elaine enjoyed looking at the countryside as they drove. The small quiet towns with their ancient church spires, the endless sweep of the fens, now transformed into agricultural land. She regretted she was seeing it now, in the fall, when everything was brown. This area was so close, why didn't they ever come here in the spring, when the tulips were blooming? She would have to make a point of it next year.

They arrived in the town of Springfield before she realized it. Dennis knew exactly where the bed and breakfast was—which surprised her a little. He had never been that good with directions. They turned into the car park next to the house. The place seemed quiet, even though it was just off the main road, but there were two other cars parked there, so someone must be at home. Elaine hoped they weren't the only guests; she would feel too conspicuous. She didn't want other people, even strangers, to sense the tension in her relationship with Dennis.

The kitchen door opened and a friendly looking woman stood in the doorway, "Hello, I'm Sue. Welcome to the Gate House."

The room that they were shown to was upstairs at the back of the house, in the old part of the building that had been the working area of the Gate House when the railway had been in operation years ago.

While Elaine exclaimed over the decor, Dennis seemed fascinated with the view and the structure of the building, checking their location from each of the two windows, and then going out into the hallway to verify their location in the building. The owner seemed pleased with their interest, although her knowledge of the building itself appeared limited.

The purchase of the new running shoes was anti-climactic after lunch with Alex. He had a boyish quality about him that Nara found appealing, yet should couldn't help feeling a little guilty when she thought of Davis. She had eagerly accepted Alex's invitation to dinner on Friday night, but Friday night seemed such a long way from Tuesday afternoon.

The clouds were moving in quickly as she pulled into car park. She slipped into the Gate House, purchase in hand. The house was silent. Her father was probably upstairs napping at this time of day. Aunt Sue's car was gone, so she was probably out somewhere. There was plenty of time for a run before tea, as long as the rain held off. She would slip quietly up to her room and change into her running clothes, and then slip out again.

Nara stifled a cry and dropped her package when she saw the strange man standing in the dining room studying the old photographs of the Gate House on the wall. She hadn't noticed a strange car outside, so she didn't think any guests were in the house.

The man turned, and with a shock Nara realized it was the man who had almost hit the car she and Micki had been riding in the day before, the man she had seen arguing outside the restaurant. *Three times and it's not a coincidence,* her father always said.

As the man turned, Nara could sense an underlying hostility towards her, although she had no idea why. "Good afternoon. I'm Dennis Maxwell." He extended his hand with the utmost courtesy. Nara automatically extended hers, as the blood drained from her face. She felt suddenly cold.

"I'm sorry I startled you. Here. Sit down." He took her arm and led her to a nearby sofa. Then he retrieved her package and set it on the table in front of her. "An athlete, I see," he said, looking at the label on the bag.

"Not exactly, I just bought some shoes," Nara answered weakly.

Dennis sat down next to her, just close enough to avoid touching her. Nara sensed that he wanted something from her, and was instantly on her guard.

"My wife and I are staying here tonight. She just went into town for a little shopping. You know how women are, always love the shopping." He glanced again at her bag.

Nara breathed deeply and felt her energy and sense of self returning. She had just been startled, but his stereotype that women were all shopaholics grated on her nerves. He didn't even know her. She knew more about him than he did about her, and that gave her a distinct advantage. She sat up straight and moved away from him a few inches.

"You startled me, that's all. We are accustomed to having guests here, but I didn't see any cars outside and had my mind on other things when I came in." She picked up her shoes from the table and stood up.

"Is there anything I can get you? Tea? A soft drink?" Nara forced herself into hostess mode.

"No thank you. I'm fine." Dennis smiled, looking around the room. "I'm fascinated by this house. Has your family lived in it a long time?"

"No. My aunt bought it just last year. My father and I moved here just two months ago."

"And your mother?"

"My mother died when I was three years old," she answered.

Dennis seemed to show suitable sympathy. "I'm sorry to hear that." He turned to the old photographs that he had been studying when Nara came in. "Do you know when these photos were taken?"

"I'm sorry, I really don't," Nara replied. "I've been here such a short time. I don't know much about the history of the place, except that it was a railroad gate house. The latest remodeling was about five years ago."

"You don't mind if I look around the outside, do you? Sometimes you can gain clues as to a building's age, and its various transformations, from studying the stonework."

"Of course," Nara answered. A little warning bell was going off in her head, but she couldn't think why, except that she had seen this man previously, and he had been angry both times. She wished her father would wake up or Aunt Sue would get back. She wanted to get away from this man, and go for her run to clear her head. Her silent prayer was answered as the kitchen door opened and Aunt Sue walked in. Nara quickly took advantage of the opportunity.

"Aunt Sue. I'm glad you're here. Mr.—" She turned toward the man, trying to remember his name.

"Dennis," he answered, smiling again. "Dennis Maxwell."

"Mr. Maxwell was just asking about the history of the house, and I know practically nothing. Maybe you can answer his questions." Before her aunt could reply, Nara was halfway up the stairs. "I'm going for a run to try out my new shoes before it rains. I'll see you in about an hour."

Ten minutes later, Nara was out the door, heading along the river path towards the town.

Nara ran along the river, enjoying the cool breeze and the sturdy, airy feel of new running shoes. Alex had told her he lived in one of the beautiful Georgians, so one of these houses along the river belonged to him. He and his ex-wife had bought it when they were married, and after the divorce he stayed on. It was too big for him, he said, but he loved the house, the town, and the view, so he decided to stay. Nara amused herself wondering which one was his. She eliminated the ones with prams and children's toys by the door, and the ones with bird feeders hanging from posts or trees. Somehow Alex didn't impress her as the bird feeding type. He was so occupied with his job.

What did he do for fun besides run? She would ask him that on Friday night. The anticipation of dinner with Alex Friday night made her smile. He had asked her out again almost as an afterthought, as they walked out of the shoe store, but she said yes immediately. She passed two women pushing prams, the women chatting companionably while their children watched the ducks on the river. Nara said "Hello," and they returned the greeting. She was feeling better. The fresh air and exercise were working their magic. That creepy little man at the house would be gone in a day or two, and she knew she could find ways to stay out of his way.

Nara was lost in her thoughts and began to leave the town on the other side. She knew the path continued on for some distance, maybe even to the next town. Other runners and cyclists passed her every few minutes. She would continue a bit farther and see where the trail led. This was one of the most fun things she had done since arriving in Springfield; she would just keep going and see where her footsteps led her.

The trail was much like the one that led past the Gate House, through tall grass and trees, and generally following the course of the river. *This will be beautiful in the spring,* Nara thought.

A flock of crows circled overhead. Fascinated, Nara slowed her pace to watch them. It was then that she noticed the car. It looked as if it were floating in the water. She stepped off the path into the brush to get a closer look, and her stomach cramped with shock. There was a car just below the surface of the water, and from the driver's window a hand waved eerily along the surface of the water. Someone was in the car and most likely dead. Nara stifled a scream. She had to notify someone. She had left her cell phone at home, as she wanted the freedom of being out of touch for a short time. She stumbled back onto the path and could see a cyclist in the distance, heading toward her from town. *Thank God!*

She stepped out into the path and waved. In a moment he reached her and stopped, looking peeved at her for interrupting his ride, but curious. He was young, probably early twenties like she was.

"I'm sorry," she stammered. "There's— there's a car in the river with a body in it."

His eyes followed her outstretched arm pointing to the riverbank. He took one look at the eerie hand waving from the submerged automobile, and said, "I'll be right back."

The young man jumped on his bicycle and sped off. Nara stayed on the path, bouncing nervously from one foot to the other, looking up and down the path for the sight of another human being. She did not look in the direction of the river, and tried not to think about what she knew was there. In the distance down the path a man and woman were walking their dog. The sight of them made her feel not quite alone.

In no more than five minutes Nara saw the cyclist returning down the path. He skidded to a stop in front of her. "I found someone to call the police. They should be here soon. I didn't think you would want to wait here alone so I hurried back."

"Thank you," Nara answered. She felt much better now that he was back.

The young man looked at his wristwatch, anxious to be on his way.

"My name's Nara, by the way."

"I'm Tom." He held out a hand, swathed in a biking glove.

"Thanks for waiting with me."

"No problem. I hated to leave you alone here but it was the fastest way to get help." He paused. "I'm just thinking my girl friend is going to be wondering where I am. She's always trying to get me to carry my cell phone, but I just have to get away from it sometimes."

Nara smiled. "I don't carry mine either, not when I run." *I sound like I run all the time*, Nara thought, *not someone who was wearing the wrong shoes only yesterday*.

The police arrived and took Nara's statement, which didn't take long since all she had done was notice the car. One of the policemen was the same one who had arrived at the Gate House just two nights before. "You seem to be a magnet for trouble," he teased Nara. She said nothing. "If you want to wait around for a bit, I can have someone drive you home."

"That's all right," she answered. "The exercise will clear my head."

The cyclist, who was still worrying about what his girl friend would think, also offered to accompany her home. "No thanks," she replied firmly, and started back down the path towards Springfield. She walked for about a minute, then broke into a slow jog and ran faster. She didn't know if she was running away from the gruesome scene at the river, or toward something else.

At the Gate House, Sue Blanchard made small talk with her guests. She had checked on her brother, and he was still napping. Dennis Maxwell, one half of the couple from Lincoln who were spending the night, had been pestering her with questions about the history of the house. Did the original building plans still exist, what about the architect's drawings of the renovation work? His wife tried to interrupt occasionally but lapsed into silence.

Sue was not in the mood for small talk today. That was one of the reasons she had agreed to have Jack and Nara come and stay with her, when she learned that Jack had cancer. They could share the burden of conversation with the guests. It wasn't that Sue didn't like talking; she certainly did. But there were times when she just needed a break, and this was one of them. She was still tired from her night out with Stan.

Sue had never been good at hiding her feelings and hoped her brusqueness wouldn't offend her guests. She was instantly relieved when she simultaneously heard Jack's footsteps upstairs, and Nara opening the back door. Nara came into the kitchen first, sweating and breathing hard from running.

Sue spoke sharply to her niece. "Nara, you look a mess. We have guests, you know."

Nara stood stock still and glared at the older woman, then she grabbed a towel from a hook behind the door and rubbed her face and neck with it.

"I just saw a car with a dead body in it, in one of the canals, all right?" She replaced the towel. "I'm going upstairs."

The other three sat in shocked silence as Nara turned the other way and headed up to the family area of the house.

Elaine spoke first. "The poor girl. What a shock! I wonder who it was?"

"Probably someone who had too much to drink and drove his car into the canal, thinking he was on the road home," Dennis said.

"You are probably right," Sue agreed. She looked up. "Jack, how good to see you. Come meet our new guests."

She made the introductions. "This is my brother Jack from St. Clare."

"St. Clare!" Dennis exclaimed. "I've heard a lot about the place. I would like to have the opportunity to talk to you about St. Clare. It always fascinated me and I think you may be the man to satisfy my curiosity.

"Speaking of a drink—and I think I was at some point—I could use one. There must be a pub nearby. What do you say, Jack? We let the ladies gab over tea and we go out for something stronger?"

"I haven't been drinking much since I started my cancer treatments, but I suppose a pint or two wouldn't hurt," Jack answered. "I'll just get my jacket."

Sue struggled to hold her composure. All she wanted was to be alone with her thoughts, and now she would be left to make chitchat with this woman from Lincoln. No use expecting Nara to come down—not in the mood she was in.

But Nara surprised her. Fifteen minutes later she was downstairs again, showered and ready to help with tea. She talked about her classes at the university in Lincoln, and Elaine spoke of her own classes there when she had studied art history years ago.

"Do you know anything about antiques?" Nara gestured around the dining room where they sat. Sue had been about to excuse herself to go upstairs, but stopped.

"I know a little bit," Elaine answered. "It looks like you have some fine pieces here."

"Do you think any of them are worth stealing?" Nara asked.

"Nara," Sue said warningly.

Nara either didn't hear or ignored her. *Probably ignoring me,* Sue thought.

"Why?" Elaine took an appreciative sip of tea. "Surely you have had them appraised and insured?" She glanced questioningly at Sue.

"The contents of the house are insured, of course," she replied in her best authoritative voice. "I've not had things individually appraised, however. You see, I bought this house complete with furnishings, after the owner died. I haven't had the time or the money to have the items valued piece by piece."

"It's not my place to say, of course," Elaine said, "but you never know what you may have here."

Sue fully expected Nara to blurt out about the break-in the other night, but she didn't. Instead, she was thoughtfully chewing a piece of lemon cake. Sue excused herself and went upstairs. She wanted badly to call Stan, but she made it a habit never to call him the day after one of their "meetings." *Some meeting*, she thought, smiling to herself at the memory. *He's probably with his wife now*, she thought with a pang, trying to make things right and family-like after his "business" trip. She wondered if his wife suspected he was having an affair? She and Stan had been seeing each other for three months now, and wives usually sensed these things. Maybe his wife didn't care?

"I would care, if he were my husband," she whispered to herself as she climbed the stairs to her room. She stopped and looked out the window at the old railroad bed and the river and fields beyond. The house had been standing on this spot for almost 200 years. What other dramas had been lived out within its walls, and were now forgotten, dead with the people who had lived here? She thought of the previous owner, whose body had been found in the very dining room where Nara and their guests sat chatting now.

Sue picked up one of the tiny porcelain figurines that lined the shelves set into an alcove on the landing. Who had collected them? Were they really worth anything? She picked up a teacup and saucer toward the back and turned over the cup to study the imprint on the bottom. It was stamped with the name of a manufacturer and a number. They must mean something, but Sue had no idea what. Maybe she should call in an appraiser, or at least take a few things to a dealer and ask about them. Maybe she could even sell a few things and make a little money.

She continued on up the stairs to her room and turned on the tap for a nice bath.

SEVENTEEN

On the train back from London, Alex turned off his laptop and closed his eyes, allowing himself to think of Nara. He had not been able to get her out of his mind. He wanted to call her, but he didn't want to seem too eager. There was a prickliness about her, a defensiveness, that he found appealing. But he wondered what was behind it. Behind the soft little girl exterior was a woman who definitely knew her own mind, and wasn't about to allow anyone else to make it up for her.

He let his thoughts wander to the curve of her small breasts beneath the sweater she had worn to lunch. His hands ached to run his hands over their softness, her slim, shapely legs. He refused to allow his thoughts to go beyond that. It was too dangerous. His emotions were still tender from his break-up with Laura. They had had such passion, and he had been fascinated by her at the beginning, too. But what she wanted out of life had proved to be far different from what he wanted. And beyond the passion, the day to day living was what made up the relationship. It wasn't as easy as it had been in his parents' generation. They still seemed slightly embarrassed when they said the word "divorced."

His reverie was interrupted when the train pulled into the Springfield station. Simultaneously, his cell phone rang. He looked at the number display. It was Harry from the police department. Harry wouldn't call unless he had some useful information.

"Hello, Harry."

"Alex, are you back from London?"

"I'm just getting off the train."

"Good. Meet me at the chip shop on Cheny Road. I have some news."

"I had chips yesterday. I don't need any fried food today."

"I don't care about your diet. Eat or don't eat." He paused to say something to someone in the background. "We found a body in a car in one of the canals, and it looks like there is a connection to the church burglary."

"I'll be there in five minutes." Alex snapped his phone shut and walked briskly to his car.

Harry was well into a platter of fish and chips when Alex walked into the shop a few minutes later. Alex sat across from him and took a chip from the plate.

"I thought you had enough chips yesterday. Get your own," Harry grumbled.

Alex's stomach was growling and he realized it had been hours since he had wolfed down the sandwich he had grabbed from Thresher's and eaten on the run in London.

"Tuna salad, please. With dark toast if you have some," he told the waitress. She jotted it down on her pad and walked back to the kitchen without a word.

"So who was in the car in the canal?" Alex snitched another chip. Harry didn't react this time.

"Don't know yet," he answered. "No ID on him, which is a mite suspicious right there. And the plates were taken off the car, so it wasn't some poor sot driving into the drink after a night at the pub. Doesn't look like it had been in the canal for more than a few hours, and the bloke had been shot in the head."

Alex winced. "So what's the connection to the burglary at the church?"

"The old tools taken from the church were in the boot." Harry wiped his mouth on a paper napkin and sat back.

The two men waited until the waitress had placed Alex's tuna salad and toast in from of him and asked cheerily if they needed anything else. When they answered in the negative, she left them to sit in a back booth with a young man with spiked blond hair and a small gold ring in his nose.

"And get this," Harry continued. "The person who saw the car and reported it is the girl from the Gate House who reported the attempted break-in there the night before."

"Nara?" Alex dropped his fork on the table with a clatter.

"You know her?" Harry asked, equally surprised.

"I'm taking her out to dinner Friday night."

Alex picked up his fork and took another bite of tuna salad. "Just a coincidence."

"Probably," Harry answered. He had finished his fish and chips and was slurping the last of his Coca-Cola. "What do you know about her?"

"I met her on the path by the river when I was out running. She was wearing the most god-awful shoes, and I stopped her to tell her she was going to end up in hospital if she ran in them, and then one thing led to another." He tried to sound casual and matter-of-fact, but wasn't sure he was succeeding with the police officer across from him.

"So you asked her to dinner."

"Something like that."

"I don't see how there could be any connection myself, but it might bear watching. She's a little too close to the action, especially now that murder is involved."

"You think she might be in danger?"

"I don't know. I just said I think it bears watching. Springfield hasn't had a murder in five years—and that time it was a domestic squabble."

"You think maybe it could be the dead guy's partner who killed him? Quarrel over the goods or the proceeds?"

"Maybe. But then why leave the tools in the boot?"

"Maybe he didn't know they were there?"

"Come on." Harry was making moves to go, and signaled to the waitress for the check. "He went to the trouble of taking the guy's ID and removing the plates from the car and the registration, by the way. Why would he leave something that connected the car to the break-in?"

"Carelessness?" Alex answered, knowing he was beaten in this discussion.

"I doubt it." Harry paid for both their meals and stood up to leave. "My treat." He shrugged on his jacket and put his hand on Alex's shoulder. "You stick to the antiquities and the girl, and I'll stick to solving the crimes. It's getting to where I'm beginning to feel like a big city policeman these days."

Alex sat at the table and finished his tea, thinking about Nara. He really didn't think she was involved in any of this, but she was a little too close to the action for his liking and he wondered how it all fit together. But, as Harry said, solving crimes was his problem.

Dennis found Jack Blake to be a companionable drinking partner, and forthcoming with the little he knew about the history of the Gate House. One pint stretched to two, then three. Although Jack was from St. Clare, he claimed to know little about antiquities smuggling. "I know it goes on. I know people who buy the stuff. But I run a clean import business. Always have. I have a daughter and I don't want to be involved in anything that could get her hurt."

Dennis wondered if the man was telling the truth, but it didn't really matter. He wasn't interested in that end of the operation—at least not yet. *Someday. Maybe.* His greed took over for a moment as he thought about running an antiquities smuggling ring with Joe and some others of his type to do the dirty work. He would be the brains of the operation and keep his hands clean.

Jack looked at his watch and declared that it was time to go back. "I don't think any of the women will appreciate us spending the evening at the pub."

"I suppose you're right. And your daughter... does she like it here?"

"She's adjusting. It's been hard for her. She left a boyfriend in St. Clare who hasn't been keeping in touch with her."

"Tough being young, when those things matter." Dennis drained the last of his beer and they got up to leave together.

EIGHTEEN

In London, Terry Clark was still in her office, talking on the phone with her contact in St. Clare. It had been a long day. She nibbled at the chicken tikka masala sandwich she had ordered two hours ago and sipped her cold coffee. The customer wanted stained glass, easy enough to acquire, but difficult to ship and easily identified. He wanted two pieces, not necessarily matching, to flank a large dining room window looking out over the ocean. Terry had one window that she had seen and knew to be genuine and valuable. Fifteenth century. Before Henry VIII's hoodlums had destroyed the monasteries and Cromwell had done his number on the churches, tramping about with his horses in the cathedrals.

But the other side was that these things were even more valuable now, since there were not so many of them. The little twerp in Lincoln had mentioned stained glass. She wondered what that piece was like. But she would have to be very careful. It had only been taken a few nights previously, he said. The police would be on the lookout for it. She decided to mention it and see if she could string the St. Clare people along while she checked it out. She started to say something when her other phone line beeped.

"Just a moment. I have another call." She quickly switched over before the man on the other line could say anymore. Didn't he realize it was four hours later in London than in the Caribbean?

"Hello?"

"Good. You're still in the office." It was her boss, the soul of tact and consideration.

"I don't consider it good," she snapped.

"Making money for the firm is always good." Terry could hear the tinkle of glass and light laughter in the background. Obviously it was she who was supposed to be working at making money for the firm.

"I had a fax from a client in St. Clare. He and his wife are willing to spend a considerable sum for the items they want for their house, but they are very particular. I'm thinking it might be worthwhile to fly out there and see the place, make some personable recommendations, from an expert, you know."

For a fleeting moment, Terry thought he meant that she would be the one to go to St. Clare, but she came back down to earth immediately. Mr. Hadley would naturally go himself.

"I have a few clients to deal with here in London, but I want to leave early next week. What I need from you is as complete a list as possible of the best items we have available." The light laughter came nearer to the other phone, and he paused to say something that was unintelligible to Terry. "We will talk about it tomorrow, but you can start thinking about it." He rang off.

Terry took a deep, angry breath. "Damn." She punched the button to go back to the other call and slapped a smile on her face. She hated this business, but she was good at it and was putting a considerable amount away in savings. One of these days she would quit... but not quite yet.

Michael Carrington on St. Clare was going through a very specific list of items his clients were interested in, besides the stained glass. Terry found his accent difficult to understand, although she had spoken with him many times. She had to concentrate to get what he was saying, and she took careful notes. She wondered if this was the same client who had faxed Mr. Hadley directly. Those wealthy types would use formal and informal channels to get what they wanted. Terry slipped her feet out of the pointy toes of her red stiletto shoes and wiggled her toes.

Finally the man was finished and the call ended. He mumbled something at the end about a drink with a beautiful lady and a walk on the beach. It seemed everyone was having fun tonight except her.

Terry crammed her weary feet back into her shoes. What was it about pointed toes that meant fashion and professionalism? She went into Mr. Hadley's office to an ancient computer that sat in a corner. She punched in the double passwords and printed a few sheets. These were the master lists of everything they had available, or that was relatively easy to obtain at any given moment. She would take them home and glance over them before going to sleep... or in the morning while she dressed for another day's work. She crammed the papers into her briefcase, locked it, and then turned out the lights in the office and set the alarm. She had the routine down, since she was usually the last one to leave. She almost took her sandwich with her, but then threw it in the trash. She could pick up something fresh from the curry place on her way home. She would be back here soon enough.

Usually Terry had her car keys out and ready, especially when she left at night, but she had been preoccupied tonight with the phone calls, the extra work Mr. Hadley had just given her, printing the lists, and then stopping to dispose of the limp sandwich. The time it took her to fumble in her small red purse for her keys was just long enough for the blow to her head to be well-aimed. She slumped against her car, releasing everything in her hands as she slid to the pavement.

NINETEEN

Dennis went to sleep a happy man. He had even made love to Elaine, and she responded to him in that grateful way she always had. It used to bother him; tonight it didn't. Tonight he almost felt as if he loved her again, as he had when they were first married. Her hair was shorter now, her body a bit fuller, but she still had a grace and an intensity that he found appealing—even erotic. At the same time, however, she had a center that he could never reach, and *that* was what had made him want her in the early years of their marriage. It was also what made him treat her the way he did now. When he discovered he could not reach that center, that part of her that she held for herself alone, it made him want to hurt her.

As they lay in the darkness together, he remembered the first time he had hit her. They had been married about six months. She had miscarried three months earlier, and then she had been emotional and needy. It was the first time he had seen how she turned inward. She didn't exactly shut him out; she just went where he could not go. His mother told him it was normal; he should let her be for now and let her know that he was there for her when she was ready to talk and that he loved her. He said the words, but the anger boiled inside him—anger at Elaine, at himself, his mother, God, even the baby. They had all ruined his life. He expected them to give to him, not the other way around. And so he struck out at the nearest flesh-and-blood victim he could find. His wife.

He had slapped her hard across the face; his ring left a red scratch on her cheek. She cried, of course, and ran and locked herself into the bathroom and cried some more. He waited; he paced. Finally after about 20 minutes he had gone out and not returned until after midnight. He had found her asleep in their bed, her eyes still puffy. The next morning she acted as if nothing had happened, and it seemed from that point on that she had gotten over losing the baby, but she still kept that part of herself hidden from him, and because of that, every so often he hit her. He even thought of other ways to torment her, like spilling coffee on the carpet so she would have to remove the stain, or ripping her blouse just before she left for work, so she would have to take the time to change.

He didn't know how much she had told his mother, but he knew that she knew something. The two women had been thick as thieves as long as they had known each other. That was another reason he hit Elaine, because he couldn't hit his mother.

But tonight, things were looking up. Elaine's breathing had slowed, and he could tell she was sleeping as she lay against him. He moved his arm carefully out from under her head and went for a glass of water. He looked out the window, where the moonlight illuminated the garden. What secrets did this house hold? What valuable artifacts were hidden here? His gut instinct told him there was something here, something that could at least allow him to be taken seriously in the antiquities smuggling business, if not make him a fortune.

He might hire another man, someone with a little more education than Joe. It was easy enough to win the confidence of people; he found that out last night with Jack Blake. A few pints at the pub and they were like old friends. Jack had promised to look up the blueprints of the Gate House in the morning, and they would see what the original structure had been like. Had the renovations left any space unaccounted for? Yesterday he had walked around outside the back of the house, but the blueprints, and an actual look from inside, would tell far more. Dennis chuckled to himself and went back to bed. Tomorrow would be a good day.

He awoke to the sound of female voices on the floor below. One of them was Elaine's. She would be enjoying a chat with the women who ran the bed and breakfast, Dennis thought. They would gossip about the men in their lives, house cleaning tips, cooking—whatever it was women talked about. He wasn't ready to face Elaine and her inevitable chatter just yet. He picked up his cell phone and called Joe's number. The computerized voice told him that the phone was turned off or out of range. Joe must be having a lie-in since Dennis was out of town.

He chuckled and then tried Joe's home number and his wife answered. Dennis had met her a couple of times. She was an ordinary sort of woman and had put on weight after having children, as they all did. *So what's Elaine's excuse?* he wondered, then he brought his mind back to the task at hand.

Joe's wife sounded upset; in fact, she said she thought it might be Joe calling since he hadn't been home all night. "And he doesn't answer his cell phone. I insisted he get it, the way he works all hours, but what good is it if he doesn't answer it?"

Dennis wondered the same thing. Maybe Joe had a little "something" going on the side, although he kept that thought to himself. *Good for him, as long as it doesn't interfere with business... and as long as business wasn't what he had going on the side.* "Have him call me as soon as he gets in. As *soon* as he gets in," he repeated and rang off.

Probably too early to get anyone at the antique house in London, but he would try Terry Clark's cell phone to tell her that there was a good possibility he would have some valuable pieces for her soon. Her cell phone rang and rang until the answering service picked it up. Dennis did not leave a message. *Odd that a businesswoman like she appeared to be would not answer her phone,* he thought. It wasn't that early. Maybe she was in the Underground or somewhere out of range. He would try again later. He pulled out a fresh set of clothes and headed for the shower.

Jack had spent a sleepless night studying the blueprints and other papers associated with the sale of the house to his sister. She had filed them meticulously in her office file cabinet, chosen to match her new computer desk that she had purchased when she opened the bed and breakfast, but now rarely used. Sue preferred dealing in cash when she could, although the bed and breakfast was set up to accept credit cards. In financial matters that were any more complicated than paying the gas bill, Sue tended to sign on the dotted line when she was instructed to and trusted the loan officer or solicitor to have her best interests at heart. Jack had always planned to go over the papers for her, but had been too sick to take care of that. But the guest's interest had given him the impetus to begin.

Jack found the blueprints intriguing for many reasons. As historical documents, they showed how the Gate House had evolved over time, from its use as a toll booth in the early railroad days in Lincolnshire, to its transformation into a family dwelling after the toll booths were no longer used, and then falling into disrepair for many years when it had been a hangout for drunks and drug users. In the 1960s the building had been purchased by a couple recently returned from the Foreign Service who wanted a project to keep them busy. They had added the rooms that now comprised the downstairs of the main part of the house, turning the upper level of the original Gate House into two bedrooms. They had also petitioned to have the building given historical status, but apparently only after they had made their renovations. There was nothing to indicate the results of their inquiry, so Jack did not know if the historical status had been granted. He made a note to try to track down the results.

Then in the late 1970s, the next owners of the Gate House had added a second story to have more bedrooms for their family of five children and had turned the upper story of the Gate House into a large playroom, installing a bathroom at the same time. Additionally they had done something Jack found very interesting. They had closed off the old stairway that led from what was now the kitchen area to the ground level of the original Gate House. Actually, it was somewhat below ground level, but had windows high on the walls to let in some light. Jack had noticed the windows, now thick with the grime of years, in one of his walks around the back of the house. He had thought nothing of it, thinking only that it must be a cellar of some sort, but now that he realized there had once been an entrance from inside the house, he was curious. He wondered if this semi-hidden section of the house had any connection with the attempted break-in. And now this stranger, a "guest" but nonetheless a stranger, was interested in the history of the house.

Jack had always told Nara *twice is a coincidence, three times is a connection.* He decided he would not show the blueprints to Dennis. He would have to come up with some reason, but he could not show them to an outsider without finding out more for himself first.

Somewhere around 2:00 in the morning Jack finally dozed off, still not resolved on how he would handle keeping the papers from Dennis. He seemed a persistent sort; the kind that could have a bit of a temper, too. And something wasn't right with his relationship with his wife. Jack had had a brief, passionate marriage to Nara's mother, which had ended with her death after only four years. His second wife had left him when she learned he had cancer, so he didn't consider himself a knowledgeable person on the subject of marriage. Even still, he could sense that there was something uneasy in the relationship between Dennis and his wife.

Jack awoke with a start around 4:00. He thought he had heard a crash. *Maybe a dream, or a lorry on the road.* He dozed again and woke when the light of dawn brightened his room. He had wanted this room, with the eastern light coming in each morning; it gave him hope. When Jack and Nara first moved in, they originally discussed their room choices and Jack had quickly made his case for claiming the room for himself. It was the largest bedroom, and as he would be spending more time in his room than either of them, and would need to rest periodically throughout the day, they agreed. Besides, both Sue and Nara liked to sleep late when they could, although they were usually up early to prepare breakfast for the guests. They didn't appreciate the dawn the same way he did.

The blueprints were lying on the night stand where he had left them. He stacked the papers carefully, replaced them in the brown manila folder and tied the cord. The morning was chilly, so he wrapped his robe around his thin frame and pushed his feet into slippers. The last thing he wanted was to catch a cold. Crossing the room, he removed a mirror that hung over the heavy wooden dresser and opened a wall safe with a combination. He placed the papers inside and closed the safe.

So much for that, he thought. He would think up something to tell Dennis later; he might possibly stay in bed for a while this morning, claiming exhaustion from his chemo treatments. But he would also confide in Nara. She would see the necessity of keeping the blueprints from a stranger and could be relied on to give some explanation to the man.

There was a knock on his bedroom door. "Dad?" She turned the knob softly. "I heard you moving around, and I thought you might like some tea."

"A large pot of it, and hot," he answered. "It's freezing in here this morning."

She walked purposefully into the room. "Then let's turn on the electric heater, no matter what Aunt Sue says. We're paying our share of the electric bill." Nara pulled the heater out of the closet and placed it so the warmth would reach her father's bed. "I'll bring your tea right up."

"Good." He settled himself back under the covers with a few pillows propped behind him, and reached for the TV remote control. "I have something I need to talk to you about."

"Oh?" Her face showed alarm.

"I'm fine, Nara. It's not related to my health. Bring the tea and we'll talk."

She gave him a disbelieving look and left the room, closing the door softly behind her.

Nara organized the breakfast things for the guests while she waited for the water to boil for her father's tea. It was early yet; she didn't know why she had awakened so early. And Aunt Sue was here this morning to help with breakfast, so there was no hurry. She wondered what her father wanted to talk to her about. She felt butterflies in her stomach every time he told her he needed to talk ever since "the talk" when he had told her he had cancer, and "the talk" when he told her they would move to England. She had been torn away from Davis, and it still hurt, but she didn't blame her father. He had been a loving, caring father all those years after her mother had died; the least she could do was be here for him. The treatments might work; he did seem better the last few days. He could live for many years yet.

And then there was Alex. What would come of that? He certainly was attractive and kind. She had only had lunch with him, but she could already make a sizeable list of his positive qualities. How many more would she add after dinner Friday night? *Slow down, girl,* she said to herself. *You're just getting over a broken heart caused by one man. There's plenty of time to get to know this one. Be open, but keep a part of yourself, for yourself.* Someone had told her that once. *And enjoy yourself.*

Nara set two cups and saucers on the tray with the teapot and carried it up the stairs, smiling to herself as she went. Whatever her father had to tell her, she knew today would be a good day.

She knocked at his bedroom door and pushed it open to find him seated at his desk going through some papers. "I thought you were cold," she said, setting the tea things on a small table in front of an easy chair.

"I'm feeling better now that the heater has taken the chill off the room." He laughed. "I'd forgotten how cold it can be here in the mornings."

Nara poured tea for both of them, adding milk and sugar to her own and only milk to her father's cup. She settled herself in the easy chair, her legs crossed beneath her tailor fashion. She was wearing dark blue leggings with a long white sweater, and her old faithful tennis shoes. They were still good for around the house. She took a sip of the hot tea.

"So what did you want to talk to me about?"

Jack stacked the papers he was going through and replaced them in a desk drawer. He turned and moved his chair closer to the tea table and picked up his cup and saucer.

"Don't keep me in suspense, Dad."

He took a sip of his tea and smiled at her. "I want you to tell our guest Dennis from Lincoln that I'm not feeling well this morning, and that I couldn't find the old blueprints of the house. Sue must have put them somewhere."

Nara set down her tea cup looking mystified. "Why? What's going on?"

"Did you know there is another staircase hidden behind the walls of the original Gate House?"

"No." Nara's eyes widened. "I never thought about it."

"I've been going through some of the house papers that Sue never bothered to read. Dennis, our current guest," Jack jerked his head in the direction of the guest bedrooms, "was asking some questions last night about the history of the place, so I pulled out the papers and spent most of the night reading."

He held up his hand when Nara opened her mouth to speak. "Don't worry," he said. "I plan on resting today to make up for the sleep I lost last night."

He paused for another sip of tea. "I have no intention of allowing our friend from Lincoln to see these papers, especially the blueprints showing the hidden staircase. I don't know who he is other than what he told me, and his interest in the house seems just a little suspicious—especially after the attempted break-in here, I think it unwise to have the plans for the house spread around. Who knows who he might talk to?"

Nara listened attentively, trying to decide if she should tell her father about the two previous times that she had seen Dennis Maxwell.

He went on. "I've locked the papers away. Sue has never looked at them. So only you and I know about the staircase. I'm sure there is no sinister meaning behind it. No dead bodies decomposed behind our walls. But I think it's better we keep this to ourselves."

Nara shivered and thought of the dead body in the car in the river the day before. Before she could speak, there was a knock at the door. "Jack? Nara?" Aunt Sue's voice called.

"Come in," called Jack.

Sue was dressed in blue jeans and a dark blue sweater, but Nara's sharp eyes noticed that her aunt was indeed losing weight. The jeans fit much more loosely than they had in the past. Nara filed her observation in the back of her brain for now.

The older woman looked at Nara. "Time to cook breakfast." She said it evenly, without the usual accusatory tone.

"Right." Nara put down her empty cup and stood. "Get some rest, Dad. I'm sure you're tired after losing sleep last night. The doctor said that might be a side effect of the treatments. You don't have any appointments scheduled for today." She bent and kissed him on the cheek as she passed and whispered, "Don't worry."

Nara closed her father's bedroom door softly behind her just as Elaine Maxwell just as softly opened her door. She wore an old pink chenille robe that had only been in fashion years ago. Nara smiled. There was something about this woman that aroused her sympathy.

"Oh, you're up. Would you like some tea? Or coffee?"

"I'd love some coffee. I'll just shower quickly and come down."

"Are you ready for breakfast? Or will you wait for your husband?"

"I'll wait a bit. I'm not hungry just yet."

Nara noticed the slight shadow that passed over Elaine's face when her husband was mentioned and wondered what that was all about. She seemed a nice woman; a little timid, perhaps.

"I'll have the coffee ready for you." She smiled and went off to the kitchen.

Sue was bustling, humming tunelessly as she worked around the kitchen. She was pulling things out of the refrigerator, tossing leftovers into the rubbish, rearranging the items on the shelves. Without looking at Nara, she said, "I won't be home for tea today, so I hope you will be."

Nara tensed. It didn't really matter, she supposed. She didn't have any plans. Still, Sue's last-minute, mysterious outings—and her assumption that Nara would always be there to take up the slack—grated on her nerves.

"As far as I know I'll be here," she answered with clenched teeth.

Sue straightened up. "Well, there's no need to get snippy, young lady. The arrangement was that you and your father would live here and you would help with the work. That means you need to be here when I have other duties." She paused. "I have a nursing conference this afternoon." Her face was flushed and Nara knew instantly that she was lying.

Nara had no plans for the afternoon, but she resented the way her aunt gave her orders. She was as sure as she could be that Sue was having an affair. All the signs pointed to it. And she really didn't care; it was her life. But it didn't mean that she should be at the older woman's beck and call whenever she wanted. She wasn't Cinderella, damn it. Nara took a deep breath and she arranged the coffee things on the tray for their guest. No use getting worked up about it. That was just what her aunt wanted. She was spoiling for a fight for some reason. She would sit down and visit with Elaine and have a cup of coffee herself. She would be hospitable; that was part of her job here, too, as well as cooking and cleaning.

"Right," she responded through clenched teeth. "I'll just take this coffee in and entertain our guest for a few minutes. It wouldn't be polite to leave her alone while her husband is upstairs having a lie-in."

She stepped into the dining room and plastered a smile onto her face. "Shall we have coffee in the sun room? We actually have some sun this morning."

Nara almost forgot to drink her coffee as she listened to Elaine speak about local history. She was so knowledgeable; maybe she would even know something about the antiques in the house. And she seemed to relax as she spoke; Elaine had looked tense... almost frightened... earlier this morning. Nara wondered again about her marriage to Dennis, to whom she had taken an instant dislike. Encouraged by Nara's rapt attention, Elaine expanded on her subject, as she shared bits of the history of Lincolnshire dating all the way back to the Romans.

"But it isn't just the history; the myths are intriguing, too. I even dreamed of one last night," she admitted. "I dreamed of the 'green man'—have you ever heard about him?" Elaine took another sip of coffee, and Nara took the opportunity to study her face. Elaine seemed to vacillate between animation and eager interest in the stories of Lincolnshire, and something like fear or secrecy.

And why did she look so uncomfortable when she spoke of her dream of the "green man?"

Elaine continued, "The green man was a grotesque, human-like face surrounded by leaves that appeared in the masonry of old churches throughout England. I have always found them sinister, with their half-human, half-plant demeanor. I was reading about them just last night, trying to study up a bit for my job, you know." Elaine set her cup back on the small table between them, and Nara saw that her hand shook, spilling coffee onto the saucer.

She quickly recovered her composure. "And then there is the imp in the Cathedral, from which the Lincoln football club took its name. Have you seen the imp?"

"I haven't even been to the Cathedral," Nara confessed.

"Then you must come," Elaine said. "I'll give you a personal tour, free of charge. And bring a friend if you like."

Nara immediately thought of her new friend. Micki had lived in Lincoln all her life and had surely visited the Cathedral numerous times, but it would be an invitation she could extend, as a sign of friendship.

"I would love it. I will be going to Lincoln three days a week for classes at the university starting next week. Maybe we could do it one day after class."

"That would be lovely," Elaine answered. "We can get to know each other a bit better."

Dennis heard the last of their conversation as he came down the stairs. *Good*, he thought. A friendship between his wife and the girl in the Gate House could only mean more opportunities for him to learn about the house. He wondered where Jack was. Then he remembered that the man had been undergoing treatments for cancer, so he probably needed extra rest. He could be patient a little while longer. He wondered again what had happened to Joe and why Terry Clark had not returned his call.

Terry Clark didn't want to open her eyes; the lights seemed incredibly bright. "Severe concussion," she heard someone say. The words were spoken by someone either inside her head or far away, she wasn't sure which. Either way it hurt. Someone groaned. "I think she's coming round."

"Good," another voice answered. "A blow like that..." The voice trailed off.

"It's just lucky she was found when she was. If she had lain there all night this could be a different story."

Terry's eyes fluttered open. As they adjusted to the lights, she was able to make out two men and a woman dressed in white, standing above her looking serious.

"Am I in hospital?" she asked, but they didn't seem to understand, and only muttered the usual comments. "Just relax. You are going to be fine."

She closed her eyes again for a moment; when she opened them she was in a dim room, and a woman sat next her bed. She turned toward the woman, obviously a nurse, and this time her voice was clear. "What happened?"

The nurse put down her magazine and smiled at Terry. "You're looking better. You had a nasty blow to the head. Lucky a night watchman found you not long afterwards." She stopped to check a dial on one of the machines to which Terry was connected. "I need to let the supervisor know that you are awake. She can tell you more."

The nurse left the room, and Terry realized that she was very young. *No more than eighteen*, she thought. Probably a student nurse sent to baby-sit until Terry awoke.

A chubby woman in her mid-thirties strode into the room with a professional air a moment later. She deftly checked Terry's vital signs, studied the same dials that the student nurse had examined, and sat down next to Terry.

"How are you feeling?"

"Like crap," Terry answered. "What happened?"

"You had a nasty blow to the head as you were getting into your car." The woman pulled some notes out of the pocket of her smock. "I'm supposed to ask you a couple of questions. It's routine with head injuries. What is your name?"

"Terry Clark." *This is exasperating*, Terry thought.

"What is today's date? Month, day, and year, please."

Terry thought for a minute. "I don't know how long I've been here, do I? If it's past midnight, it's 25 September 2007."

"Who is the Prime Minister?"

"Gordon Brown."

"Good," the woman answered, making a note.

"Do you remember what happened to you?"

Terry thought again. She remembered being in her office late at night, and the sandwich sitting on her desk, which reminded her that she was hungry. She must have set the office alarm system; she always did. "No," she said finally. "I don't remember."

The woman made another note, then patted Terry's arm in that condescending manner medical people used that Terry despised. "That's normal with a head injury. I'm going to give you something to help you sleep. You'll be right as rain in a day or two, I'm sure."

What is right about rain? Terry thought. She couldn't seem to keep her mind focused. She needed to ask this woman some questions and demand answers herself.

"The doctor will be in to see you in the morning, which is only a few hours from now." She glanced at her watch. "I'm sure you will be feeling better than, and he can give you all the information you need."

Before Terry could protest, a needle pricked her arm. *I'm hungry!* she thought, as she faded back to sleep.

When she woke again her head hurt terrifically. Had someone hit her? Had she fallen? She couldn't remember that part of it. All she could remember was leaving work late, which was not unusual, locking up as usual and walking to her car, and then what? Bright lights? She was obviously in a hospital, so she must have been hurt. She searched with her left hand for the nurse's call button, and found it dangling just within reach. She pressed the button.

A woman about her own age, but with mousy hair pulled back into a ponytail and a few more pounds on her came quickly into the room. "How are you feeling?" she asked, and without waiting for an answer, began checking the various dials on the machines attached to Terry's body. She took out a blood pressure cuff, wrapped it around Terry's arm, and stuck a thermometer into her ear. "Vital signs normal," she said more to herself than to anyone else.

"I feel fine, except for a headache." Terry tried to make her voice sound strong and assertive. She wasn't accustomed to being ignored.

"Do you remember what happened last night?"

Terry went back over what she remembered from the night before. She could see her car in the dark. It always looked black when she came out at night, although it was bright red. But there it stopped.

"No," she admitted. "I don't remember."

"The doctor will be in soon. He can answer your questions. Would you like some breakfast?"

"Just some tea right now and I do have to use the bathroom."

"Right. I'll send someone to help you."

Great, thought Terry. *Now I need help to use the bathroom.* She closed her eyes and tried to escape into sleep again, but now that she had sent the message to her bladder that it would be emptied soon, it wouldn't allow her to sleep.

A large woman with a name badge reading "Ella, Nurse's Aide" bustled into the room and literally picked Terry up out of the bed. "I was about to get a bed pan," she said cheerily, "but the duty nurse said 'See if she can made it to the toilet.' I'm here mainly to see you don't fall and hit that head again. You feel all right? Not dizzy or anything?"

To tell the truth Terry did feel dizzy, but didn't want to admit it. She tried to take a step on her own and the room began to spin. She started to slump. Ella placed her back on the bed with a surprisingly gentle movement. "I'd best get the bed pan." It was probably the most humiliating episode in her entire life, but afterwards she was able to close her eyes. She was almost asleep again when another nurse's aide who looked to be about sixteen came in with her tea. She set the tray carefully on the moveable table and adjusted Terry's bed to a sitting position. She moved the table into a convenient position and asked quietly, "Would you like me to pour it for you?"

"Yes, please," Terry answered, amazed at how weak she felt. She only hoped she had the energy to raise the cup to her lips.

"Call me if you need anything," the girl said, then left the room without a sound. *Why can't everyone here be quiet like that?* Terry thought. She tentatively lifted the cup and her hand cooperated by carrying the cup to her mouth without a mishap. Just a sip of the hot liquid began to revive her. She experienced a flash of memory of printing out a list the night before. A list of ---? A list of items—where was it? Where was her briefcase? Panicking—she pressed the nurse's button again. The quiet aide opened the door just a moment later. "Yes?"

"Do you know what happened to my briefcase?"

The girl's eyes widened. "I'll find out." She disappeared.

It was the efficient but dowdy nurse who returned a few moments later. "I'm sorry to say there was no briefcase when you were found, or a purse. We were only able to tentatively identify you through your car registration. The police found your keys on the ground. Is there someone we should notify for you? I know the police tried to call your phone number but there was no answer."

"My boss. Hadley's Antiques in Bond Street."

"Is your boss Mr. Hadley?"

"Yes." Terry had momentarily been afraid that she would not be able to remember where she worked, but that part of her brain seemed to be functioning. But what was that at the edge of her memory about a list? And what exactly had happened to her last night?

Five minutes later the nurse came back into her room, a concerned look on her face. "I just spoke with your boss. He said he would be over later today to see if you needed anything, but he is very concerned about some list you were supposed to have had." She took a deep breath as if she were trying to reconcile something within herself. "I explained the nature of your injuries, but he is quite insistent on speaking with you."

Terry said nothing. *The list. It had been in her briefcase*. Maybe talking to Mr. Hadley would jog her memory.

"I'll give you three minutes," the nurse said, having made up her mind. "Then I want you to rest until the doctor gets here."

Terry nodded her assent, and the nurse went back out to transfer the call.

The phone by the bed rang.

"Terry. Hadley here. Heard you had a nasty spill."

"I'm really not sure what happened, and they haven't told me much yet."

"I'm sure you'll be fine in a day or two. Problem is—I found your note saying you printed a copy of the master list. Did you have it with you?"

Terry thought. Did she?

"Yes, it was in my briefcase." She felt a rising sense of panic, of something being horribly wrong, but she lacked the energy to deal with it.

"In your briefcase? Damn it, Terry. If that list should fall into the wrong hands..."

"I'm sorry, Mr. Hadley. I just... I don't know what happened."

"The three minutes are up, I'm afraid." The nurse stood at the door, looking stern. She walked over and took the phone from Terry's hand.

"I'm afraid you will have to talk to Ms. Clark later, sir. She needs rest now. I'm sure she will be in touch with you later."

She hung up the phone.

Terry sank back onto her pillow. "He's angry with me."

"He'll get over it," the nurse said soothingly. "What's important is for you to get well. Let your injuries heal themselves." She settled Terry and left the room. Terry could hear her speaking with someone in a soft voice outside her door and wondered if they were talking about her. She closed her eyes and went back to sleep.

While Terry slept, Mr. Hadley made some discreet phone calls. Chances are that whoever robbed Terry had only been looking for money or credit cards, and the lists would end up in a dustbin somewhere.

But then again, the theft might have been deliberate. If those lists fell into the hands of the police, Hadley's could be in trouble. Some of the items on the list had been reported stolen years ago and were being held in warehouses around Britain and in other countries. And other "less than scrupulous" dealers could also benefit from the lists.

But it didn't make sense. How would anyone know that Terry was carrying such a list in her briefcase? Beside, if the list was what they were after, why would they take her purse as well? He slowly placed a call to St. Clare, knowing the result could make or break him, depending on the mood of the person on the other end.

TWENTY

Dennis paced the floor of the Gate House. The breakfast had been delicious—a traditional English breakfast of eggs with bacon, sausage, tomatoes, mushrooms and beans, along with toast and jam. And he had washed it all down with three cups of coffee. Maybe that was why he was pacing the floor.

Jack was still sleeping. Lovely little Nara had told him her father wasn't feeling well and was planning to rest for at least the morning. She knew nothing about any papers related to the history of the house. Yes, she would ask her father about them when he woke up, but the chemotherapy treatments left him terribly exhausted, you know. Her wide, steady eyes revealed nothing. She was extremely protective of her father, of that there was no doubt, but did she know any more? It was impossible to say.

Dennis decided to try calling Joe again. It was strange that he had not returned his call by mid-morning. He tried the cell phone again, still no answer. If he wasn't answering his cell phone, he probably wasn't at home, either. Dennis couldn't sit still. Maybe some fresh air would help. The sun was out and the day looked fine. He went upstairs for his jacket, where Elaine sat reading, looking out at the garden. "I'm going out for a walk." He grabbed his jacket and left quickly, before she could suggest coming with him. He had had enough togetherness. Maybe he could check the outside of the house again and get an idea of what he was looking for—if there was something to look for. There had to be.

He slipped out the French doors leading to the garden. A round table surrounded by white wrought iron chairs was set up on the small patio. Flower pots were neatly stacked along the side of the house, waiting for next spring, and some chrysanthemums still nodded in window boxes. Beyond the patio the back garden narrowed to a v-shape where a garden shed stood. Nothing looked interesting in that direction.

Dennis stepped out into the grass and looked up at the back of the house. Elaine was still sitting by the window reading. He didn't know where everyone else was. He and Elaine had been the last guests to eat breakfast, and the other guests had gone out already. Only one car besides his was in the car park, so Nara or her aunt must be out as well. He continued around the back of the house, to the side where the railroad had once been. This side of the garden was much narrower, as the house took up most of the lot, and a wooden fence separated the property from the common trail behind it. Some lavender still waved in the slight breeze from boxes hung on the fence. Dennis picked a sprig of it and held it to his nose. He had always loved the scent of lavender. It reminded him of his childhood; his mother had used it then, but stopped sometime after his father had died. Elaine never used it.

He tossed the sprig on the ground and continued around the house. The walls of the original gate house rose high above him. The lowest level was half below ground and the window on this level was filthy, probably used for storage. Dennis tried to peer through the glass but could see very little. It might be worth investigating. He knew that the two floors above contained guest rooms.

He rounded the building to the corner of the lot and stopped. There were fresh footprints in the mud leading to the door of the storage area. This had just happened last night, after the rain. Had Joe been here, sneaking around, trying to get something on his own? Was that why he wasn't answering his calls? Anger rose inside Dennis and he kicked the wooden door. It rattled in its frame; it wouldn't take much to kick it open. He tried the knob, but it was locked. *I wonder,* he thought, and pulled a credit card out of his wallet. He slipped it between the door and the jamb and pushed. The door stuck in its frame for a moment and then gave way.

Dennis entered the dim cellar and closed the door. Only the most meager bit of light came through the dirt-encrusted windows, and he waited for his eyes to adjust. His torch was in the car but he didn't want to risk going back for it just now. Wooden crates were piled against the walls, nailed shut. They could contain something or nothing. Strange that whoever had left the footprints had not taken anything... or maybe they had? One box was open. Dennis looked inside to find a set of old china. The plates were delicate blue with a raised white design—Wedgewood. He turned over a cup but could not read the bottom in the dim light. *Probably valuable*, he thought, *but risky to take out of here without breaking anything. Maybe whoever was here last night is coming back.* His eyes had adjusted somewhat now and he inspected the floor just inside the door. The muddy footprints continued inside the door, showing up clearly on the dusty floor, and leading to the same boxes he was inspecting.

He looked around the small room. Just to his left he noticed an opening. A narrow stairway rose to the next floor. Dennis tentatively put his foot on the first step, testing its strength and noise potential. He didn't want to fall through and be trapped here in the cellar, or risk anyone in the house hearing his footsteps and raising an alarm. The step seemed to be solid, so he continued, feeling his way along the dirty walls as he climbed. He counted fourteen steps, then the staircase ended at a locked door. It was pitch dark here; no light reached from above or below.

Dennis heard voices and leaned his ear against the door. This door must be right near the kitchen. Elaine was saying that he had gone out for a walk. "Can I get you anything?" Nara asked politely.

"No," Elaine answered, "I was just admiring your selection of books on the area. I like to read as much as possible to help me in my work in the tourist office."

Their voices trailed away as they turned into the lounge area.

Dennis didn't need the blueprints anymore. He picked his way carefully back down the stairs and out into the sunlight. He squinted as his eyes readjusted. He wouldn't say anything about what he had found, of course. He picked up a few handfuls of dead leaves and piled them over the muddy footprints by the door. His own shoes were muddy, but a walk by the river would explain that.

He walked back to the garden, where he could be seen from the house, at a leisurely pace. He took out his cell phone and dialed Joe once again. No answer. He tried the home number. A woman's voice answered, but it did not sound like Joe's wife.

"Could I speak to Joe please?"

"Who is calling and what is your business with Joe?"

"Who are you and what business is it of yours? I'd like to speak to Joe." *Impudent biddy*, he thought.

"Well, you will have to speak to him in the spirit because he's dead, Joe is. You can call St. Agnes Church to find out when the services will be. Otherwise the family will thank you to leave us alone."

"Wait. I'm a friend of his. What happened?" Joe paced toward the back corner of the garden where the potting shed stood. Several large shovels were leaning neatly in a row against the outside wall.

The woman on the other end of the line seemed to be discussing something with someone in the background. She came back to the phone.

"Who are you, please?" She asked in a more civil voice this time.

"My name is Dennis Maxwell. I'm a friend of Joe's. His wife knows me." She repeated the information, probably to Joe's wife.

He paced back toward the house. One of the cars had returned to the car park, but he could see no movement in the house from where he stood.

The voice returned. "Yes, she remembers you. He was found dead in his car, sunk into one of the canals outside Springfield. Shot in the head."

"My God," was all Dennis could manage.

"Yes. It makes no sense." The woman seemed full of talk now that she had been given leave to talk to Dennis. "Must have been kidnapped, is all we can think. But who would kidnap poor Joe?"

"The police are on it, of course."

"Of course. But that won't bring him back. Lonnie is without her man no matter what now. I'm her sister. I'll do what I can for her. It's going to be a hard time."

"Thank you for telling me." Was there any way the police would connect this with him? He had an alibi. He had been here at the bed and breakfast. "Thank you for telling me. Give my condolences to... *What was her name?...* to Lonnie."

"I will do that." He rang off.

Dennis went inside to find Elaine. It was time to go back to Lincoln. There was nothing more to do here.

TWENTY-ONE

The plane touched down at Heathrow about ten minutes ahead of schedule. The two men and the woman cleared customs easily as citizens of St. Clare, a former British colony. They spotted the sign, Hadley Antiques, among the crowd of tour companies and drivers meeting the international flights. The person holding the sign was no ordinary cab driver, but the handsome son of Mr. Hadley, the owner and manager of the enterprise. William Hadley was every bit the modern businessman, although he knew the antique trade inside and out. He shook hands formally with the three visitors, then flipped open his cell phone to contact his father. "Just picked them up, Dad. We're leaving the airport now."

He flipped the phone closed and led them to the taxi that was waiting outside. "I'll take you to your hotel first. Let you rest a bit. We'll send a car round for you about 4:00." He looked at each of them in turn. None of the three looked like antique dealers, which was all the better. Michael Carrington, the warehouse manager, was of medium build, olive skin and dark hair. He had the muscular build of a man who had done physical work all his life. While he had no formal education, he seemed well-schooled in moving goods from one place to another—and making a profit for himself on the side.

The young woman with him was introduced as his cousin, Lily. She was petite with long dark hair and wide, dark eyes. *A real beauty,* William thought appreciably. She had spoken little beyond a basic greeting and stared raptly out the window as the London suburbs flew by. The third member of the group was tall and dark, elegantly dressed in linen trousers and an open neck shirt, with a dark sweater swung casually over his shoulders. He had introduced himself as Dr. Davis Jarrett.

Nara left for class that afternoon with plans to ask Micki if she wanted to explore the Cathedral afterwards. But Micki seemed distracted during class and afterwards told Nara that she couldn't go to the Cathedral because her youngest child had a fever. She had promised she would only go to class and come right back, but she wished Nara good luck on her Friday night date with Alex, and promised to go with her on Monday for a tour of the Cathedral with Elaine.

It was an overcast, blustery afternoon, raining off and on. Nara maneuvered her car into a narrow space in a crowded car park a short way down the hill and climbed up Steep Hill. There was no other way to walk up the hill except slowly, so she looked in the shop windows as she climbed. The narrow, cobblestoned street was lined with book shops, art galleries, and tea shops and restaurants. Nara was fascinated and promised herself she would come back when she had more time and some money to spend.

She was freezing when she arrived at the Cathedral, and the old Gothic building didn't feel much warmer than the outdoors. Nevertheless, she was awed by the grandeur of the architecture. Lincoln was the first Gothic cathedral Nara had visited. She and her father did not take time to visit any of the historic sites in London when they arrived in the country due to his illness. Aunt Sue had met them at Heathrow and zipped them up to Springfield in her car to hot tea, food and rest. Her father had slept for almost two days straight.

Nara walked quietly inside the cathedral, her eyes drawn upward to the vaulting of the great building. She had never been in any place so old, and the feeling of antiquity was overwhelming. She looked down at the stone floor, and realized she was walking on the graves of people who had been dead for 400 years or more. Confusion overcame her for a moment as she heard, or rather felt, the voices of visitors to the cathedral over the centuries. She put her hands over her ears and snapped herself back to reality.

There was a visitor's desk where tickets were being sold for guided and self-guided tours. She had half-hoped that Elaine could show her around, but was out on a city tour that afternoon. Nara paid the few pounds for a self-guided tour, knowing full well that her money wouldn't go very far on the upkeep of so grand and ancient a place, but it was something. She thanked the woman at the desk and opened her pamphlet, starting in the direction of the first stop on the tour.

She dutifully studied a few portraits and statues, and then wandered off on her own. She found "the imp" on his perch at the top of a column in the Angel Choir and smiled at her memory of the story that Elaine had told her just that morning. One version of the legend was that the imp had been sent by the devil to wreak havoc in the Lincoln Cathedral. The little creature was throwing things around the building, making a general mess when an angel caught him at it and turned him into stone.

Nara shivered with the cold, thinking that Lincolnshire would be a truly wonderful place if it weren't for the climate. She made herself shrug off the thought and walked toward the other side of the cathedral, where small side chapels lined the outer wall. As she stepped into the first chapel, she suddenly had the eerie feeling that someone was watching her. Her eyes adjusted to the gloom, and she looked around the small room. The stained glass windows let in little light on this overcast day. The chapel was empty except for a wooden bench placed at the rear. "For quiet prayer and meditation," the sign read.

Nara turned toward the doorway to return to the main church and tripped on a loose stone in the floor. She caught herself with a hand outstretched to the prayer bench, and as she stood upright she could have sworn she heard someone breathing. When she turned back to the doorway, Dennis Maxwell stood blocking her way.

"My father died in this chapel," he said.

"I'm sorry. I didn't know." Nara wanted to leave the chapel but he continued to stand there.

"He fell and hit his head on the stones, and when they found him the next morning, he was dead. Cold as the stones."

Nara couldn't think what to say, and even if she could, she was sure she had no voice with which to speak.

Dennis continued. "They said he must have tripped on the stones in the floor, just like you did. I didn't believe them. What do you think?"

He stepped part way back from the doorway, as if indicating she could pass, but not allowing her enough room. "Come on out of there. It's deadly cold." She walked toward Dennis and the doorway, desperate to get out but repulsed by being so close to the strange little man. He stepped back to allow her to pass, then quickly stepped behind her and grabbed her shoulders, moving close behind her. He bent his face close to her right ear, his lips brushing her cheek and whispered, "Be careful."

Nara could hear tourists' voices not far away. Dennis dropped his hands and strode quickly in the opposite direction.

Nara walked back into the choir area, her knees shaking. She tried to study the needlepoint designs on the kneelers, pretending to be fascinated by the stitches and workmanship while her heart rate returned to normal. When she felt steadier she began to walk around again. She needed to get out in the open air and think, but she did not want to be seen running out in a fright—by Dennis or anyone else. Neither would she let that evil man spoil her enjoyment of this beautiful, spiritual place. She believed he was trying to frighten her, but she didn't know why.

She stopped to examine a face carved into the bottom of a large wooden frame. This must be the "green man" Elaine had talked about. She reached out her hand to touch the features.

"So you've discovered our green man." The voice was gentle and familiar, with a hint of humor, but in Nara's nervous state she jumped nonetheless and stepped back against Alex's solid masculine form.

"Steady," he laughed, and now it was his hands on her shoulders. "I didn't mean to frighten you."

"You scared the life out of me."

"Sorry. I was just glad to see you."

"What are you doing here?" she snapped. Her head was beginning to ache and she felt dizzy.

"It's part of my job. I stop in here every couple of weeks."

"Oh, right. I forgot. I'm sorry."

Alex looked carefully at her face. "What's wrong? You're white as a sheet."

"I tripped in one of the chapels and almost fell. I guess it scared me. And it's really cold in here." She rubbed her arms, thinking that Alex's hands had just touched the same spots.

"How about some tea?" he said gently.

"The English panacea for any trouble, a cup of tea." She smiled up at him and then glanced at her watch. "I really should be getting back home."

"Nonsense." He took her arm, tucking one cold hand in his. "You will be better off driving after you've warmed up. Tea just takes a few minutes."

She acquiesced, partly because his touch felt so good—so warm. She had never appreciated warmth so much when she lived on St. Clare! As they passed out of the main door into the dreary afternoon, Dennis Maxwell stood just outside smoking a cigarette. He glanced up, catching Nara's eye for just a split second, before moving on to Alex. Did a spark of recognition flash between the two of them? Nara couldn't say, but there might have been.

It was beginning to rain. Alex put his arm around her shoulders and said, "Let's run." Together they ran out of the Cathedral Close and out into Castle Square. "Some tea is what we need."

The rain came down harder as they ran, changing in a few moments from a soft mist to a downpour. They reached the doorway of a cafe just before they would have been thoroughly soaked. "Come." Alex pulled her inside and led her down a stairway to the main room of the restaurant. Although below ground level, the walls were painted white, and colorful works of art hung on the walls. A fire crackled in the fireplace. Alex seated Nara where she could feel the warmth of the flames and helped her out of her wet jacket. "I'll go order tea," he said. "Would you like something to eat?"

"Yes, please." Suddenly she felt hungry. "A scone would be nice."

"A scone it is."

Nara ran her fingers through her hair. She must look a mess. She shivered. She rubbed her hands together to warm them. A shiver ran through her entire body.

By the time Alex returned she was shivering violently and couldn't stop.

"Nara! What's wrong?"

She clenched her fists to try to stop the shivering, but to no avail. "I—I don't know," she answered through chattering teeth. "It... it must be the cold, and the rain. I'm not used to it."

Alex's frown made it clear that he believed it was more than that, but he said nothing. He removed his jacket, draped it around her shoulders and moved his chair close to hers, putting his arm around her. "It's all right. Breathe deeply." The warmth of his arm, the feel of his jacket still warm from his body, his closeness, began to calm her shivering, and give her different and more pleasant sensation altogether. She took in another deep breath. His chin rested on the top of her head, and she could feel the warmth of his breath. She raised her head to look at his face, and his brown eyes caught hers. Their faces were just inches apart, and there was nothing to do but meet his lips in a kiss. It was a gentle kiss that deepened, surprising her with its intensity. It seemed less a beginning than a culmination of something that had begun long ago.

They were interrupted with the sound of footsteps descending from the shop above. They moved apart as the waitress entered with a tray of tea and scones. "Here you are then. Nice and hot." She arranged the things on the table. "Enjoy your tea. It's a good day to be in drinking tea. You made it just in time." She indicated the downpour that was still going on outside.

They both poured milk into their tea, and Alex added two spoonfuls of sugar to her cup. They took their first sips of the hot liquid silently, and as Nara reached for her scone, richly filled with marmalade and double cream, Alex covered her outstretched hand with his.

"What's wrong, Nara?"

She looked up at him, her eyes suddenly brimming with tears. "I don't know. All of a sudden everything just hit me."

For the next half hour, Nara found herself pouring out her distress to Alex—her fears about her father's health, Aunt Sue's strange and secretive behavior, her loneliness for St. Clare, the strangeness of living in England. Added to those worries was the break-in the other night, which only she seemed to take seriously. Her father was too sick and Aunt Sue too preoccupied. She even told him how Dennis Maxwell had frightened her in the Cathedral. The only thing she left out, in fact, was Davis.

It was still raining when they left the tea shop. Alex put his arm around Nara to steady her through the cold, rainy weather. In spite of the cold wind and rain, Nara felt a sense of warmth this last hour with Alex that she had not felt since her earliest memories of childhood, when her mother was still alive. Even though she had known Alex only a few days, she felt comfortable with him. He held her close as they fought their way through the wind and rain back down the hill to her car in the car park near the Usher Gallery.

"Will you be all right now?" he asked when she was settled behind the steering wheel.

"Of course. I'm just going back to Springfield." She laughed lightly, her independent spirit still stung by the stress of the afternoon.

"I'll call you tonight," he said. He then started back up the hill toward his own car, parked below the Cathedral next to the Old Bishop's Palace .

TWENTY-TWO

In the London hospital, Terry Clark was thinking of her parents when she woke up. The room was almost dark, with the hum of voices from the hall. *I really should call and let them know I'm in the hospital.* The nurses kept offering to call for her, but she refused. She rarely spoke to them these days. There was a tiny part of her that was ashamed of the dishonesty of her work, and she knew her parents would be horrified if they knew the whole truth.

Terry had gone her own way after high school. She was ambitious and smart but not a student, so university was not for her. Her parents hadn't minded as long as she worked hard and stayed out of trouble, and she did. She was good at selling and had started out at the local Marks & Spencer in the lingerie department when she was 18 years old. She became interested in antiques when her friend's grandmother's house and its contents had been put up for sale after the woman's death. Terry was amazed that the trinkets and household items from the twenties and thirties had gone for such high prices at auction. To Terry it looked like a much better way to make a living than selling lingerie.

She took a few courses in art history and business. She visited museums and took notes. Eventually she felt confident enough to apply for a position as a floor girl at Hadley's Antiques in Regent Street, and Mr. Hadley had noticed her potential, her drive and determination. She had gone from floor girl to one of the firm's top antiques buyers, entrusted not only with the legitimate buying from individuals and estates, but also the under-the-table purchases, where the firm looked the other way as to how and from what source the purchases were made.

At 26, Terry was the firm's top salesperson and field worker. She knew the merchandise, and, even more importantly, she knew how to handle people to get the most profit for Hadley's.

She was accustomed to dealing with people like Dennis Maxwell—small time thieves who had a little bit of knowledge and some luck. Knowledge and luck. That was what was required in the antiques business, especially if you didn't look too closely into the background of the pieces you acquired. Turn over the merchandise quickly and keep two sets of records. That was the motto at Hadley's, and Terry had done very well living and working by it.

Now she was in hospital with a concussion, she was told. And she honestly did not remember what had happened. Someone had hit her from behind and taken her briefcase and purse. Her briefcase contained a copy of the master list of all the merchandise Hadley's had available for sale. None of the items had turned up so far. It was impossible to know if her assailant was a petty thief merely after cash, credit cards and other personal valuables, or if it was someone who knew that she might be carrying the list and was after it. And although Scotland Yard was involved in the case, anyone with the right knowledge and background would recognize that a number of the items on the list in the briefcase had been stolen over the past two years. This was what worried Terry the most as she lay in her hospital bed, and this was what worried her boss as well as he wined and dined his buyers and potential customers from St. Clare.

She looked at the phone on the table next to the bed. All she had to do was dial and the phone would be ringing in her parent's house in Golders Green. She closed her eyes and fell asleep again.

In Regent Street, Michael, Lily and Davis were just finishing tea with the Hadley executives. Davis Jarrett knew what his wealthy friends on the island wanted. With their backing, he was willing to pay whatever it took to bring the best, the oldest, the rarest pieces to decorate their luxurious homes high above the white sand beaches. Since his was a name that was not well-known, he could act in their stead and help them achieve their dreams of bringing more than a little bit of English history to their palatial island homes. They wanted the best, the rarest. And these beautiful pieces of England would stay in their homes, hidden, locked away from the eyes of the public. The people who would possess these treasures wanted to do just that, possess them. It was the pride of ownership that drove them, the value of the material things that were worth only money to them—and they had money in abundance. Davis would be one of them in a few years; his idealism and his thoughts of running a pediatric clinic for island children were all swept away in his desire to possess.

Michael Carrington was the manager of Blake Imports, Ltd., where he handled the day-to-day business for the owner, Jack Blake. Michael was hard-working and intelligent; he had been at the firm since he was a teenager. Now in his thirties, he knew the business inside and out. Increasingly over the years, Jack had turned the management of the company over to Michael, who hoped to take over the company someday—or at least attain the position of executive manager. Jack's health was declining, and his daughter Nara had no interest in the family business. Yet even when Jack and Nara moved to England, he received no promotion or raise in salary. He supplemented his income with the smuggled antiquities that passed through the firm—as he had done for at least the past five years.

Lily was Michael's cousin, but they had been raised under the same roof by their grandmother. Lily was an artist, and that gave her a certain aptitude when it came to evaluating antique works of art. Michael had learned to recognize and admire good pieces, too—as well as junk when poor imitations occasionally slipped through. They rarely did, at least not from Hadley's, and he did business almost exclusively with Hadley's now. Michael wanted to be rich. It was as simple as that. He had grown up in poverty on the island. He wasn't sure who his father was, though his mother had hinted before she died that he was someone important on the island. Michael thought for a while that it might be Jack Blake, but that idea just didn't feel right. He had watched Jack carefully and detected no sign that he knew anything, and saw no father/son resemblance. But it was during this time, when he thought Jack might be his father, that he caught hold of the idea of taking over the company.

Nara had been away at school in Miami for several years, only returning for holidays. While it was clear that she idolized her father, she showed no interest in the business, there for a visit and then gone again. She was of no consequence to Michael and the plans he had for his life. He worked hard every day, both for himself and for Blake Imports. In time, Michael came to realize that Jack ran the business as if he were in his sleep; only making minor adjustments from time to time while leaving most of the decisions to him. Jack was weak—he had been since the death of his first wife.

Michael communicated with Jack by e-mail daily, giving him facts and figures about the business that were sometimes phony, sometimes real. He had told Jack that he would be away for a few days visiting an aunt and uncle in Miami, but would still be in touch by e-mail. Jack had not replied, and Michael had no fears that he would encounter Jack, sick as he was, in London.

TWENTY-THREE

Nara drove home from Lincoln in a daze. She was later than she had expected to be, so she knew that Aunt Sue would be upset. And the events of the afternoon had left her confused. Her feelings for Alex surprised her. She hadn't really gotten over Davis; she had not expected to feel so strongly attracted to another man, but, as she drove along, she kept thinking of the way it felt when she leaned her head against Alex's shoulder. It had felt so right. And he had kissed her. Nara caught her breath and felt a melting softness inside. *He is attractive, kind, intelligent, funny. What more can I ask?* Another part of her brain argued: You don't know him that well. *But I'm getting to know him. We are having dinner tomorrow night.* That thought caused her to catch her breath again, and then her thoughts wandered to thinking about what she would wear. *Maybe the female mind turns to clothes to protect it from thinking about the deeper questions–like what am I doing letting myself be attracted to this man I barely know?*

Nara had slowed down her driving while she was daydreaming, passing through the brown fields dotted with villages and farmhouses off in the distance in the Lincolnshire countryside with barely a glance. A small car roared past her and disappeared ahead towards Springfield, and it made her think of Dennis Maxwell again. The first time she had seen him had been when he had almost hit her and Micki the day they registered at the college. Since then he seemed to turn up every time she turned around.

He had been outside the restaurant where she and Micki were having tea, and at the bed and breakfast with his wife, and then at the Cathedral. Why had he tried to frighten her—and why had he succeeded? She was sure that Alex knew him on some level, and that thought gave her a chill. *What have I gotten myself into?* Was everything as it seemed? Was anything ever as it seemed? Nara arrived home thinking there were too many mysteries in her life right now and maybe it was time to get to the bottom of at least one of them.

Aunt Sue was in a tizzy, as usual. She was getting dressed to go out, in an expensive designer black dress that just skimmed her knees.

"Oh, great. You're here. I was just about to start your father's tea. Were you caught in the rain?"

"Yes. I was." Nara felt slightly out of breath as she set her bag down on the counter, removed her raincoat and hung it on the peg by the door, and slipped her feet out of her still sodden shoes. She considered running upstairs to quickly get another pair of shoes, but decided against it since she didn't want to lose the moment to talk to Aunt Sue. She hoped she wouldn't catch cold walking around on the cold stone floor in her damp socks, but at the moment it couldn't be helped.

She reached for a knife and started to slice an apple for the plate of fruit and cheese that Sue was preparing.

"Aunt Sue?"

The older woman turned toward her absently as she poured the boiling water into the teapot. "Hmm?"

"May I say you are looking wonderful these days? Have you been going to the gym? That dress looks smashing on you." Nara carefully watched the look on her aunt's face. She saw conflicting emotions flit across her eyes, and a slight smile spread to her lips, but just as quickly the older woman brought it under control. In that instant Nara saw pleasure at the compliment and a kind of secret joy before she closed herself up again.

Nara seized the moment. "Aunt Sue." She put down the knife and spoke quietly, with all the sympathy and woman-to-woman emotion she could muster. "Whoever he is, he seems to be making you very happy."

A heartbeat passed. Sue turned toward her niece. "What did you say?" she asked weakly.

Nara kept her voice soft. "I think it's wonderful. When are we going to meet him?"

The emotion on Sue's face this time was something like shock, and it had gone very white. "I... I don't know. He works long hours. I usually meet him in Lincoln."

"Where did you meet him?" Nara asked, in what she hoped was a genuine female-to-female question of interest.

"I... I've know him for a long time. We just... just started seeing each other a couple of months ago."

"What's his name?"

Sue stared at Nara for a long moment before she started to turn away. "I don't have time to talk now, Nara. I'm running late as it is."

"He's married, isn't he?"

Sue stopped in her tracks and turned back to Nara. For a moment the younger woman thought she was going to strike out at her, the anger in her face was so intense, and then it softened and tears began to roll down her cheeks.

"Yes, he's married."

Nara went to her aunt and put her arms around her. She could not see her aunt's face, but she could feel her crying. Tears dripped onto Nara's neck, and she could feel her aunt's breath shaking her body.

After a couple of minutes, Sue pulled away and reached for a kitchen towel to dry her eyes. Her mascara was smeared, creating dark raccoon-like circles around her eyes. Nara took the towel from her hands and wiped it away as best she could.

"He has made me feel younger, more alive, than I have in years. Maybe than I ever have. I've never been a young, carefree person. I've always had someone to take care of. I thought he really loved me. But lately—I don't think he is going to leave his wife." She laughed sadly. "I think that's why I have lost so much weight lately. I know it's going to end, and I don't want it to."

They heard footsteps on the stairs. Jack was coming down for his tea. At the same time the sounds of a car tires on the gravel of the car park intruded on the moment.

"Go fix your face and take off," Nara said quietly. "Enjoy your evening and then tell the bastard to get lost. You're too good for him. Break up with him before he breaks up with you."

"I don't know if I can," Sue responded, her voice still full of tears and barely above a whisper.

"Sure you can. It will give you power."

"I'm afraid I'll gain the weight back."

"Come running with me," Nara grinned impishly.

Jack walked into the kitchen. "Tea ready?" He noticed the two women in an obvious tete-a-tete. "Sorry. I didn't mean to intrude on girl talk."

"It's okay, Dad. We've sorted things out."

He looked from the calm, to the tear stains on the face of his sister, taking in the sexy dress.

"I'll see you later. I won't be late." Sue left just as the door opened and two guests walked in.

Jack looked questioningly at Nara. "I'll tell you later," she whispered.

TWENTY-FOUR

In Lincoln, Micki placed plates of melted cheese on toast in front of her two small children. She cut the toast into small squares the way they liked it.

"Tony, eat the food. Don't stick your fingers in it." Small Tony, six years old with his father's ready smile, was poking his index finger into the melted cheese, watching the little dents that were left behind. He glanced at his mother, picked up a square, and stuffed it whole into his mouth. Micki sighed and said nothing; she had told him to eat it.

Micki was thinking of bringing the children along to visit the Cathedral on Monday. Or maybe she would just bring Tony; he was old enough to learn to appreciate some of the history of the city where he lived. Christy was only a year old; it might be better if she stayed with Grandma. She was sure Nara wouldn't mind if Tony came along. She would call and ask if she thought Elaine would have a problem with it. She thought it would be okay, but it was always a nice gesture to ask first.

She smiled to herself as she picked up her own toast and cheese and chewed thoughtfully while she leaned against the kitchen counter. She was content with her life, which was more than most people could say, and she thanked God for it every day, even if she hadn't been inside a church in years. Well, she would be in the Cathedral on Monday, but that was different. That was more history than religion. She more easily saw God in the faces of her children than the stones of a church, but that was just her. And she had a new friend—Nara. Life was good. She was truly blessed.

Her husband came back into the kitchen telling her he just checked in two couples and a single businessman. "Everyone out there is settled. How's everyone here?" He tousled the children's hair, then came over to Micki and pulled her close. "Why don't you sit down, luv? Take a break."

"I will. I have studying to do."

"That's not a break," he teased.

"It is for me." She looked at the children who were tearing their last pieces of toast into tiny pieces and eating them one at a time. Tony had started it, and Christy imitated him as best she could with her clumsy fingers.

"You are an amazing woman. I love you," he whispered into her hair, sending chills down her spine.

"I love you, too." She moved closer.

"I'll clean up here. You study. Once these two are in bed we'll have some time together."

Micki kissed his lips, leaving the taste of cheese behind, then kissed the children and headed for her bedroom. She would study hard and then spend time some romantic time with her husband. She couldn't think of a better reward.

Terry Clark insisted on coming in to the office Friday morning. She had been released from the hospital the day before and was feeling much better. The headache was almost gone and she could remember everything except for the actual moment when she was attacked. Retrograde amnesia, the doctor called it—it was common in such situations, he said, and her memory of the actual moment she had been struck would probably never come back. Her purse had been found in a dustbin a few blocks away, minus the cash and credit cards, of course, but still containing her ID. She was going to get the locks changed on her flat just the same. Terry's cell phone was gone, too, and the contacts on it were cause for concern.

Her briefcase had not turned up, and that was where the lists were. Only the police would see any significance to the lists, and only if antiquities experts happened to look at it. Mr. Hadley told her it was fortunate she had amnesia, because it gave her an excuse not to tell the police about the contents of the briefcase. Anyone connected with Scotland Yard would surely recognize some of the items on the list. Most of them were on their list too—their list of stolen historical treasures. In the meantime, it was back to business as usual at Hadley's Antiques, Ltd. They would limit contact with "questionable" dealers for a few weeks, but they had customers ready to buy, and would be foolish to turn them away.

After receiving the sympathy from her co-workers, Terry set about going through her calls and messages of the past few days. Most were from business associates expressing concern about her accident, another group were business calls from people who knew nothing about the accident, and there were several from Dennis Maxwell in Lincoln.

Maybe he had something for her. He was an unknown contact, and maybe she could redeem herself if she could bring in some new business. She dialed his cell number. He answered immediately, and she spoke quickly in the cold, business-like manner she reserved for vermin like him.

"It's Terry Clark from Hadley's. What do you have for me?"

"I—hold on a minute."

She could hear muffled voices, a woman and Dennis were shouting. *He really is a little twit,* Terry thought. There was the sound of a door slamming.

"Okay. I'm back."

"So what do you have for me?" Terry tapped a pen impatiently on her desk.

"Maybe something besides the church stuff. I've gotten access to an old house with a lot of antiques in it."

"What kind of things?"

"I haven't had a chance to go through everything, but there are boxes of things in storage, plus the things on display."

Terry still didn't have the energy to deal with this man. "You need something better than that. I don't have time for 'things.' I need specific pieces. And I need to know when you can get them to me. If you can't do that, then don't bother me." She rang off.

TWENTY-FIVE

Nara was restless. Her father had gone upstairs to read, the guests were all out, and Aunt Sue had gone out with her married man. Nara wondered if he was someone from Springfield? This was a small town. She could imagine the gossip if the news leaked out and the embarrassment to the man's wife. *I hope Sue is careful,* she thought. *And I hope she sticks to her guns and breaks up with him before he breaks up with her.* Sue was a very giving person, but Nara knew there was a fine line between "giving" and "doormat."

Idly, Nara picked up some of the objects on the shelves in the hallway just outside the kitchen. They didn't look as if they were worth much. She really wished she knew more about antiques. Maybe she could buy some books or take a class. And that brought her thoughts back to her studies at Lincoln College. She was enrolled in two business classes. She was doing it to please her father, who had dreams of her taking over the import business in St. Clare one day. When he had been diagnosed with cancer, it looked as if that day might come sooner than later. But Nara had absolutely no interest in business. She was sure she would make a mess of things if she ever were in charge of the business that her father, and her grandfather before him, had worked so hard to build up. Besides, they had a capable manager, who would surely resent Nara coming in and trying to manage something that he had done so well over the years.

Nara knew that if her father died, she would sell the business. But beyond that, she didn't know what she wanted to do with her life. She had been a teacher for a short time after college, but that had been a disaster. And she was already wondering if she would really want to go back to St. Clare. Davis was there, and it was a small island. She wasn't sure she could bear running into him on a regular basis, and she knew now that their relationship was over. Even if he wanted her back, she had moved on. *But moved on to what?*

As she thought, she picked up items of bric-a-brac from the shelves. There were cups and saucers, and little figurines of china and porcelain. She turned some of them over to study the markings on the bottoms. Some had none; some had numbers or words that meant nothing to her. *I would recognize the name Wedgewood, but that's about it,* she thought.

She picked up a mug with a small town market scene painted on it. When she turned it over, a small key fell to the floor. Nara bent to pick it up, remembering now that she had found the key on the linen shelf the other day and had placed it in the mug. She had completely forgotten about it. Now was a good time to do some investigating and try to find out what, if anything, the key fit. She looked around on the nearby shelves and saw nothing. She noticed a dusty wooden box on one of the higher shelves, and stood on tiptoe trying to reach it. How many times had see wished she were just two inches taller than five feet two inches? She was too lazy, or stubborn, to go get a step stool from the kitchen, so she held onto the shelves and jumped. She was able to touch the box, but not get a grip on it. She tried again. This time she succeeded in pushing the box back farther on the shelf, but something else happened. The entire set of shelves seemed to move. *Weird,* she thought, and then stood flat and jiggled the shelves. Yes, they definitely moved. She pushed, and heard a faint clicking sound, like a latch locking or unlocking. She pushed again and nothing happened, and stood still for a moment, thinking.

The house was perfectly silent. A car slowed on the road in front, but did not turn in. Nara looked at her watch. It was ten o'clock. The guests could be back from dinner at any minute. She didn't get opportunities like this very often, with the house to herself. She took a deep breath and pushed again, heard the click and pulled the shelves toward her. The shelves swung open like a door, revealing a dusty stairway leading downward. *This is the staircase her father had found on the blueprints!* She simply stared for a moment, allowing her eyes to adjust to the dimness. A cobweb-covered string dangled a few inches in front of her face. Looking up, Nara saw that it connected to a grimy light bulb. She gingerly pulled the string with the tips of her fingers and was rewarded with illumination. The staircase looked sturdy enough, and at the bottom she could see boxes piled in the gloom.

She propped the entry way open with one of Aunt Sue's old shoes that was sitting in the hallway. The last thing she wanted was to be trapped down there. She put her weight down on the first step, which creaked softly, then she went on more confidently down the steps. There were stacks and stacks of boxes—some were wooden crates, some pasteboard, and one of the pasteboard boxes stood open. *That's odd,* she thought. Nara looked inside and saw what looked like a full set of porcelain dinnerware. She picked up a cup. *Odd that's not dusty.* Suddenly she realized that this box had been opened recently. Someone had been here!

Nara's heart began to pound as she looked around the silent, gloomy room. The musty smell and dust made her want to sneeze. She left the open box as it was; whoever had been here needn't know that someone else had been there as well. She went over to one of the wooden crates and lifted the lid. There were several boxes inside, some looked like the kind people used to use to store letters, back when people actually wrote letters and saved them. There was also a wooden box that looked identical to the one she had seen on the shelf upstairs. She took it out and studied it. A dark wood, carved with some intricate pattern, possibly from India. A small padlock hung from it. Where was the key she had found? She slid her hand into her pants pocket and found it. A perfect fit. The box was full of what looked like junk jewelry. But who knew if it was junk? Nara used her finger to poke around at the pieces, fascinated.

She heard footsteps above her. She quickly closed the crate, tucking the box under her arm, and ran up the steps. She turned off the light and emerged into the hallway, pushing the bookcase door closed behind her.

"Hello?"

It was some of the guests returning.

Nara steadied herself and walked calmly into the lounge. "I was just checking some supplies downstairs. How was your dinner?"

"It was lovely. The hotel you recommended was wonderful. Have you ever had their stuffed peppers? The best I've ever eaten." The woman was enthusiastic.

Her husband stood quietly. "My steak was a bit overdone, I'd say."

"Now, Geoff. You know you take a chance when you order meat well-done."

Nara smiled slightly. There was nothing like embarrassing yourself in front of your spouse. Still, she made a mental note to suggest to her dad and Aunt Sue that they give the Woodbridge a try for dinner one night, since she hadn't actually been there.

"Can I get anything for you? Tea?" Nara was amazed at how quickly she had picked up the English habit of offering tea for any occasion, from a lag in the conversation to a death in the family.

"No thank you," the wife answered. "I think we will go on to our room."
"Good night, then."

Nara checked the front and back door locks, and headed to her own room, the box of jewelry under her arm.

TWENTY-SIX

Alex read the e-mail over again, not wanting to believe what he saw. Scotland Yard had informed them that three people, two men and a woman, had arrived from St. Clare, had been met by a driver sent by Hadley's Antiques, and had spent the day in meetings with Mr. Hadley himself.

It was a coincidence, surely. But then a second message had come, verifying that one of the two men, one Michael Carrington, was the manager of Blake Imports. Still—a coincidence. No reason to think that Nara knew anything, or was involved in any way, or even her father, for that matter. Alex took a sip of the glass of wine he had poured for himself and grimaced. He was drinking less and less since his break-up with Laura. He found he had less desire, less need, fewer occasions to drink, and the stuff tasted nasty. He wondered if he should give it up altogether. Would it matter? He wondered if Nara drank. Most people did these days, but not everyone.

His thoughts came back to Nara and the smuggling ring. He just couldn't believe she could be involved in smuggling stolen antiquities, but why not? He was allowing his heart to rule his head, and he couldn't do his job if he thought that way. Or maybe she wasn't involved, but knew what was going on? How much did she know about her father's business? He realized that he barely knew Nara. Dinner tomorrow night was to be their first real "date." He hadn't expected to feel the strong attraction that was already burgeoning in him. Was it just that he felt sorry for her after the incident with Dennis at the Cathedral? And what had that been all about? Why was she even there?

He shook his head. This line of thinking was getting him nowhere. Lots of people visited the medieval cathedrals in England. Why not Nara, who was, in fact, new to the country.

Finally alone in her room, Nara gently opened the wooden box. She removed several pieces and placed them on her desk, lining up the pieces of tarnished metal with sparkling stones. Some of them were gold, certainly, but of what quality? A brooch caught her eye. It was gold, an antique style with a clumsily fashioned clasp on the back. It reminded her of the pins some people in St. Clare made to sell to the tourists, with a safety pin for a clasp. But this brooch was something she had never seen before, at least not on a piece of jewelry. The dark red and white stones formed the figure of the imp from the Lincoln Cathedral. She studied the gold backing. The piece was heavy, whatever that meant. When she held the brooch up to the light, the stones blazed blood red and fiery white light. Could they be diamonds and rubies? And if this was real, what about the rest of the pieces in the box, and the rest of the boxes in the Gate House store room, for that matter? Nara realized she should tell someone, but whom? Legally everything in the house belonged to Aunt Sue, but she was so unpredictable these days. She could tell Alex; this was his line of work, after all, but she didn't really know him that well. What if he wasn't really who he said he was?

She looked at the imp again, his face sparkling in the artificial light of her bedroom. He looked sinister now, behind the mischievous grin. Perhaps the best thing to do would be to take the jewelry, or at least the brooch, to London to be appraised. She could ask around and see if she could get a recommendation. Maybe Elaine would know someone.

Terry Clark could not believe her luck. It was beginning to look like whoever had knocked her out and stolen her briefcase had only been after money and valuables; the precious list of Hadley's acquisitions had not turned up anywhere. The police hadn't found it; no blackmailers had contacted them. They had watched all their sources and contacts, and no unusual interest was being shown in any of the items. It looked as if she was in the clear. And now that she was feeling better, Mr. Hadley had asked her to take a trip up to Lincolnshire and to bring along the handsome doctor from St. Clare for company.

To tell the truth, he wasn't exactly for company. He was representing a wealthy client in St. Clare who was furnishing a new house. She had seen photographs of it and they were breathtaking. Perched high on a cliff above the sea, the house was built to look like an eighteenth century English manor house. The owner was sparing no expense to create an English garden surrounding the house and was furnishing the interior with authentic antiques. And he wasn't limiting himself to only items from the eighteenth century. He was willing to look at anything old and valuable, from medieval up to the end of the nineteenth century. "Before the First World War changed everything. I was born in the wrong century," he was fond of saying. "Before that war having a title in front of your name meant something."

Terry had never met the man, and neither had Mr. Hadley. But he was known by reputation and by the size of the retainer he had paid the Hadley firm to search for, purchase, and deliver the antiques he desired. Now all Terry had to do was follow up. She had the name of a new contact from Mr. Hadley, and she would get in touch with that funny little man she had met in Lincoln. She was wondering if it would be more to her advantage to bring the handsome doctor along to that interview, when she pulled up in front of his Oxford Street hotel.

He was standing at the hotel door, dressed in dark casual pants and a red shirt that made his dark skin look like burnished bronze. He ran a hand across his close-cropped hair, unsure for a moment if this was the car he was waiting for. When he recognized Terry from their meeting the day before, he smiled, showing very white, even teeth. He walked round to the passenger side, carefully watching for traffic as he did so, and climbed into the seat next to her. Terry was immediately aware of a subtle aftershave scent, and the scent, or just the presence, of the man next to her. *It has been too long,* she thought. *My heart pounds when a good-looking male sits next to me in the car. For all I know, he's married.*

"Good morning." He turned the dazzling smile on Terry full force.

"Good morning." Her voice came out softer and more feminine than it usually did. *Get it together, Terry,* she told herself.

By the time Terry had guided the car through London traffic and they were out of the city and headed north, she was totally captivated. She would do anything for this man. He was a doctor, getting ready to open his own clinic, with the financial backing of the investor who was purchasing antiques for his house. He had come to England as a favor. He was trusted to make the right decisions about spending money, and he had friends in Lincolnshire that he planned to visit.

"Are you married?" Terry's heart pounded, waiting for the answer.

He laughed. "No. I almost was once." There was a heartbeat pause. "I'm not ready for marriage."

"I'm not either. I'm too independent." She concentrated on the road ahead as a lorry pulled in front of them onto the motorway. She laughed. "So now that we have that settled, maybe we should get down to business." She put on her turn signal and pulled around the slow moving lorry. "What exactly are you looking for in England? For your client, that is?"

"He isn't exactly a client. I'm a doctor, not an antiques dealer. He's a friend, an associate. I'm doing him a favor, and he does favors for me. It's a mutual arrangement."

"All right." Terry could be patient when it came to dealing with clients with money. "Does he have any specific idea of what kind of antiques he wants?"

"Oh, absolutely." Davis fished in his briefcase and came up with a list, neatly printed. For a heart-stopping moment Terry thought of the list that had been stolen along with her briefcase, but of course this was different altogether.

Davis put on a pair of reading glasses, which gave him a very sexy look, Terry thought, as she pulled her eyes back to the road. He skimmed the list and then read some of the items.

"Stained glass of any kind as long as it is good quality. Ceramic ware, anything before 1900. Wooden beams, old ones. Fireplace mantel."

Terry looked at him. She had been concentrating on what he read, trying to think what she had or could acquire. "Fireplace mantel? What does he need a fireplace for in St. Clare?"

"Atmosphere."

"Oh." She turned her eyes back to the road. "Go ahead. What else?"

"He is most interested in medieval pieces. I know those are hard to come by, so he will take anything made in that style up to 1800. Any gold or silver religious pieces."

Terry thought of Lincoln Cathedral looming above the town. Most of the treasures had been stolen centuries ago, and the pieces remaining were well-secured. But what about the village churches? They were less secure and always in need of money. What was available from those sources? She knew many of the pieces Hadley's acquired were stolen, but she tried not to think about it. She simply approached the suppliers her boss sent her to. She dealt with customers and the occasional individuals who approached them with pieces, sometimes real and sometimes not. Sometimes the pieces were acquired legitimately and sometimes not. It might be worth talking to the contact in Lincoln, much as Terry hated the idea. But she would bring Davis with her, and that should make the meeting more comfortable.

"Oh, one more thing. My friend's wife apparently spent some time in Lincolnshire when she was a girl. She remembers the little stone imp in the Cathedral. If you could find an antique piece of jewelry with the imp on it, she would pay whatever the price is. I realize it's a long shot, but you never know."

"No, you never know." Terry answered abstractedly. The only such piece she knew of was in the Usher Gallery in Lincoln. But surely more must have been made.

"I've booked rooms for us in a hotel in Lincoln. I have a dealer I will contact when we get there. He has an inventory that changes constantly, but he can be relied on for quality, genuine pieces. There are also some smaller dealers in Lincoln who sell to us occasionally. We are often willing to offer them higher prices than the tourists." She glanced at him as she spoke. He had put on sunglasses against the rare sunshine that had brightened the morning, and she couldn't see his eyes to glean any reaction to what she was saying. "And there is another individual who contacted me recently. A strange little man. He may or may not have anything worth looking at. But we can talk to him if we have time."

"Are we going anywhere near Springfield?"

That was one of the villages with a medieval church, Terry thought. It might be worth a look... but why would he want to go there?

"Nothing in this country is very far from anything else. Why do you ask?"

"A couple of people I know moved there a few months ago." His eyes were still shrouded by the dark glasses, even though the clouds had moved in and hidden the sun.

"Moved to Springfield? There isn't much there that I know of, although I do remember reading something about it being a popular retirement destination. Quiet small town and all that. But why would someone leave St. Clare for a small town in Lincolnshire?"

"Health reasons. The man had cancer. He may be dead now, although I probably would have heard if he was. I think they live in an old gate house of some sort."

"I wonder if they have any antiques they would be willing to sell?" Terry pictured an older couple, the man suffering from a terminal illness, the wife dutifully caring for him.

TWENTY-SEVEN

Nara had a busy day ahead of her. Aunt Sue had come in very late the night before, and although her alarm had gone off shortly after Nara's, not another sound had come from her bedroom. It didn't bother Nara as much as it had in the past. She would get up and start breakfast on her own. She wondered if Sue had broken up with her married lover last night. If she had, she deserved a lie-in. If she hadn't, well... it was her life.

Nara started the kettle for tea or coffee. Coffee was much more popular in England than she had expected. She began slicing tomatoes and mushrooms for frying. There was some sliced fruit in covered bowls all ready in the fridge. She set out eggs and bacon, took out the loaf of white bread for toast and stared at it. Nara hated white bread, but it was *de rigueur* for an English breakfast. She wondered what people would do if she offered a nice whole grain alternative. Have her burned for a witch? No, probably just look at her funny. It was worth a try, just for the fun of it. She would pick up a loaf at one of the bakeries in Lincoln later in the day when she went for her classes.

She could hear someone in the guest bathroom. The day had begun. A day of household chores, classes at the college, and finally, her date with Alex tonight.

This morning her suspicions of the night before seemed ridiculous. He was a nice, attractive man. He was not involved in anything sinister, illegal or underhanded, and he was interested enough to ask her out. She would enjoy the evening, the process of getting to know him, his conversation—and whatever else the evening might bring.

The American couple came down first for breakfast and surprised her by asking for tea. It just proved that you could never make assumptions about people. She was spooning the dark leaves, her favorite breakfast blend from Fortnum & Mason's, when Aunt Sue came into the kitchen. She was dressed in jeans and a pink wool sweater that Nara had not seen before, but which brightened Sue's fair complexion. She poured herself a cup of coffee.

"I couldn't do it." She took a slug of the strong brew and sighed. "I tried. But I wasn't strong enough."

Nara finished pouring the boiling water over the tea leaves and replaced the cover on the pot. She looked directly at her aunt, feeling sympathy for her predicament. She would never have been able to break up with Davis. Or would she if she had found out he was married?

Sue continued. "I tried. And I made it as far as telling him that I can't spend the night away anymore. I told him it was too hard on you, with going to college and taking care of your father. It's partly true." She smiled.

"But that's great," Nara stepped forward as if to hug her aunt, but stopped short, unsure how the physical expression of support would be received. "That's a big step. And he may get the idea, now that you aren't at his beck and call anymore."

"Maybe." She took another sip of coffee. "I feel better. I feel as if I've done something for myself. I did the right thing."

"If you feel right about it, then you did the right thing."

Nara heard footsteps and conversation in the dining room. "I'll take the tea in." Sue picked up the tray with the pot and the milk and sugar. Another couple with their young son, on holiday from Scotland, had joined the Americans at the table. And Jack Blake stood visiting with the group, talking about the history of the house to the American woman, who, it turned out, was a history professor at a university in Washington, DC.

When Sue brought the tea in, Jack excused himself and joined Nara in the kitchen. She was arranging individual bowls of mixed fruit, complete with slices of mango, her touch of the tropics.

"You're up early." She smiled and stopped her work to give him a quick hug and kiss on the cheek.

"I smelled the coffee brewing, so here I am." He poured himself a cup of coffee and asked for some milk. Nara took a small pitcher out of the microwave where she had warmed the milk and handed it to him,

"I have a request to make, Nara."

"Anything you want." She had started frying tomatoes and mushrooms, which she would keep warm while she cooked the rest of the breakfast to individual orders.

"Don't say 'anything,' Nara. You are grown up now and you don't have to agree with everything your dad asks. And I have a feeling I'm not going to die soon, so you don't have to feel guilty."

She waited, stirring the tomatoes and mushrooms in the pan. The smell was stimulating her appetite.

"I would like to ride along with you into Lincoln when you go to class today, if you don't mind."

She put down the wooden spoon on the tile square she used for a spoon holder on the stove. "That would be great. And we could go have tea somewhere afterwards. And maybe you can meet my friend Micki."

Jack laughed. "Yes. I'm sure we can do both of those things." He sipped his coffee, and stepped out of the way of his busy daughter who was moving the vegetables to a plate to keep warm in the oven.

"I know there are some good used books stores in the old part of Lincoln. I can browse there while you are at class. I just need to get out."

"But they are on Steep Hill, Dad. Are you sure you are up to it?" Nara thought of the old medieval cobblestone street that climbed from the market area up to the Cathedral and castle on the top of the hill.

Jack laughed. "I'll take it slow. I promise." He held up his hand as if he were swearing an oath. "A little exercise will be good for me."

Sue came back into the kitchen. "The Scottish couple would like coffee and just milk for the little boy. The Americans want the full English breakfast and the Scots just want scrambled eggs on toast with bacon."

Nara began cracking eggs into a bowl. "Well, they are all getting fruit and mushrooms and tomatoes with their eggs."

"Yes, ma'am." Sue answered teasingly.

"Anything I can do to help?" Jack asked.

Nara paused and looked around. "Sure. You can start making the toast."

"I should be able to handle that." He picked up the loaf of bread. "White bread," he muttered. "You would think they could produce a decent baguette. We aren't that far from France."

Nara smiled but said nothing. It was just so good to see her father back in his old good humor, and taking an interest in life outside his bedroom.

An hour later breakfast was finished. Sue was doing the washing up while Nara showered and dressed for class. The wooden box she had found in the storeroom the night before was still snugly hidden in her lingerie drawer. She knew she should tell her father and Aunt Sue about her find, but she wasn't ready, not just yet. She was afraid it would spoil the fragile serenity and good humor that had appeared in the house that morning. There was no harm in just holding onto it for a day or two. But she really wondered about the imp brooch. Should she show it to Elaine? Would she say anything to her husband about it? She did not want that weird little man to know. Maybe she would tell Micki. She might have an idea, and she knew that Micki could be trusted to keep it confidential.

Alex was eating a bowl of American rice cereal, watching the BBC news, and talking on the phone. He had put in a call to the Springfield police chief, wondering if they had any more leads to the killer or killers of the man whose body had been found in the car. He waited. The chief had apparently just come in but was in conference with someone at the moment. "If you would like to wait a moment, I'll catch him for you as soon as he is free." Somehow the secretary made it sound like catching a fish. She came back on the line every minute or so, to tell him the chief was still busy but would be with him shortly. At least it was reassuring to know he had not been forgotten, but she usually caught him just putting a bite of cereal into his mouth, or just as his attention was caught by an interesting news story on the telly.

Finally the chief's voice came over the line. "Good morning, Alex. How's everything?"

"Fine. Great." He quickly swallowed his mouthful of cereal. "Just wondered if you have any news on the guy in the car."

The chief sighed. "Nothing yet. Whoever did it covered their tracks pretty well. He was a workman at the Cathedral in Lincoln. No one knew him well. Kept to himself and didn't cause any trouble. Left a wife and a couple of kids. We're working on the connection with the burglaries just now. Best guess would be that's why he was killed. Funny thing is, there haven't been any more attempts in Springfield since those first two."

"Maybe the thieves are lying low for a while." Alex took a sip of his tea. It had gone cold.

"I need to go down to London today but..." He started to say, "I'll be back this evening," but stopped himself. He didn't want any interruptions of his dinner with Nara. "I don't know when I'll be back."

"I'll get in touch if there is any news." Alex heard him speaking to someone in the background. "Gotta go."

"Thanks. Good-bye." Alex hung up the phone and sat sipping his cold tea and finishing his soggy cereal. He used to do that when he was a boy, and his mother would chide him for trying to do too many things at once. She and his father had retired to southern Spain a few years ago, and he only saw them once or twice a year. *They would like Nara,* he thought, *more than they liked Laura.* They had accepted Laura into the family because she was his wife, but he knew they thought she treated him shabbily. She treated them all shabbily, in fact. She always made a point of being better dressed than his sisters, or dropping names of celebrities she met at parties in London. And she was always too busy with her career to attend family gatherings. Yes, they would like Nara.

Alex shook himself. What was he thinking? He hardly knew her. She might be just as selfish as Laura had been, but his intuition told him that wasn't so.

She might not care for him once they became better acquainted. "Snap out of it," he told himself. He stood up from the table and gathered up his few dishes to carry to the sink. The news on the telly caught his eye. Another church in a village in Lincolnshire had been burglarized the night before. The thieves had entered through a small door leading into the Lady Chapel. Working from inside the church, they had stolen a small but valuable stained glass window. It was a rare stained glass depiction of the "green man," the mythical figure that appeared in many medieval wood carvings.

Alex picked up his phone and dialed his boss at the museum.

"I was going to come in to London today, but do you want me to go check this out instead?"

"No," Mrs. Lawton answered firmly. "The police are handling that for now. I have something I want you to see."

Alex checked his watch. "I'll be there by 10:30."

He turned off the telly, swigged the last of his cold tea, grabbed his jacket and briefcase, and was out the door.

TWENTY-EIGHT

Terry and Davis checked into their hotel in Lincoln. Terry informed him that they would have a quick lunch and then meet with one of her contacts who ran an export business. Their warehouse was in a small town where rents were cheaper, so they usually met in Lincoln.

Terry glanced at her watch several times as they walked from their hotel over to the main street. The street was crowded with shoppers, students, and a few tourists carrying knapsacks. Terry looked up and down the street before leading him into an arcade lined with shops, mostly the kind that catered to teenage girls. The shop windows displayed mannequins in high-heeled boots with hip-hugging skinny pants and tee shirt tops short enough to show off a belly button ring or tattoo; Terry walked on without so much as a glance at the shops.

In the center of the building was a food court, which besides the ubiquitous American hamburgers and pizza, held a shop selling traditional English fish and chips and one selling Middle Eastern sandwiches such as falafel and donar. The smells reminded Davis that he had not eaten since breakfast at the hotel in London hours ago. Stopping for a morning break during the trip had not been on Terry's agenda.

Terry waved her arm, taking in the full array of fast food available. "Take your choice."

"Is this where we are meeting your contact?"

"Yes." She looked at her watch again. "Go on. Order your food."

Davis was intrigued by her nervousness, but his hunger took precedence. He headed toward the fish and chips.

When he returned with his food, Terry was sitting at a table at the far side of the food court, stirring a cup of coffee and talking with a heavily built man who was dressed in dark work pants and an open necked white shirt, covered by a thick multi-colored sweater. His longish black hair fell in his eyes as he moved his head. He wasn't talking much right now because he was giving his attention to a huge sandwich on pita bread. Pieces of filling fell out and the man stopped to pick them up with his fingers and shove them into his mouth. He washed it down with a soft drink from a large paper cup.

Davis set his plate of fish and chips down on the table and sat down. He thought Terry looked tired and a little uncomfortable. He wondered why. She took a sip of her black coffee. "Davis, this is Charles Ludley. He is the... he is from the antique dealer I told you about. Charles, this is Dr. Davis Jarrett from St. Clare."

Charles Ludley merely nodded at Davis. "I hear you are interested in some stained glass."

"Among other things."

"Are these items for yourself?" Davis felt Ludley's scrutiny, as if he were being judged on his ability to come up with a suitable amount of cash. He self-consciously unbuttoned the cuffs of his new leather jacket.

"No. They are for an associate." Davis took a sip of his soda. "In a few years, when my business gets going, I'll probably be looking for items for myself."

"I see." Ludley had finished his sandwich and swallowed the last of his drink. His hand moved toward the pack of cigarettes in his pocket, until Terry reminded him that smoking was not allowed in the shopping mall.

"How much are you, or is your associate, prepared to spend?"

"It depends upon the items, and the guarantee of its authenticity."

Ludley barked a laugh. "Our Hadley representative here will vouch for the authenticity. I'll quote you a price."

"Fair enough."

Terry had been watching and listening to the exchange, "Stained glass." She said it as if she were reading a list, "Anything religious or medieval, which amounts to the same thing. And apparently the man's wife wants a Lincolnshire imp brooch, a jeweled one."

Ludley looked sharply at Terry. "We don't run across those very often. At least not the real thing. The only one I know of is in the Usher Gallery, and their security is tight."

Terry glowered at him. "I'm not asking you to steal it from the Usher Gallery. Just keep a look-out. Things turn up."

"Sure, maybe I can nick it off some old bird's dressing table."

"If you have the opportunity." Terry met his gaze, then calmly dabbed her lips with a paper napkin.

Ludley ignored the bait and turned back to Davis, who had just polished off his fish and chips. "I think I have some of the items you are looking for, but I have to have them moved from my warehouse to the show room. I don't have the more valuable items on display for the general public—I'm sure you understand what I mean."

"Of course." Davis did not know which of his two companions to look at, since they were both staring at him, so he continued to look into his empty fish and chips basket. "I understand." He raised his eyes and met Terry's. The brilliant blue depths of her eyes were difficult to fathom. He pulled his eyes away from hers and turned to Ludley. "When can we see them?"

"Let's make it this evening about 7:00."

"That will be fine." Terry took charge again. "That will give us time to contact the client in St. Clare and discuss some of the details."

"I'll see you at 7:00, then." Charles Ludley stood, nodded perfunctorily to the two of them, and left the shopping mall by the nearest exit.

"Strange man," Davis said, to break the silence.

"Yes. But he knows his business." Terry was once again in control and all business. "You have crumbs on your shirt."

"What?" He looked down at his shirt beneath the open jacket.

"You've crumbs on your shirt." There was a bit of a giggle in her voice the second time.

He brushed them off and looked into the blue eyes again, seeing humor for the first time.

Quickly she broke the connection and stood up. "There is another contact I would like you to meet. Not as professional as Charles Ludley, and not as well established. But he could have something valuable nonetheless."

She pulled out her cell phone and punched in a number. She turned away from Davis when the person answered, and Davis had to be content with looking at her long slim legs beneath the professional business suit. Before his imagination could get carried away, she turned back, flipping her phone shut and stowing it in her bag. "He'll meet us in an hour. In the meantime, let's go to the Usher Gallery and I'll show you the brooch."

TWENTY-NINE

Nara felt happier than she had in a long time as she drove with her father across the Lincolnshire farm country to the city of Lincoln. The sky was gray and there was a hint of rain, but the weather could do nothing to dampen her mood. Her father was animated, talking about the scenery as they passed, the people they saw going about their daily routines on the streets of the villages. Was he really getting well? Were the treatments working? All of a sudden she had a thought that frightened her. *What if he wants to go back to St. Clare?* She wasn't sure now that she wanted to go. She was beginning to like her life in England. It seemed to be leading somewhere, although she wasn't sure yet where it was leading. She had not wanted to come here, and now she didn't want to leave, and the fear she suddenly had at the thought of leaving frightened her even more. With an effort she turned her attention back to her father's conversation.

"It must be 40 years since I've been to Lincoln. I remember visiting the Cathedral as a boy with my mother. She showed me the imp, and she asked someone if I could use their binoculars so I could see it." Jack's voice dropped off. He rarely talked about his childhood, and it surprised Nara to hear him speak of his mother.

"I didn't know you came here with Grandma." Nara's voice was quiet. She kept her eyes on the road in front of her.

"I spent a school year here when I was about ten. My parents were separated at the time, and we came back here to stay with my grandparents. I became quite familiar with the area, or as well as small boys do, and I was sad to leave."

"Grandma and Grandpa were back together then?" Nara turned her head slightly to look at her father.

"Yes. He was devastated without her. I remember she received letters from him almost every day, and sometimes she would tear them up."

"Why did she leave him?"

"I really have no idea. I think there might have been another woman. She always seemed very watchful when they were around attractive women, and she worried a lot about her appearance. She was always dieting."

"Were they happy once they were back together?" Nara increased her speed to overtake a slow-moving lorry, and then pulled back into her lane.

"I don't know. I didn't think that much about such things. I readjusted to my life in St. Clare, going to school and learning the import business from my father. And Sue was born not long after that time. But I didn't pay much attention to how my parents treated each other. I don't remember them fighting, but no; I wouldn't say they were happy. They were indifferent. Marriage can be good, bad, or indifferent. Theirs was indifferent, which is often the worst. A bad marriage gives you reason to leave. An indifferent marriage, well, you just go along day to day and suddenly realize 20 years have past."

"What about you and my mother?" Nara's heart pounded as she asked the question, although she had asked it so softly she wasn't sure he heard. He didn't answer for a moment.

"Your mother and I were very happy."

"But you weren't happy with some of the things she did."

"No." Jack shifted in his seat so he could look directly at Nara as she drove. "But the love was there. She was mixed up in things..." His voice trailed off.

Nara knew some of the rest of the story, about how her mother would go to the villages to bring gifts to the children. How she spent time with the shaman of the village, learning native healing and participating in rituals. She would go for days at a time, leaving baby Nara in the care of Clara, her capable and loving nanny. On one of those trips, when Nara was three years old, her mother had visited another little girl who had contracted what they later found out was meningitis. Nara's mother also became infected and died a week later. Nara knew her father had never recovered from her loss, or the anger that he felt that she had given her life for a native child, and left her own small daughter without a mother. The child she had gone to help had survived.

Father and daughter rode in silence for a few moments. They had always been close, but there were certain things they rarely discussed; the pain was too raw, even after 20 years. He had married again when Nara was 16 years old, but Kelly had never liked the day-to-day life on the island. She wanted a more active social life and eventually spent more and more time in Europe. When he was diagnosed with cancer, she left for good.

"Look." Nara indicated the landscape ahead, where the thick clouds were breaking and sunlight shone on the hill that was Lincoln. The Cathedral towered above the city and the surrounding countryside. The sunlight hit the massive building and the color seemed to change from gray to an almost luminous white.

"I've never been a religious man, Nara, as you know, but there is something about that sight that is spiritual. It lifts me up. I don't know if it is the work of the hands that crafted it, all the people of faith who have prayed there, but there is something about it."

Nara said nothing but smiled and nodded her agreement. She skillfully navigated a round-about and headed toward the center of the town and up the hill.

"I can drop you in the Cathedral Close, and you can walk to wherever you want to from there."

Nara slowed to allow pedestrians to cross from the Cathedral to the medieval bishop's palace. She stopped the car just at the Cathedral entrance. "Don't tire yourself out, Dad. Stop and have a cup of tea."

He laughed. "I was waiting for you to say something like that."

"I'll see you in about two hours." She leaned over and kissed his cheek.

After he closed the car door, Nara reached into the back seat for her purse. She checked that the clasp was tightly closed. She had brought the imp brooch with her. She had decided to show it to Micki.

Elaine had just finished leading a tour of the Cathedral when she noticed him—the man from the Gate House bed and breakfast in Springfield. He stood just inside the Cathedral doors, hands in the pockets of his jacket. His head was tilted up as he scanned the arched ceiling, and he had a smile on his face. The Cathedral often had that effect on people. It was, without doubt, one of the finest medieval buildings in Europe. But more than the architecture, there was the sense of wonder that the building never failed to evoke. There was a sensation of timelessness. It had withstood desecration by rival factions of soldiers, the onslaught of Cromwell's men, and the neglect of more modern times. The high Gothic arches were designed to lead men's thoughts upward to heaven, and after 800 years, they still did just that. The man lowered his head and looked around. He saw Elaine and she smiled, unsure if he recognized her or not. It was her job to make visitors to the Cathedral welcome, so she walked over to him.

"It's beautiful, isn't it?"

"The last time I was here I was ten years old. I was here with my mother. I thought after all those years it would not seem as awe-inspiring as it did to me at that age, but it still is."

"Yes. I'm struck by its beauty every time I come here."

He brought his gaze back to her. "You look familiar."

"My name is Elaine," she said, holding out her hand." I'm a docent here. And I was a guest in your bed and breakfast earlier this week."

"Ah, yes. I remember you now. You and your husband. I don't believe I saw much of you; I was feeling tired. The bed and breakfast belongs to my sister, and my daughter helps her out." He ran his hand over his bald head a little self-consciously. "I'm Jack Blake."

"Would you like me to show you around? I'm not officially working now, but we could walk around and I can point out some of the things you might not remember from your last visit."

"That would be nice." He smiled, and Elaine was touched by a vulnerability in his smile. "I am really very, very glad to be here." He once again tilted his head upward to take in the vastness of the Cathedral.

Elaine walked slowly with Jack, appreciating the way he gazed around him, as if he didn't want to miss a single point in the Cathedral. He stopped to run his fingers over the carved wood and laughed at the humorous and decidedly irreligious figures on the choir stalls. Elaine related the story of St. Hugh, and how his head had rolled away when his body was being buried. This was taken as a sign that a special shrine should be built in his honor, and it was done with his head covered in gold. But the gold had been too tempting for Cromwell's men, and it had been pillaged, along with the brasses on the floor and many other precious items. Poor St. Hugh's head had disappeared in the mists of history.

Elaine pointed out the imp, "I always called my daughter an imp when she was small."

"Do you just have one child?" Elaine asked.

"Yes. Only one. And you?"

"We don't have any children."

"I didn't mean to pry."

"Asking a question isn't prying," she answered with a smile. "I let people know if they are prying."

They walked on in silence for a few moments. Around them groups of visitors moved from place to place, marveling at the carved masonry, the way the building itself told the story of all that had happened here, and the faith of the people who had been a part of its construction and maintenance over the centuries.

Elaine paused by a tomb set along the outside of the angel choir. She placed her hand on the cool marble. "This is the tomb of Katherine Swynford, mistress of John of Gaunt. Our current queen can trace her lineage to them."

"I don't know much of English history, I'm afraid," Jack answered.

"I've learned a lot since I started this job, and I find Katherine fascinating. Everything we know about her, and the historical evidence is sketchy, points to the fact that she did what she did out of love. Otherwise her life would make no sense. And he married her in the end. Why would they have married if it weren't for love?"

"Why, indeed," Jack wondered. "Many people marry for reasons other than love, although not, as you say, in the end."

Elaine seemed about to speak, then moved on as a group of noisy school children crowded around them, trying to look at the inscriptions on the tombs in the floor as they scribbled notes.

"This is St. Blaise's Chapel." She turned just before they reached the doorway. "Mind the step. These old stones are quite worn."

Jack did mind the step as she suggested and found himself in a cool, bare room. A mural on one wall celebrated the wool trade that had been a mainstay of the area for many centuries. Painted butterflies and flowers decorated the lower edge of one wall, while geese in flight were shown above.

"It's lovely," Jack commented, admiring the painting. "I know very little about art, but I enjoy color. There seems to be very little color in most of these old buildings."

"That's only because the colors have faded, worn away, or been destroyed, as the brasses that were stolen from the floor by Cromwell's men." Elaine was enjoying sharing her knowledge with someone who seemed to appreciate it. "The Cathedral was actually a very colorful place. There were paintings, bright woven tapestries, and of course the men and ladies who visited dressed in bright clothing of the day."

"I never thought of that," Jack answered. "These paintings can't be as old as the Cathedral, then."

"Oh, no. These were added in the nineteenth century, although they are in the style of an earlier period."

They left St. Blaise's Chapel and continued back down the nave of the Cathedral. Far above them, at the back of the building, a group of people stood looking down from a balcony. "What an incredible view they must have from up there!" Jack remarked. "Is that area open to the public?"

"It is for special roof tours. The view is quite amazing. Come." She led him to a spot in the center of the nave, where they could look up toward the area where the people were standing. "Look up at the arches." She pointed above the heads of the tourists. "Do you see where the points of the arches don't quite line up? The front part is what's left of the Norman church, built by William the Conqueror just a few years after 1066. Most of it was destroyed in an earthquake. "When it was rebuilt, the construction was begun at the back, at St. Hugh's shrine, and, as you can see, they didn't match up. It's created a nightmare for maintaining the structural integrity of the building."

"It's a wonder they didn't just tear it down. That's what they would do today."

"They couldn't afford to. And I suspect they wanted to get it finished. There was politics involved, as there is in everything today as well."

Elaine watched as Jack looked around him, taking in the arches, the clerestory along the side designed to let in sunlight, the columns supporting the roof from the inside, as the flying buttresses did on the outside. "Sometime I would like to take that roof tour, when I'm feeling a little stronger."

"I'm so sorry. I didn't mean to tire you with my jabbering on. I get so involved, and I do love sharing the tidbits about this place. My husband says I need to learn when to be quiet." Elaine stopped, embarrassed that the last bit had slipped out.

"I've enjoying every bit of your narrative. It's my feet and my back that are tired, not my ears. Can I invite you for a cup of tea? That way I can rest and listen to more stories about Lincoln."

Elaine glanced quickly at her watch. There was just enough time for a quick cup of tea before she would need to get home to prepare lunch for Dennis. "All right. There are several lovely places just a few minutes' walk from here."

"That sounds perfect."

They emerged out of the Cathedral Close onto the cobbled street at the top of Steep Hill.

"There is a lovely place just a few steps down the Hill," Elaine commented, regaining her jaunty tour guide persona. Jack followed her down the narrow center of the street.

"There are several good tea shops up and down this street, but I like this one in particular. They have a huge variety of teas and coffees. I like to try something different each time I come. And the pastries are delicious." When Jack didn't answer, Elaine stopped and turned around. He had stopped and was staring down the hill, and the color had drained from his face. Elaine looked in that direction and could only see the crowds of shoppers, some huffing and puffing from their climb up the hill.

"Jack? Are you all right?"

He shook his head, as if shaking out thoughts that had no business being there. "I just thought I saw someone I knew in St. Clare. But that's impossible. If he were going to be here, he would surely let us know."

Davis buried himself in a used book shop, idly scanning titles, picking up books randomly without seeing the words. Jack Blake was in Lincoln, and had seen him and recognized him. Davis couldn't believe it. The man was supposed to be on his death bed. It was one thing to jilt Nara; she was a foolish, romantic young girl and would get over it. It was another thing to be caught in his duplicity by her father—especially a father who seemed to have regained his health.

To his credit, he had tried to call Nara last week, and she had been out. But he hadn't known at the time that he was going to be in England, not to mention Lincoln. And what was Jack doing in Lincoln? They lived in a small town some miles away, and Jack was sick. He had come to England for chemotherapy treatments for lung cancer. Davis realized that he would have to call Nara now; this was turning into just too big of a mess. A healthy Jack Blake could be a formidable enemy. And if he came back to St. Clare and took over the daily management of his business again, all of Davis' plans could fall apart. There was no avoiding it; he would have to see Nara.

Elaine did her best to pull Jack out of his state of shock. She ordered Darjeeling tea and carrot cake for both of them. She asked him about life in St. Clare and about his daughter. His face brightened when he spoke of her. It was obvious that she was the joy of his life.

"She has always had a mind of her own. There's no persuading her once she has decided to do something. I guess she gets that from both her mother and me."

"What is she studying at the university?" Elaine asked. The tea and cake arrived just as she asked the question, and he waited until the things were arranged on the table.

"No tea bags here," Elaine commented with a smile as she poured the tea.

Jack took a bite of carrot cake and chewed thoughtfully. "She's studying business, but I know she is doing it for me."

Elaine looked at him questioningly and took another bite of her own carrot cake, making sure to combine a generous bite of icing with the cake. She let the flavors blend in her mouth.

"What do you mean?"

"I own an importing business that I inherited from my father. I always expected Nara to join me in the business and take it over when I retire. She was engaged to a young man in St. Clare, a doctor, and those were their plans. He would run a pediatric clinic and she would manage the importing business." Jack sipped the tea appreciatively. "Nara would love this tea. She won't use tea bags either."

"What happened?"

"I found out I have lung cancer, and we came here so I could stay with my sister in Springfield and take chemotherapy treatments. My sister Sue is a nurse. I insisted that Nara come with me. Selfish of me, I know." Jack finished the last bite of his cake and wiped his mouth with a paper napkin that he wadded up into a small ball, and then smoothed out again with his hand.

"I thought I was dying, you see. I still might be. But I feel well these past couple of weeks, and I'm seeing things more clearly. Then again..." Jack folded the napkin in half, in quarters, and smoothed it again. "I'm not sure it wasn't for the best. Nara has a big date tonight with someone she met in Springfield. The doctor from St. Clare has only called once, and she was out. But the truth of the matter is—Nara is not a businesswoman. She has no real interest in a business that imports appliances and furniture for the island. She likes antiques and art. I know she would rather study art than business."

"So what are you going to do?" Elaine finished her cake and placed her fork diagonally across her plate. She put her hands in her lap so she would not be tempted to fidget with her napkin, a trick she had learned long ago when Dennis had criticized her for playing nervously with napkins and cutlery. She could twist the fabric of her skirt or trousers without anyone being the wiser.

"I'm not sure. Try to stay out of her life, for one thing. Let her know that whatever she chooses is fine with me. I have a capable manager at the company. He's taking care of things now. I can give him more authority. Or I could sell the company." He drained the last of his tea. "But it's too early to make decisions right now."

Jack checked his watch. "I need to meet Nara in 15 minutes. She'll panic if I'm not there. Think I've passed out somewhere." He was at the counter paying the bill before Elaine could say a word.

They left the tea shop to feel a few drops of rain. "Where are you meeting her?"

"Back at the Cathedral by the main door."

"I'll walk back with you. My car is parked down by the old Bishop's Palace."

The pedestrian traffic thinned as they passed under the archway leading into the Cathedral Close. Jack paused. "Thank you, Elaine."

"For what?" she laughed.

"For listening."

"Any time." The words came out too flippantly. "Any time," she said again.

THIRTY

Alex arrived at his superior's office just after 10:00. *Thank God for the British Rail Service.* As much as people complained about it, it always took him where he needed to go, and in a timely fashion.

"Mrs. Lawton, good morning." Cornelia Lawton was an elegant woman in her mid-forties. Although her dark hair was pulled back into a severe bun, the sparkle in her eyes and her ready smile belied her serious appearance. She took no nonsense, but she appreciated hard work and responsible people, and Alex knew that he was one of the people she appreciated most.

"Good morning, Alex." She glanced up and then back to something she was going over on her desk. "Have a seat. I'll be right with you."

Alex watched her use an expensive pen to skim the words on a document with the V&A Museum letterhead. She finished quickly and affixed her signature. She had elegant hands, long slim fingers, but never decorated with nail polish. The only ornaments were a large diamond engagement ring with matching gold wedding band. Mr. Lawton, whom Alex had met once at a reception, was some years older than his wife and a Member of Parliament. They had been married only a few years, and it was obviously a love match.

She placed the document into a basket and put down her pen, looking at Alex. "Remember the box of William Morris tiles that went missing from the holding area last month?"

"Of course." The severe side of Mrs. Lawton had certainly come to the forefront during that incident. Alex had only been happy that it had not been directed at him.

"Well, a bright young Scotland Yard agent spotted it on a cargo trolley at King's Cross. Thought it a bit unusual that the V&A would be shipping things by rail cargo."

"There were some other items in the crate as well, if I remember correctly. A Burgess tulip vase. Quite remarkable. Some nineteenth century stained glass."

"Right." She picked up the pen again and tapped it on the desk. Alex always wondered how she managed to keep her working area so immaculate. Not an ink smudge or a scrap of paper out of place. "Everything was intact. The interesting thing was where the shipment was going." Her dark eyes held his and she paused. "It was addressed to the Gate House, Springfield, Lincolnshire."

Alex caught his breath. "No name of an individual?"

"No name. No date. Just the Gate House."

Alex continued to stare at Mrs. Lawton while his mind worked frantically. Nara just couldn't be involved. She was too open, too real. And her father? He was sick, wasn't he? But Alex had never seen him. It was impossible. He realized that Mrs. Lawton was staring back at him.

"In a dream world, Alex?" She laughed. "What do you know about the Gate House? You've been living in Springfield for a few years now." She waited, pen tapping again.

Annoying habit in such an elegant woman, Alex thought.

"I've lived there but I've spent a hell of a lot of time on the train commuting to London. The only investigation I've done in the town itself was at the church earlier this week, and . . ." His voice trailed off as the possible connections fell too neatly into place.

"And what?" Damn, she was quick.

Alex pulled his thoughts together and pushed his emotions into the back of his mind for the moment. "The Gate House was broken into the same night as the church, although nothing was taken. The burglar—or burglars—were surprised by one of the residents. It turns out it was the same burglar as the one at the church. The police found footprints that matched. A few days later a body was found in a car submerged in the river just outside of town. The tools that were taken from the church were in the boot. The shoes on the dead man's feet matched the footprints. There haven't been any more attempted burglaries in Springfield since that night."

"But that doesn't mean there won't be." She stopped tapping her pen and began doodling on a small sheet of paper. "Was the body identified?"

"A semi-skilled laborer from the Lincoln Cathedral."

"Hmmm. Very unlikely he was in it alone. I don't suppose any of the stolen items have been found? No, of course not. You would have reported it." She stopped doodling and stared at the wall behind Alex and above his head. He could almost hear the wheels spinning in her brain. "Who lives at the Gate House?"

Alex's heart rate sped up ever so slightly, and he tried to breathe evenly so he wouldn't give away his feelings. "A new owner took over several months ago, a single woman, Springfield native. And her brother and his daughter moved in with her about two months ago."

Cornelia Lawton looked at him with interest. "Oh? Where did they move from?"

"St. Clare."

"If stolen British antiquities end up in St. Clare, it won't be the first time. This is too much of a coincidence. I would suggest you get to know these people from St. Clare. Maybe book a night at the bed and breakfast."

"That won't be necessary."

"What won't be necessary?" Alex knew Cornelia Lawton hated obtuseness. That was why her conversations were always direct and to the point.

"I have a dinner date with the daughter tonight."

Cornelia laughed and slapped her hands on her desk, causing her pen to roll toward the edge, where she deftly caught it. Her face changed entirely when she laughed, and a few tendrils of brown hair slipped down across her forehead. "I thought there was something you weren't telling me, Alex. And I knew it would come out. And here I was picturing the daughter as a six year old school girl, which she obviously is not." She pushed her hair back and replaced the smile with a business-like gaze. "They could be involved, Alex. All the signs point to it. When did you meet the girl?"

"Just a few days ago."

"Good. You haven't had time to get involved yet. And I know you to be the cautious type anyway. Just don't lose your objectivity."

"I won't."

"Good. Enjoy your dinner." A flicker of a smile crossed her face as she indicated their meeting was over.

THIRTY-ONE

Nara and Micki took their seats together in the fourth row from the front in the Business Practices class. They had already established a routine. They chatted a few minutes before the professor walked in to begin the class. Micki's little girl was coming down with a cold, and she was sure that both children would have it before the end of the week. Nara told her about her dinner date, and Micki wanted to know what she was going to wear, a detail that had completely escaped Nara until that moment, there had been so much else going on to occupy her mind.

When the professor began going over the reading assignment from the preceding class, Nara tried hard to concentrate. She had read the assignment, and even taken notes, but she found it devilishly difficult to make it mean anything to her. She raised her hand and answered a simple question that she was sure of and then relaxed. It only seemed to have made the professor aware of her presence, for five minutes later he unexpectedly called on "Miss Blake" to explain a concept. Nara took a quick look at her notes and gave what she hoped was the right answer.

"That's part of it." He looked at her as if he had expected more. "Who can add to Miss Blake's answer?" A tall young man with blond hair and broad shoulders, and utter self-confidence, completed the answer, and the class moved on. Nara felt embarrassed. She always felt that way when she knew she was out of her depth or in the wrong place. And, except for her friendship with Micki, she was out of place in this class. She felt hot tears in her eyes and pulled out a tissue to blow her nose. When she finished she saw that Micki was looking at her with concern. Nara picked up her pen and tried to focus on the lecture.

Midway through the class, the professor called a ten minute break. "Are you okay?" Micki's motherly voice held deep concern for her new friend.

I'm okay. Just allergies, I think."

Micki gave her a look that clearly said, I don't believe you, but she refrained from saying any more.

The two women went out to the corridor with the rest of the class. Some stepped outside the main building door to have a smoke in the chilly fall air. Nara headed for the ladies' to wash her face, while Micki pulled out her cell phone to call and check on her children. Nara rejoined Micki a few minutes later, with lipstick freshened and hair combed and pulled back in a short ponytail.

"Everything okay at home?"

"They're fine." Micki smiled the way she always did when she talked about her family, a smile that seemed to hold a special secret. Nara hoped someday to feel that way, to experience that sense of belonging, of being part of something. She loved her father but it had always, or as long as she could remember, been the two of them. Two was a family, but then it wasn't.

"Tony is sniffling, and Christy has a cough and is cranky. Looks like we will be in for a rough weekend."

"Is there anything I can do to help?" The words were out before Nara realized it, wondering at the same time what she could possibly do.

Micki cocked her head to the side and looked at Nara, a smile skittering over her face as if Nara had said something cute. "YOU–have a date tonight."

"Yes–I do," Nara answered, wondering what that had to do with it.

"You can help me by having a wonderful time and telling me all about it on Monday. And you haven't told me yet what you are going to wear. Don't tell me you haven't even decided yet."

"I haven't decided yet." Nara smiled sheepishly.

"Speaking of Monday." Micki thoughts had clearly taken another turn, as they often did. She tended to jump from subject to subject. According to her, that was the only way she could keep track of all the things going on in her life. "Are we still on for the Cathedral tour with Elaine?"

"As far as I know," Nara answered absently. Now that Micki had brought up the subject of her date with Alex tonight, her thoughts had turned to what to wear. He has not yet seen me at my best, she thought. Too bad she hadn't had time for a haircut.

"Do you have her phone number? I'll give her a call and check on it." Micki was already pulling a small notebook out of her purse.

"I'll call her. You have enough on your plate this weekend."

Micki grinned. "But I don't have a 'big date' tonight. And I'm used to multi-tasking."

Nara placed her hand on her purse, as if to protect the phone number from Micki's responsible hands. "I'll do it."

"Okay." Micki laughed. "I trust you. I do."

Speaking of the Cathedral brought the imp to Nara's mind, and she remembered that she had brought the brooch along for the express purpose of showing it to Micki. She was about to take it out when the professor returned, walking briskly, mug of coffee in hand. The students followed him obediently into the classroom, and they returned to their discussion of Business Practices. Nara tried hard to pay attention and glean something meaningful from the class. She thought about how the information could help her to help her father at their company in the future. As hard as she tried, she just couldn't see it as her future. The class concluded with the professor distributing instructions for a project that would be due in two weeks. They each needed to describe a product and devise a marketing plan. Nara was thinking as the class ended that she would ask her father for help. He would enjoy working with her, seeing her interest, and, frankly, she wasn't sure she could motivate herself to do it alone.

Then she remembered the imp again. "Micki, I want to show you something. Ask your opinion."

"Sure." Micki already had her car keys in her hand; clearly her thoughts were on her children and their needs.

"Let's sit down." Nara led the way to the student lounge, where students were milling about chatting and buying coffee from the vending machines. Nara sat down at a table near the window, away from the crowd. "It will just take a minute." Micki sat down on the chair next to Nara and gave her full attention.

Nara opened her purse and pulled out the brooch, which she had wrapped in tissue paper. "I was nosing around in the house the other night. You know I told you how it's full of antiques, and Aunt Sue doesn't seem to know anything about them, or even care. I came across this." For expediency's sake, Nara didn't tell Micki about the hidden staircase and the storeroom she had found. She unwrapped the brooch and held it in her open palm.

"The imp!" Micki exclaimed. She picked it up and let the sunlight play on the gems. "This is beautiful." Her face grew more serious. "These look real, not that I'm an expert. And it's old." She turned it over and examined the clasp. "I don't know much about these things, but you should get this appraised." She placed the brooch gently back on the square of tissue paper. "Maybe the things in the Gate House are more valuable than any of you realize. You really need to talk your aunt into getting the things appraised. And you need an alarm system, I would think."

"I think I'll have to start with this. Aunt Sue doesn't know I found it. Do you know where I could get it appraised?"

"I really don't. There are several antique dealers in town. I know there are several up the hill near the Cathedral. I could ask my parents. They know a little about antiques. Or maybe Elaine would know. Why don't you ask her when you call her?"

"I really don't want anyone to know about it."

"Well, don't tell her what you want to have appraised; just ask her if she knows a reputable dealer."

"But surely she will ask what I want appraised." Nara rewrapped the imp in his paper and stowed in carefully in the bottom of her purse.

"True." Micki glanced at her watch. "Tell her it's something you brought from St. Clare."

"I'm not a good liar."

Micki looked at Nara, at her deep dark eyes. "No, I can see that. And as a general rule that's a good thing. I can always tell when little Tony is lying–or trying to."

Micki efficiently tore a half sheet of paper out of her notebook and jotted down a name and a phone number. She pushed the sheet across the table to Nara. "Call my parents. I've already told them about you. They will suggest someone and won't ask any questions. They are great respecters of privacy."

"Thank you." Nara folded the paper neatly in fourths and slipped it into her purse.

"I have to go." Micki stood, car keys again in her hand.

"I know. Sorry I kept you."

"It's all right. It was important to you." She turned to leave. "Let me know what Elaine says, and have fun tonight." She was gone, deftly weaving her way between groups of students as she headed for the exit.

Nara sat for a moment, then gathered up her things and left to pick up her father. She was hungry; she wondered if he had already had tea.

THIRTY-TWO

Jack Blake's eyes followed Elaine as she walked toward the stone steps that led down to the car park. He found her attractive and wondered what she saw in her mousy little husband. She was tall, well-proportioned although not skinny, and carried herself well. Her short brown hair, sprinkled with gray, blew every which way in the wind, but Jack liked the effect. It seemed to give her a waifish, vulnerable quality, although she seemed anything but that after an afternoon of conversation. She disappeared in a crowd of people as they passed through an old stone archway. When Jack turned around, Nara had just driven round the corner. "Been waiting long?" He slipped in next to her and fastened his seat belt.

"Just arrived. Perfect timing."

"Have you had tea?"

"As a matter of fact I have."

"I'm starving. Do you mind if we stop?"

"Of course not. I can watch you eat."

"How was class?"

Nara launched into a funny story that Micki had told her about her children. Jack listened, smiling at his daughter. He wondered if she realized what she was doing. He had asked her about class, and she told a story about her friend's children.

It was time to bring things out in the open. "You don't like the business classes, do you?"

Nara gaped. "I like them okay." The waitress brought Nara a steaming jacket potato with beans and cheese melting on the top, along with a pot of Earl Gray tea.

"I asked you about class and you told me about Micki and her children."

Nara took a bite of steaming potato, gooey with cheese. She chewed, swallowed, and met her father's eyes.

"No, I'm not that interested in business. I can't lie to you, Dad."

"You never could." He smiled lovingly at his daughter.

"I'm doing it for you, Dad. I have a responsibility to you and our company."

"No, you don't, Nara."

Nara set down her fork. "What are you trying to say, Dad?"

Jack placed both his hands flat on the table and looked his daughter directly in the eye. "I'm trying to say, Nara dear, that I want you to do what interests you. I think we have both been pretending that this was what you wanted. It gave us a familiar dream to hold on to. But things have changed, Nara. Our lives are very different from what they were when we arrived here from St. Clare."

Nara set down her fork and sipped her tea. "What do you think I should do, Dad?" she asked in a small voice.

"It's not what I think you should do; it's what, you think you should do. You are more of an artist than a business woman." He stopped. He was almost on the verge of suggesting that she study art, but he wanted her to make her own choice.

"Think about it, Nara. You have only attended three classes. You could drop the business class and take something else."

Nara took another bite of potato and chewed thoughtfully. "I could. But I think I will stick it out."

Her father started to speak but she touched his hand and he waited. "For one thing, I think I will do better in the class knowing that I don't have to take it. A basic business course never hurt anyone. And Micki is in the class. We are just becoming friends, and I don't want to abandon her."

Jack smiled. "It's your decision. Just remember that. You make the choices and I'll back you up one hundred percent." Jack wonder if he should mention that he thought he had seen Davis that morning. No. Better not. It would only upset her, whether he had seen him or only thought he had seen him.

"I would like to meet Micki," he said after a moment.

"I'm sure you will," Nara answered, as she swallowed the last of her potato with her usual gusto. "I know." She put down her fork as her eyes sparkled with an idea. "Why don't you come with us Monday when we tour the Cathedral with Elaine?"

Jack realized that he had not told Nara that Elaine had given him a personalized tour just that afternoon. "Sounds like a good idea. We'll plan on it."

Jack picked up the bill when the waitress brought it to the table before Nara could argue.

"Dad? You're feeling a lot better lately, aren't you?"

"Yes, I am. Knock on wood." He looked around for some wood to rap his knuckles on, and settled for the back of the chair. As he turned around, Jack once again glimpsed someone who looked like Davis walk by the restaurant window, then disappear into the crowd. He turned back around to see Nara looking at him strangely.

"You look like you've seen a ghost, Dad. Are you okay?"

He shook his head. "I just saw someone who looked like a person I used to know. Must be déjà vu."

"That happens to me, too." Nara smiled And Jack felt relieved. After all, they never lied to each other.

Jack paid the bill and stood up. "Time to get home. You have a big date tonight."

When they arrived back at the Gate House, Sue was in the midst of cleaning and organizing the kitchen cupboards. She had a scarf tied around her head and was singing along with the oldies radio station.

"There's some left-over roast beef if you want sandwiches for lunch."

"We already ate." Nara stared at her aunt, and at the disarray in the kitchen, in wonder. "What's going on?"

"I just decided it was time to bring some order into the chaos of my life. And I thought I would start with the kitchen."

"Is there anything I can do to help?" Out of the corner of her eye, Nara saw her father stepping quietly out of the kitchen and toward the stairs. This was a conversation he wanted to be far away from.

"No. No. I know what I want to do. And you have a date to get ready for."

"Aren't you going out tonight?" Nara tried to ask casually.

"No. I told him I had to stay with your father because you were going out." Nara was about to protest that it wasn't necessary, when she understood what Sue was saying. Sue stopped her work and turned down the radio.

"Nara, one of these days I will have the courage to tell him I can't see him anymore. I don't have it yet."

"Don't you want to see him anymore?"

"No, I don't." She wiped her hands on a kitchen towel and tossed it across the room to a pile of dirty towels on the floor. "I don't want to be hurt anymore than I already have been," she said softly. "In some ways, I feel better about myself than I did before. I lost weight. I bought new clothes. I learned to feel attractive. And I did it for him. But I really did it for me." She pulled the scarf off her head and ran her fingers through her short hair. "I just don't have the courage to tell him it's over. Isn't that crazy?"

"So are you going to tell him when you get the courage? Or are you going to just wait until he figures it out?" Nara picked up a salt and pepper shaker set shaped like a hen and a rooster.

"I don't know. I think that is what this flurry of cleaning is all about. The activity will help me figure it out."

"Good idea." Nara wondered if that was Davis's plan, to let her figure out that he no longer considered them a couple. If it was, he had done a good job of it.

Sue tied her scarf and picked up a stack of plates to return to their cupboard.

"What are you planning on wearing tonight?"

"I haven't decided yet. A dress or pants do you think? How fancy is dinner out in Springfield?"

"Don't go too fancy. But men like to see women in dresses. We dress so casually most of the time that it surprises them."

Nara laughed at her aunt's advice on men. "I wore skirts all the time in St. Clare, but then it is the tropics and skirts are comfortable."

"Why don't you pick out a few outfits and come down and show me? It will be fun picking out date clothes for someone else for a change."

"I'll be down in a little while then." Nara bounced up the stairs, feeling once again that life was settling into a routine that wasn't turning out to be half bad.

THIRTY-THREE

Lily sat cross-legged on her bed in her London hotel room flipping absently through the TV channels. She had been told to stay there until they called her. Her brother had gone off with someone from the antique dealers, and Davis had gone to Lincoln.

Lily sat. She wondered why they had agreed to bring her along, although the two men assured her that her presence was necessary. She was an artist, had studied art, and somehow Davis in particular believed her presence lent some legitimacy to their journey. She supposed they would trot her out and show her off at the proper moment, or what they assumed was the proper moment. Her grandmother had insisted that she go, saying that Lily would know what to do when the time came, but she couldn't see how she could do anything stuck in a hotel room. She flipped the channels again through the same news stories and the same serial dramas she could not get into. This was ridiculous.

Lily flicked off the television and stood up, stretching her arms over her head. She would show them. She wasn't going to wait around just to be at their beck and call. She went into the bathroom and ran her fingers through her curly brown hair. She studied her face and added a touch of blush and some pink lipstick. She figured her blue jeans, boots, and black tee shirt were appropriate anywhere. She grabbed the all-weather jacket she had picked up that morning and her small black purse and left the room. It was time to see a bit of London. She didn't hear the phone ringing as she walked down the hall toward the lift.

Lily walked for what seemed like hours. She stopped at a souvenir shop to pick up a map of London. She walked down Oxford Street and down Regent Street to Piccadilly Circus. She held tight to her purse, as she had been warned to do, but otherwise enjoyed looking in shop windows and watching people. She had never seen so many types of people, or heard so many languages. There were men and women from the Middle East, the women in long robes and heads covered with scarves. She heard people of African origin speaking English, French and languages that Lily did not recognize. Occasionally she heard the lilt of a Caribbean accent.

She continued on to Trafalgar Square and watched the pigeons on Lord Nelson's statue. The square was crowded with tourists from all over the world, and everyone seemed to be taking pictures of each other. Lily realized that she had not brought a camera. Maybe she could buy one of those disposable ones.

Her brother and Davis had brought her along at the last minute, and she hardly had time to think about what she would need for the trip besides clothes.

Lily consulted her map, considering going to the Design Museum, but it was on the other side of the Thames, across Tower Bridge. A little bit of guilt was nagging at the edge of her conscience. She wished she could be independent and sure of herself like Michael and Davis, but she wasn't. She had been brought up to be meek and subservient to her brother and his friend. Her art had never been important to them. Even when the handbags and clothing that she designed began to sell well in the tourist shops on the island, she hadn't been taken seriously. She had been raised by her grandmother, after her mother died when she was five years old. She had never known who her father was, and it had ceased being important by the time she turned eighteen. She enjoyed a certain sense of independence within the female world on the island, like her grandmother did, but Michael was the important one in the family. Michael had the important job at the Blake import company.

Lily refolded her map and started toward the Charing Cross tube station. She would be back on Oxford Street, and the hotel, in twenty minutes if there were no delays. She held her bag tightly and allowed the crowd to move her along. She wasn't afraid; it was just all so new. She found the city exhilarating—so many people, such color, so much variety. She slipped her day pass into the turnstile expertly and followed the signs to the Bakerloo line. A large crowd stood on the platform, and Lily wondered if she would be able to board the next train.

She was beginning to get a little nervous about being gone for so long. After all, Michael had told her to wait in the hotel room until he called her. But it just hadn't seemed fair. An announcement came over the loudspeaker saying that there had been a problem at the Waterloo station, and a train would be arriving as soon as possible. A few people in the crowd grumbled, but most seemed to take it in stride. It was hot in the station in the midst of all those pressing bodies, and Lily suddenly began to feel claustrophobic.

It was only two stops back to Oxford Circus. Maybe she could walk or take a bus or a taxi if she had enough money. She had no idea how much a taxi would cost in London. In St. Clare taxis were a cheap form of transportation that everyone used, but she knew that wasn't the case here. She began to work her way back out of the crowd on the platform and back to the escalator. Once again, she was able to let the crowd carry her along, because she wasn't the only one who had decided not to wait for the train from Waterloo. Her feet hurt, and she didn't really want to walk back. A line of taxis stood in front of the station, and people were rushing to grab them. Somehow Lily reached one before anyone else and asked the driver, "How much would it cost to go to Oxford Street?"

"Depends on what the meter says, Miss. It's all on the meter."

"I know. But I'm not sure I have enough money."

He must have sensed her inexperience and naiveté, because the driver looked at her, mentally labeling her as a tourist, but unwilling to take advantage of her.

"How much do you have?"

"I think I have about 20 pounds."

"You have enough." He reached back, opening the door for her. As she seated herself on the smooth black seat, a professionally dressed man, in a white shirt and a tie hanging loosely around his neck, grabbed the door handle before it could close. "Where are you going? Do you mind if we share? I'll never get another cab in the mess."

He indicated behind him where people were pouring out of the station. "Accident at Waterloo. Someone jumped on the track. Committed suicide." He was already seated in the cab and it had begun to move into traffic.

"Poor bloke. Never could see the sense in suicide. There's always a way." The taxi driver commented, glancing at the two of them as he maneuvered up Charing Cross Road. "Still going to Oxford Street?"

Before Lily could answer, her companion replied for her. "Oxford Street. Perfect. I can get home easily from there." He settled back and smiled at Lily.

Lily smiled tentatively and then turned to look out the window as the sights and sounds of London whizzed past them.

"What's the name of your hotel, Miss?" the driver asked. Lily hadn't even noticed that they were now traveling down Oxford Street, the driver expertly weaving in and out around cars and buses that blocked their path.

"The Sussex."

"Right." He moved over one lane to the left, just in front of a double decker bus. Lily gasped.

The taxi stopped and Lily started digging for money in her bag. "I'll take care of it." Her companion was already giving instructions to the driver. Lily jumped out just in time and watched the cab speed away through the traffic.

Alex caught the 3:15 train from King's Cross station. With the change at Peterborough, he would be in Springfield by 5. It was the weekend, or he would not have been able to get away from the museum, and Mrs. Lawton, that early. She had left at the same time he did, with plans to meet her husband at their country house in Kent. They had house guests arriving for the weekend from

America whom they were anxious to impress with the beauty of their home and their British hospitality.

Alex picked up a newspaper just before boarding the train, but after glancing at the headlines, he left it folded on his lap. He kept working over what he had learned today. Stolen antiquities were being sent to St. Clare; Nara and her father were from St. Clare. A shipment of items stolen from the museum was found on its way to the Gate House in Springfield, the house where Nara and her father lived. It was too much to be a coincidence. At the least, the police would want to question the residents of the Gate House about the shipment.

"Nara can't be involved." The words repeated themselves over and over in his head. But even if she wasn't, what if her father was? From the way she spoke, he was too sick to be actively involved in any business dealings, legitimate or not. Or was he? As devoted as Nara was to her father, she would be devastated if he were arrested. Or was it all a set-up? Or was it all perfectly innocent? And here he was, the investigator of stolen antiquities for the Victoria and Albert Museum, on the verge of falling in love with someone who could be a suspect in one of the most serious series of thefts of British antiques in recent years.

The train pulled into Peterborough, and Alex changed to the platform to wait for the Springfield train. He felt as if he were in a daze. He couldn't reconcile his emotions and his excitement about dinner with Nara tonight with the clear-headedness he cultivated in order to do his job. He found a seat on the little one car train that would take him to Springfield while his mind continued to whirl. What about the attempted break-in at the Gate House? Could that have been staged? But the footprints had belonged to the same man who had broken into the church, the man who was found dead in the car in the river. It just didn't make sense. He was still missing some pieces to the puzzle, so there was no way he was going to be able to solve the mystery with the knowledge that he had. The question was: Would he be able to keep a clear head and learn what he could from Nara tonight, without spoiling his pleasure in the evening? He cared enough for Nara, with her big dark, intense eyes, her slim figure, her energy, that he didn't want to see her hurt. His gut instinct told him that she was not involved with the thefts. But was it his instinct, or his developing feelings for her? This had never happened before. He wasn't sure he could keep both parts of himself balanced without someone getting hurt.

Nara thought of all the lovely summer dresses that she would have worn for a dinner date in the tropics. They were packed in boxes in the back recesses of her closet in the Gate House. She wondered fleetingly if she would ever wear them again. Instead she pulled out a simple dark red knit dress that she had purchased at Springfield's one department store soon after their arrival in England.

The A-line skirt just skimmed her knees, and the fabric clung to her body just enough to reveal the curves of her slim figure. No one would say she looked like a boy tonight. The dress was topped by a black bolero jacket that relieved the red, and, Nara thought, brought out her dark eyes. Not bad, she smiled into the antique full length mirror in her bedroom and turned on her bedside lamp to get a better view. The overhead light did little to illuminate the room.

There was a knock on the door. "Nara, it's me."

"Come in, Aunt Sue." Nara continued to hold the dress and jacket in front of her body as she scrutinized herself in the mirror.

"I thought you might like some tea." Sue set the tray with teapot, two cups and saucers, milk, sugar, and some biscuits on a low table. "You are going to look great. I could never wear that color." A flicker of sadness came and went in Sue's eyes.

"I could never wear some of the colors you wear. That soft pink that makes your skin glow? Makes me look like I've spent my life in a cave." Nara laid the dress on the bed and picked up a biscuit. "Thanks for the tea. Maybe it will calm me down."

"It's going to be wonderful. What shoes are you wearing?"

"I'm not sure. I bought these when I bought the dress." Nara rummaged in her closet and came out with a pair of black spike heels with a slim ankle strap.

"Yes, definitely." Sue helped herself to a biscuit and poured tea for both of them. But Nara giggled.

"Sexy if I don't fall on my face. I'm not a spike heels kind of person."

"You will be when you put them on. Just step carefully and slow down."

"You think I need to slow down?" Nara poured a bit of milk in her tea, added about a half teaspoon of sugar, and took a sip.

"Sometimes. Maybe tonight is the night."

"Don't say that. It just makes me nervous." Nara set down her cup and twirled around the room, finally landing in front of her window looking out at the back garden. It was already almost dark.

Sue started to take another biscuit, but put it down. "Nara."

Nara brought her thoughts back into the room and her smile faded at the serious look on her aunt's face. "What is it?" Her voice held concern.

"Nothing." Sue shook her head, as if to shake away the thoughts she was about to put into words. "I just wanted to say that I am happy that you and your dad are here." Before Nara could answer she continued. "I wasn't at first, you know. I had just started going out with—the man I have been seeing, and I was worried that having the two of you here would interfere with my love life. It had been so long since I had a love life."

"We did interfere." Nara sat down on a hassock close to her aunt. "At least I did."

"Yes, you did. But now I'm grateful for the interference. Seeing a married man, especially at my age, would only lead to trouble. And especially in a small town like Springfield." She tried to laugh but it came out more like a cry.

"Now you are staying home and I'm going out." Nara spoke quietly.

"That's probably as it should be. If I don't find someone else, that's okay. I still have a life." She looked at Nara without speaking for a moment, and something in her eyes prevented Nara from speaking. "You look very much like your mother, do you know that? I never met her, but your father sent me pictures. The dark hair and eyes, the quick smile."

"That's what I've been told. I barely remember her, but I remember her smile. But I also remember that she wasn't always smiling."

"No one smiles all the time and I guess neither of us really knew her."

They sat in silence for a moment, before Nara broke the spell. "I'd better get dressed. He will be here in half an hour."

"You're right. Sorry." Sue stood up to go, gathering up the tea things as she went.

"Don't be sorry." Nara did not know what to say next, so she settled for lightening the tone. "Thanks for the fashion advice."

Sue smiled. "Always willing to help."

Alex had barely had time to stop at his house, take a quick shower, and change clothes before going to pick up Nara. A light rain had been falling as he arrived and retrieved his car from the station car park, but it had stopped now. At least he had the presence of mind earlier in the day to call ahead to the Woodbridge House for a dinner reservation. He pulled into the small car park next to the Gate House and put his suspicions about Nara and her father, and the shipment found in the King's Cross Station, firmly in the back of his mind. He was going to enjoy the evening. Nara was an attractive, personable young woman. She didn't fit the profile of a smuggler. Her father? But she wasn't her father. *One step at a time, Alex old boy*, he said to himself as he stepped out of the car.

The vision Alex had carried around in his head all day, of the petite, dark-haired girl in running shorts, disappeared in an instant when he saw the sophisticated version in red and black, slim legs covered in dark tights and emphasized even more by high heels. Her hair was swept up, lengthening her neck and bringing out her cheekbones. Makeup brightened her eyes and lips, but was not overdone. Her only jewelry was a pair of small red stones that dangled from her ears.

"You look beautiful." What had happened to his voice? It came out all husky.

"You look pretty good yourself." The impish smile he was already half in love with played across her face.

He bent down and kissed her gently on the cheek, smelling the light scent of jasmine, a hint of the tropics that he had noticed before. She still only reached his shoulder, even in the high heels. He wanted to touch her. He put his hands on her shoulders, drawing her just a little nearer. He could feel goose bumps spreading under the touch of his hands. She shivered.

"Are you cold?" His face was very close to hers when he spoke.

"No." Her dark eyes met his. They were smoldering now; the impishness was gone. Her full lips, with the hint of red color, invited him. Alex bent his head and brushed his lips against hers, intending to only taste. But her response was not what he expected. Her lips parted and the kiss deepened, their tongues meeting and caressing. He pulled her closer, so their bodies were in contact. The effect was electrical. Heart pounding, Alex broke the contact and stepped back, although his hands remained firmly on her shoulders. He felt himself sinking again into the depths of her eyes, the dark tropical eyes, now full of desire. He wondered if the desire he felt was as apparent.

Alex took a deep breath and let it out slowly. "We have a dinner reservation." What had happened to his voice?

"Yes. We do." The impishness was back, combined with something else, something deep and wanting.

The Woodbridge House was a small hotel that had once been the home of one of Springfield's most renowned families in the early 1900s. The family had sold the house in the 50s, and it had gone through a series of owners and a slide downhill as it became more expensive to keep up a home of the sort, until the mid-70s when the present owners had purchased it, turned it into a hotel, and added a fine restaurant and bar. A large portrait of Joshua Beekman, the original owner, hung in the entryway where an elegantly dressed hostess stood at her podium checking dinner reservations.

"Collier. Reservation for two."

She consulted her list. "Yes." She drew a line efficiently through his name and picked up two menus. "This way please."

She seated them at a table in the back, near the fireplace. The walls were decorated with antiques from the late nineteenth and early twentieth centuries. Alex looked around appreciably. He wondered if the pieces were originals that had been in the house, or if they had been purchased later to carry out the theme.

The light was too dim, and his close examination would be too obvious for him to distinguish the genuine articles from copies right now. Alex turned his attention back to Nara, which wasn't difficult. In the firelight her eyes had taken on a deep glow, and the reflected flames seemed to burn in their depths. If Alex believed in witchcraft, he would have considered this a spell that she had cast. She smiled, showing very white, even teeth. "This is lovely. I didn't know Springfield had a place so elegant."

"It's my first time here, too. But I've heard it recommended."

Nara pulled her eyes away from his and slipped off the black jacket that covered her shoulders, revealing long olive-skinned arms that moved gracefully as she draped the jacket on the back of her chair. Now the solid red of her dress stood in vivid contrast to the darkness of her eyes and hair, and her breasts rose and fell beneath the shapeliness of the dress. Suddenly Alex felt shy and unsure of himself. He had dated a number of women before his marriage to Laura, and a few since and had never felt as disconcerted as he did at that moment.

"Shall we order some wine?" That seemed like a good place to start.

"I–don't drink. I've just never developed a taste for it, and I've seen it ruin too many lives on the island. But go ahead if you want."

Alex smiled. Her honest, forthright answer put him at ease, and he felt more truly himself. "I drink very little myself these days. I don't know why. Let's see what their best mineral water is."

The disappointed waiter took the wine list away and relief flooded over Nara's face.

"Thank you, Alex, for understanding."

He covered her small hand with his, surprised at the electricity that coursed through his body when he touched her. "If we can't be honest with each other on our first date, what's the point?"

She laughed, a light, musical laugh that had heads turning at a couple of nearby tables.

"I've never had much of a problem with honesty. I just seem to blurt things out and deal with the consequences later. Like when I resigned from my teaching job in St. Clare. I went in early one morning, cleaned out my desk, and left a note for the principal." Nara sipped her water, a sparkling one from Scotland called Highland Spring, appropriately enough. "Of course then I went home and stayed in my room and let my dad deal with her when she came looking for me."

"Did he know what you did?"

"Not until later. But she deserved it. She was a tyrant. And Dad always knew I did what I did for a good reason. He backed me up."

Alex took a moment to sip the mineral water that had arrived. He did not relinquish his grip on her hand while he asked, "What kind of work does your dad do, or did he do in St. Clare, if you don't mind my asking?"

"He has an importing company. His father started it. It does quite well, since almost everything has to be imported on the island."

The dark eyes never wavered. She was either a very good liar, or she was telling the truth as she claimed, or he was bewitched and already half in love with her. Whichever it was, Alex sensed his life was about to change.

They took their time with dinner, taking turns talking about their childhoods, hers on a tropical island being raised by her father, and his in southern England with two active parents, a sister, and two brothers. Nara told him about Davis and about how she had changed since coming to England. It had felt so strange at the beginning, and now she wasn't sure she wanted to go back to St. Clare to live. She told him about her conversation earlier that day with her father, when he encouraged her to study art instead of business. All the while Alex was unable to take his eyes off her, the graceful movements of her hands as she ate, the way her dark eyes could go from smoldering to sparkling and back again in an instant. The smooth lines of her throat, her breasts beneath the knit of her red dress. She was exquisite. He had known that from the moment he had seen her running on the path along the river.

She asked about his work and expressed her fears after the attempted break-in at the Gate House. "The newspaper said the man who was in the car in the river had the same footprints as the burglar at the Gate House and at the church."

"That's right," Alex agreed. He didn't realize the information had been published in the local paper, but it would be just the kind of connection that a local reporter would seize on, and it would put people's minds at ease.

Nara seemed about to say something, but then shifted her eyes away from his. After a moment she spoke, but Alex had the definite impression that what she said was not what she was thinking a moment ago. "I still worry about the antiques in the Gate House. I know many of them aren't worth much, but some of them might be. But I haven't been able to talk Aunt Sue into my way of thinking, or into installing an alarm system."

"You should get them appraised, and you should have an alarm system for your own safety. I would feel better if you had an alarm system."

The smile and the musical laugh again. "Do you worry about me?"

Alex flushed. "I guess I do."

Their eyes held, Alex reached out and gently brushed the line of her cheek bone with his fingers. She raised her own hand and held his against her face. "You are very nice to me, Alex. You are making me forget."

"I hope I do more than make you forget."

At that moment the waitress brought the bill, and Alex pulled his attention away from Nara to deal with it. As he searched for his credit card, a well-dressed gentleman approached the table. "Good evening. I'm Stan Beckly, owner of the Woodbridge. I trust you had an enjoyable dinner?"

"Yes, it was very nice," Nara answered, and Alex smiled his agreement.

"I happened to hear you mention living at the Gate House. You must be Nara."

Alex was surprised at his assumption. By the look on Nara's face she was shocked as well. The man laughed a chuckle that began in his throat and ended there. "I'm a friend of your aunt's. I've been unable to get in touch with her and I wondered if you would give this to her." He handed her a small yellow envelope, unsealed, but fastened with metal clasp.

Nara took the envelope from him, holding it gingerly with her thumb and forefinger. "I can't imagine why you wouldn't be able to contact her. She is home most of the time, and when she isn't she has her cell phone."

"Yes, I thought it was odd, too. I've been calling her on her cell phone. And as we are neighbors and both in the hospitality business, I thought it odd that she did not return my calls."

Alex said nothing, but watched the faces of Nara and Stan Beckly as they conversed. Beckly continued. "Would you also convey a message to her?"

"Of course." Nara answered quickly, but Alex detected the slight wariness in her voice.

"Please tell her I'm interested in purchasing the Gate House. I'm looking to expand my business, and I think I could do something with it."

Nara's eyes were steel. "I'll tell her."

"Thank you. I hope you enjoyed your dinner." He glanced briefly at Alex and left the table to join a slim, attractively dressed woman standing near the kitchen door. Alex had seen her watching the man as he and Nara conversed. He put his arm around her and bent to brush her cheek with his lips, guiding her back through the kitchen door as he spoke to her.

"Is he gone?" Nara asked, since her back was to the kitchen.

"He's gone."

Nara unhesitatingly opened the envelope and found a pair of earrings inside, tiny silver filigree loops with a turquoise stone suspended from each loop. Nara held them in her hand a second, then returned them to the envelope, closed the clasp, and placed the envelope in her purse. Then she covered her face with her hands. She told Alex, "These are my aunt's favorite earrings."

Alex reached out to her, his warm fingers caressing her arm. When she lowered her hands he saw tears in her eyes. "Oh, Alex. Everything is such a mess."

Caught unaware by her reaction, Alex took a moment to respond, and his shock at her tears elicited the typical male response. He didn't know what to do and thought of resorting to logic, which he knew wouldn't work.

"Do you want to tell me about it?" His hand continued to caress her arm.

"Yes." Her voice was almost inaudible. "But not here."

"How about my house? I can make you a nice cup of tea."

"All right."

THIRTY-FOUR

As they drove the short distance to Alex's house by the river, he tried to remember if he had left any clothing lying around in his rush to get out this evening. The cleaning lady was due on Monday, so the house wasn't spotless. Why was he worrying about these things? It had been too long since he had invited a woman back to his house, and Nara certainly wouldn't be evaluating his housekeeping skills, would she?

Although the air was chilly and held the scent of autumn rain, the sound of the water of the river lapped peacefully as Alex showed Nara into his house. He wondered briefly if any of his well-meaning but nevertheless nosy neighbors saw him bringing a female to his house at 10:00 p.m. *Well, let them talk*, he thought. He turned on the lights and quickly surveyed the living room. There were a few papers lying around but nothing to embarrass him. Nara went straight to the painting behind the sitting area. It was large, about six feet by six feet, unframed. Splashes of brilliant color appeared to have been spilled down the canvas from the top and dissolved to pastels by the time they reached the bottom.

"This is beautiful. I've never seen anything like it before." She walked around the room, admiring the painting from all angles. Alex, for his part, admired her shapely calves above the high heels. High heels definitely did something for a woman's legs, but they looked damned uncomfortable. He moved to stand close behind her, as close as he could without their bodies touching.

"My brother painted it. He would be pleased that you like it. He says he likes to play with color."

"And he does it wonderfully." She turned her head to him, favoring him with a smile. The movement brought her shoulders in contact with his chest, and it was an easy progression for her to turn into his arms. He pulled her close, skimming his hands down from her shoulders to her back, so warm beneath the fabric of her dress. Her arms reached up and around his neck, and their lips came together as naturally as if they had been doing this all their lives. Just as naturally, the kiss deepened, as their bodies melded together.

Alex sensed Nara's breathing increase its pace and knew his was doing the same. All he could think of was the pleasure and marvel of holding this woman. He could lead her to the bedroom, and he felt his body react to the thought. She must have felt it too because she eased herself back from him just enough to look into his eyes. "I thought you were going to make us some tea." Her eyes had a dark, languid look he had never seen before, and he wanted to drown in them.

"Would you like some?"

"I think it would be a good idea, right now."

"I'm sure you're right." Reluctantly, Alex pulled himself away, but their eyes remained locked.

Nara spoke first. "I've been feeling a lot of things tonight, Alex. But this is the best."

"Do you still want that tea?" Conflicting feelings raced through Alex's mind and body, his desire for Nara, his realization that she was too special to just jump into bed, her need to tell him why she was upset, and the whole bloody mess about the connection of stolen antiquities, the Gate House and St. Clare. And right now Nara herself, and her happiness, were what mattered to him most.

She raised her hands as if to touch him again, and then pulled back, balling them into fists at her sides. "Yes. I'd like tea. There will be time–for other things–later." She took just one step back but continued to look into his eyes. "I think we should start with tea."

She followed him into the kitchen and watched him fill the kettle with water and take out cups and tea bags. "Would you like Earl Grey?"

"I love Earl Grey."

"Should I be jealous?"

She cocked her head and smiled, her eyes sparkling. When the tea was ready, Alex started to carry their two mugs into the living room, when Nara stopped him. "Let's sit here." She indicated the kitchen table, partially covered with papers since Alex often used it as his home work space. "Kitchens are always cozy places for conversation."

"All right." Alex set the mugs on the table and stacked the papers into one pile which he moved to an extra chair already piled with papers. He put a sugar bowl, a small pitcher of milk, and two spoons on the table. They sat in silence, spooning and stirring.

He waited for her to begin. The physical contact with Nara had changed his priorities, and he wondered if she felt the same, and was having difficulty deciding how to begin. Alex helped her by reaching out his hand to hers. "So what's going on? Beckly had your aunt's earrings."

Nara took a deep breath. "Yes. I know now that he is the man she's been having an affair with."

Alex stared. "Your aunt? Stan Beckly?" These were pieces of the puzzles that didn't fit. Or the puzzle was not what he thought.

Nara took another deep breath and stirred her tea. She had yet to drink any of it. "She told me she was seeing a married man. I didn't know who. Then she said she wasn't going to see him anymore. It was hard for her. I think he made her feel desirable for the first time in years. She's lost weight, started to care about how she dresses, and all that."

Nara ran a finger up and down along the handle of the mug. "But she wants a real relationship. She deserves one." Nara looked up, the defiance she felt in her defense of her aunt blazing in her eyes. "And of course he won't leave his wife. He just wanted Aunt Sue to meet him at a hotel whenever he felt like calling her." Nara took a sip of tea. "The nerve of him to say he wants to buy the Gate House. And to ask me to pass along the message with her earrings." Nara stared out into the darkness through the window, not able to see Alex's sympathetic eyes.

He wanted to touch her, to tell her it was all right, that he admired her empathy for her aunt, but he sensed there was more. There was more that Nara had left unsaid.

She turned back and faced him, her eyes brimming with tears. "Alex, promise me something."

"Anything." He handed her his handkerchief for the tears and waited. He was overwhelmed that she was willing to confide in him. All he knew was that he wanted to be in her life, to support her through whatever it was that was making her cry.

Nara wiped her eyes and took another sip of tea. Her words caught him completely off-guard. "Alex, I think I know why someone tried to break into the Gate House. I found boxes of things in a store room that look like they might be valuable."

Alex could not move a muscle. If she was telling him this, then she couldn't be involved, could she?

He found his voice. "What makes you think this?" Did his voice sound too official? He hadn't meant for it to.

"Just a minute." Nara stood up and went back to the living room. She was back in an instant with her purse. She opened it and took out a small object wrapped in tissue paper and placed it on the table in front of Alex. "Maybe it doesn't mean anything, but tell me what you think."

Alex opened the tissue and found himself faced with the smiling, yet somehow sinister face of the Lincoln imp. He knew the original, of course, sitting high between two arches in the Choir of Lincoln Cathedral. He had seen the jeweled brooch in the Usher Gallery, and a myriad of cheap tourist copies on everything from shoe horns from the early twentieth century to modern day coffee mugs. Jewels sparkled at him in the kitchen light, although the stones could use a good cleaning. On first glance the jewels looked real. He turned the brooch over to see the antique backing and closure. He looked up at Nara. "Where did you get this?"

She took a deep breath. "I found it in the Gate House. In the store room in the lower level of the old part of the house, the part that was the original gate house."

"You found it? How?"

Nara took another deep breath, as if she were debating what, and how much, to confide in him. "With a lot of other things. It was in a wooden box with other jewelry. I really haven't looked at the other stuff yet, and I wouldn't know if it was real or not anyway. Is–is that real? Is it old?"

Alex turned it over in his hand. "My guess is yes. It is real and old." He looked up at her. "Was there anything else? Besides the box of jewelry?"

"Boxes and boxes," she answered.

"How long do they look like they have been there?" he asked carefully.

"Long enough to be pretty dirty and covered with cobwebs, but not centuries, if that's what you mean. The boxes and crates are modern."

Now it was Alex's turn to stare into his tea mug, watching the liquid swirl as he turned the cup around, thinking. There was a part of him that was experiencing profound relief. Nara was not involved. She couldn't be or she wouldn't have told him about the boxes, wouldn't have shown him the brooch. He picked up the brooch and turned it over in his hand. He wasn't a jeweler, but he could tell the stones in the brooch were genuine, the setting was antique. He knew the brooch on exhibit in the Usher Gallery in Lincoln wasn't the only one in existence, but this was the first one he had seen.

He hadn't seen any reports of a brooch being stolen, but there were so many reports of stolen items, he could be forgiven for having missed one small piece of jewelry. Nara is not involved, he thought again, but someone at the Gate House is, and it could be just as traumatic for her if it were her father or her aunt. Somehow her aunt sounded too flighty to be part of a theft scheme, unless her lover, Stan Beckly, were the mastermind; she might do it for him. That left Nara's father. Maybe his illness was just a ploy. But that would be difficult to fake. Maybe he just took advantage of the fact that he was spending time in England to expedite some shipments of stolen goods. It would need to be investigated, but not tonight. Tonight it was enough to know that Nara was not involved. And he would be here for her with whatever happened in the future.

When he looked up from his tea, he saw her watching him, her big dark eyes serious.

"You are going to have to report this to the police."

"Why?" Her eyes widened.

Why indeed, he thought. "The goods in the boxes are probably stolen."

"I hadn't thought of that. I thought maybe they had been stored there by the previous owner. You know he died, and then the house was sold to my aunt with all the furnishings. Apparently his son didn't want the bother of going through everything, and didn't think the contents of the house were worth very much."

"How long ago did your aunt buy the house?"

"About six months ago."

The box of pieces stolen from the Victoria and Albert Museum had disappeared about six months ago and turned up at King's Cross with a shipment date of about one month ago. It was possible the sender hadn't known that the Gate House had changed hands, but it seemed unlikely. And then there was the St. Clare connection. He looked again at the concern in Nara's eyes. She was waiting for him to do something. She trusted him. He had intended this to be a romantic evening, a chance for them to get to know each other, to see if the burgeoning feelings they had for each other would continue to grow. Alex forced himself to put the thoughts of what lay in the store room of the Gate House out of his mind. He could deal with it tomorrow in the light of day.

He reached over and smoothed a stray lock of hair behind her ear. "I'll have to give it some thought. It's obvious you didn't steal this." He held up the brooch. "Or anything else."

"Is it worth a lot?"

"I don't know. I'm not a jeweler. The jewels are genuine, I believe, and the setting is antique, but I couldn't say how much it is worth. A jeweler would have to appraise it."

He pushed the brooch across the table to her. Nara wrapped the brooch back in the tissue paper and put it back in her purse. She could still see the imp's smile in her mind and felt somehow that he was laughing at her.

Nara finished her tea, stood up from the cluttered table, and stretched her arms over her head. "So are you going to show me around your beautiful house? Do you have an office somewhere, or do you work from here?"

Alex laughed and joined her in the lounge, with the large window facing the river, in darkness now. "I have an office in the museum in London, which I rarely use. I mostly work from my laptop and phone, wherever I happen to be."

"Wouldn't it be more convenient to live in London?" Nara stood at the window looking out. The room behind her was not totally dark, and she thought that anyone who happened to be watching could probably see her. But who would be watching from the river banks at this time of night? She was getting paranoid.

"It might be more convenient, but Lincolnshire has become my specialty, so I would be up here a good part of the time anyway. And I prefer the small town atmosphere, the friendly people and the quiet life."

"I like it, too." Nara turned from the window to Alex, who stood close behind her. Impulsively, she took his hand. He drew her into his arms and she felt the electricity of his touch throughout her body. She turned her head upward for his kiss. As the kiss deepened, the thoughts that went through her mind said, "This is right. It's so right." Alex's hands caressed her shoulders and moved down her spine. The touch of his fingertips sent chills from the top of her head back down to her toes. It was more than right.

After a moment, he stepped back slightly to look down at her face. With one hand, he smoothed the dark hair back from her face, delighting in the softness of her skin. "Nara." His voice was low. "I've been thinking all day about what it would be like to do that."

"So have I." With a forefinger she touched the crinkles at the side of his eye. "But I was distracted by figuring what to wear and what to do with my hair."

"You look beautiful." He drew her close again, touching his cheek to hers, before finding her lips again with his. This kiss was even more intense than the first, and Nara found herself giving in to feelings she hadn't felt with Davis. But, at the same time, she felt as if she were about to head down a slope that she wasn't quite ready for. She pulled away from Alex's embrace, ever so gently.

"Alex." She put her hands to her face, feeling the warmth on her cheeks. "I'm not ready for this."

"I know. I'm sorry." He looked so repentant, his eyes burning, his head down.

"I'm just not ready, Alex. I didn't say I didn't want it. I'm just not ready."

He smiled and reached for her hand, and brought it to his lips. "What is it that you want, but aren't ready for?"

"You, Alex."

Before either of them could speak again, Nara's phone began to ring. She extricated her hand from his to return to the kitchen for her purse.

Alex stayed in the lounge, listening to the concern in her voice as she answered. After a few brief words, she returned, bag over her shoulder and her eyes wide with anxiety. "Alex, can you take me to the hospital? My dad is having chest pains so they took him there."

"Of course."

Alex picked up his jacket and car keys, and turned off the light as they left the house. On the opposite back of the River Wegland, a car motor started and moved slowly off down the quiet street, unnoticed .

The hospital was less than ten minutes away at that time of night, with no traffic at all. To Nara the journey seemed to take an hour. She stared straight ahead, saying nothing, lost in her own world.

Finally Alex spoke to her. "Chest pains can be caused by a lot of things, Nara. Some of them very minor."

She seemed to come back to the present and turned to him. "I know. I guess I know. I just worry about him so much."

"Worrying isn't going to make him better."

"I know. I really do know that. I just don't want him to die. I want things to be the way they always have been. We've always been there for each other."

The hospital lights came into view, and Alex found a parking space close to the casualty entrance. He put his arm around her shoulders as they walked from the car, pulling her close. The bright lights of the emergency room hurt her eyes, and Nara followed Alex to the emergency desk.

"This is Jack Blake's daughter. He was brought in with chest pains a short time ago," Alex said.

"Oh, yes." The nurse consulted a list. "He is still in Room 7, just down the hall to the right. I think they are going to keep him overnight for observation." She looked from Nara to Alex, sizing up the situation. "Just relatives in the emergency room, I'm afraid. You'll have to wait here," she said to Alex.

Nara felt torn, and afraid again. "Please?" she said, looking at the nurse but reaching for Alex's hand.

The nurse said nothing, but looked around as if searching for someone to help her or back up her decision. "All right. There is no one else here tonight anyway so no one will know."

Nara continued to hold Alex's hand and practically dragged him down the hall to Room 7. Then she stopped and looked up at his face again when they reached the door. "Thank you," she whispered.

The door was open a few inches, and she pushed it open, and went in, still holding onto Alex's hand. Jack Blake lay on a gurney, tube in his nose and a monitor bleeping at his side. His face was pale, but his smile was warm when he saw his daughter. Sue sat in a chair next to him. She was dressed in a pair of bright blue sweat pants and shirt that was at least two sizes too big for her, a remnant from her "fat days" that she had thrown on to accompany her brother to the hospital. She looked up when Nara and Alex entered the room, her eyes darting from Nara's face to Alex's, to their joined hands and back to Nara, a slight smile growing on her face as she sized up the situation.

"Dad! What happened?" She bent to kiss his cheek.

"I don't think it's anything serious, Nara. I had some chest pains and the doctor thought I should come over here just as a precaution. Probably something I ate," he laughed. Jack's voice was strong, and his color was returning to normal even as he spoke. He looked over his daughter's shoulder at the young man standing behind her. "And who is the visitor you have brought with you?" He smiled as he spoke.

"Oh!" Nara had momentarily forgotten that Alex was there, so preoccupied had she been with her father's condition. "Dad, this is Alex Collier, the one who helped me buy my new running shoes. Alex, my dad." She spoke the last two words with a love and devotion that was unmistakable. The simple words "my dad" revealed a universe of shared lives and emotions. Then she turned, took Alex's hand, and smiled at both of them. "You two should get to know each other."

As Nara turned to introduce Alex to Aunt Sue, there was a quick knock on the door and a woman entered. She was about Nara's height, with long black hair twisted into a bun at the nape of her neck. She wore green medical scrubs and a stethoscope around her neck. She looked around at the small crowd that had gathered in the tiny room. "I'm Doctor Vidri."

"I'm Nara Blake. I'm the daughter." Nara extended her hand.

Dr. Vidri greeted Nara and looked expectantly at Alex. Nara jumped in to include him in the family group. "This is Alex Collier. I asked him to come with me when I heard Dad was in hospital."

Dr. Vidri looked as if she were about to remind them that only family members were allowed in emergency.The patient was doing well, and was obviously pleased with the company in the room. She turned to Jack. "Mr. Blake, you did not have a heart attack, or anything of a serious nature that we can determine. Most likely it was caused by stress or muscle tension. I want to keep you overnight for observation, but we can probably send you home tomorrow." There was another knock on the door. "Ah, that must be the orderly, here to move you up to your room." She turned to the three people clustered around Jack's bed. "You are free to go up to his room with him, but I think everyone could use some sleep. I'll be in around 10 tomorrow morning and can see about releasing him then."

Before anyone else could speak, Jack made the decision. "Alex, can you take Sue and Nara home? Sue came in the ambulance with me. The doctor is right, we all need some sleep. I don't need people sitting around trying to make conversation when what I really need is sleep. I'll see all of you tomorrow."

"All right, Dad." Nara leaned over to give her father another kiss on the cheek, and he held her briefly with the arm that was not connected to an IV. "Sleep well."

"Sleep well, sir." Alex added.

Nara, Alex, and Sue walked to the car park in silence, each lost in their own thoughts. Alex gallantly held the car doors for each of the women, and they drove to the Gate House. The rain clouds that had threatened earlier in the evening had dissipated, and stars shone in the black sky. As they crossed the bridge, Nara saw a shooting star streak across the blackness, then disappear over the trees. "Oh," she exclaimed.

"What?" Sue said quickly, thinking something was wrong.

"I just saw a shooting star, the first one I've seen in England."

"It must be your lucky night," Alex said, grasping her hand in his.

"It's definitely my lucky night," Nara answered, giving his hand a return squeeze.

"Some people are born lucky," Sue commented. Nara turned around to smile at her aunt. She knew how she must be feeling, to see the happiness that was so obvious between Nara and Alex. She turned back around to Alex and was surprised at his frowning face as they traveled through the dark streets.

"Alex, is something wrong?" she asked softly.

He shook his head as if to clear away unpleasant thoughts. "No, just happened to think of something I'm working on."

"One of the burglaries?"

"Yes," he answered. "One of the burglaries."

Dennis Maxwell had not bothered to wait to see who Nara and Alex were visiting in the hospital. He had guessed it was Nara's father. He had gone directly to the Gate House, thinking it might be a good time to get into the store room, with everyone away from the place. But lights burned brightly in the house, and he could see several people moving around on both the first and second floors. Damn them for using the place as a bed and breakfast! It was too risky. Those boxes weren't going anywhere. Dennis turned the car toward Lincoln and home.

Davis paced in his hotel room, unable to sleep. He wished he had bought a bottle of something while he was out. He supposed he could call room service, but that would mean explaining to Terry why there was a bottle of whisky on the bill. And even if he paid for it himself, he could just see her elegantly raised eyebrow when she saw it on the bill. He didn't have enough British cash to cover it; he hadn't thought he would need much since everything was being taken care of.

He was attracted to Terry, and thought maybe they could at least spend the evening together. She was the exact opposite of Nara. Terry was tall, blonde, and elegant, and she knew how to dress to show off her best features. Nara was a "natural" girl; her hair was usually falling in her face, and she wore sundresses or jeans with sandals. At least, that was what she wore on the island. She never tried to look sexy; she just *was* sexy... at least, he had thought so at one time.

He didn't feel particularly attracted to her now, and was not necessarily looking forward to seeing her again, but he also realized that he needed her. Well, at least he needed their partnership. With him running a high-priced clinic, and her in charge of her father's import company—at least nominally—they could make millions. And so he had made up his mind to call her tomorrow and apologize. He still wished he had had a night with the sophisticated, lanky Terry, but she had told him a brusque good night and gone to her room.

Davis lay back down on the bed and turned on the TV. There was nothing at all that he could do until morning. Might as well see what was on the BBC. A good solid history program on some castle that no one cared about would be just the ticket to lull him off to sleep.

Elaine, too, was wakeful. Dennis was rarely out this late, and she was in the habit of listening for him to come home at night—like waiting for the other shoe to drop. Their bedroom was upstairs and at the back of the house, so she could have the light on and still have time to turn it off, get under the covers and feign sleep when she heard him come in. She was flipping the channels on the telly and nibbling a little bit of the Belgian chocolate that she kept hidden in her underwear drawer. She stopped when she caught sight of the parish church in Long Sutton in the south of Lincolnshire.

The reporter was interviewing a young man about a theft that had occurred at the church. From the clothes the people were wearing, Elaine guessed the program had been made at least seven or eight years ago. Still, it was interesting historically. The young expert was from the Victoria and Albert Museum, and although he looked not a day over 25, he was very knowledgeable about the subject of stolen antiquities. Elaine wondered idly if she could contact him for more information, find out the current situation. There might be some facts she could throw into her spiel to the tourists. She watched the program through to the end to catch his name—Alexander Collier. She jotted down on a piece of paper on her night stand and then turned the light off. The program had been just enough to take her mind off Dennis's whereabouts and make her sleepy.

THIRTY-FIVE

Nara woke the next morning feeling as if something had happened, good or bad, or maybe both, that would change her life. She could hear her aunt moving around downstairs, talking to guests as she prepared breakfast. *My God!* She thought. *What time is it?* She groped for her alarm clock. 7:00 a.m. She had forgotten to set it when she came home last night, and for some reason Aunt Sue had let her sleep. Then it all came back in a rush—her date with Alex, the lingering kisses and caresses and the promise of more, followed by the phone call and the rush to the hospital, where her dad was even now.

Nara leapt out of bed and headed for the bathroom. She would shower later, better get downstairs and help Sue with breakfast. A few weeks ago, Sue would have been livid if Nara had overslept, but the "new" Sue seems much more tolerant and patient and she seemed to genuinely like Alex. But who wouldn't like Alex? He was handsome, charming, considerate, and his touch made her tingle. Nara felt her body responding just at the thought of Alex's hands, his lips. She pulled off the tee shirt she had slept in and dressed in jeans and a sweater, and the old shoes she had been wearing the day Alex stopped her on the path behind the house. She would keep those shoes forever, as a memento of how they met. If she had been wearing good running shoes like she had now, he would never have stopped her, would never have given her a second look. Or was it fate, as some people on the island would say? Were they destined to meet, somewhere, sometime, no matter what? Was it all out of their hands and in the hands of some unseen force? Nara really didn't know, and at the moment didn't care. She only cared that they had met and had been so strongly attracted to each other. She ran a brush quickly through her hair, and at the last minute, tied it back in a ponytail to keep it out of her eyes at least through breakfast. Maybe she would see if she could get it trimmed today. But with her father coming home there might not be time. Oh, well.

Nara ran downstairs to the kitchen where the scent of frying sausages and coffee filled the air. Two middle-aged couples sat at the dining room table, sipping coffee. One of the men, a short, bald man who spoke with a French accent, was telling about his recent heart attack and the symptoms he had experienced. Sue had evidently told the guests about their midnight journey to the hospital.

"They can do so much these days. They have medicine they give you right away and they monitor everything that goes on in your body. If you get help quickly, you can survive a heart attack. I'm living proof." He thumped his chest as if to demonstrate the strength of the organ beating within it. His wife, an attractive woman with neatly coiffed grey hair, sipped her coffee, looking slightly embarrassed. They reminded her a little of Elaine and her husband Dennis. Why did short men often act so pompous, as if they needed to compensate for the lack of height by acting obnoxious? Was there really such a thing as a Napoleon complex? And why were the wives of those men often quiet little mice, at least on the surface? At least Alex is tall, and he would never be pompous and obnoxious. *I'm certainly questioning everything this morning,* she thought. *And it always leads back to Alex.* She greeted Aunt Sue with a cheery "Good morning."

"Thanks for letting me sleep in. What can I do?"

"You needed your sleep, and we only have two couples here." Sue deftly turned the sausages in the pan and added the tomatoes and mushrooms. "You could start the toast. I'm almost ready to do the eggs."

"Right." Nara put the bread in the toaster and poured herself a cup of coffee. "Have you heard from Dad yet this morning?"

"Not yet." Sue looked sideways at Nara as she handled the frying pan. "Sorry to interrupt your date last night."

Nara felt herself blushing, as she wondered what would have happened if she had not received that phone call. "It's all right. Alex was very nice about it."

"He seems like quite a nice young man. He works for a museum, did you say?" She moved the sausages and vegetables onto a platter and cracked eggs into the grease in the pan.

Nara sipped her coffee, trying to keep her voice even and casual. "Yes. He works for the Victoria and Albert Museum, something to do with investigating stolen art work."

"Is he working on the thefts at the church?"

"That and other things. We didn't talk about his work all that much."

"I'm sure you didn't." Sue gave her a meaningful look and a quick smile, and she moved the eggs to individual plates, adding the sausages, tomatoes and mushrooms. Nara placed the toast on a rack and the two women carried the food into the dining room, where it was welcomed by comments on the delicious smells and the excellence of the food. Nara was glad of the distraction and prepared to change the subject when she and Sue returned to the kitchen.

As it turned out, there was no need. When they returned to the kitchen, Sue said, "If you can do the washing up here, I'll run up and take a quick shower, then start some laundry. Do you want me to go with you to collect your dad from the hospital?"

"You don't need to, but we would enjoy your company if you want to come." Nara still felt that she was walking on eggshells around Sue, although she was much less touchy than she was when she was going out with her married lover. But now Nara was the one with a man in her life, and she didn't want Sue to feel shut out.

Sue paused as she was about to leave the kitchen. "It's all right, Nara. You're not shutting me out. It's only a trip to the hospital."

Nara stood open-mouthed, surprised that her intentions had been so transparent.

She went upstairs for her purse and jacket, and as she opened her purse to check that she had everything she needed, she remembered Sue's earrings that she had been given the night before. She might as well get it over with.

Nara had the earrings in her hand when she went back downstairs. Sue was just adding washing powder to the dishwasher. "There. That's done." She straightened up at looked at Nara's grim face. "What's wrong?"

Nara opened her hand to reveal the earrings. Sue's face went white as she reached out for them. "Where...?"

"We had dinner at the Woodbridge last night."

"He gave them to you?" Sue's voice caught in her throat.

"Yes. Along with this note."

Sue took the note offering to buy the Gate House and took in the contents in an instant. "That swine." She cleared her throat. "That SWINE!!" She crumpled the note and tossed it in the open dustbin. "If I had any feelings left for him, that ends it. I can't believe he gave this to you, to give to me."

"You deserve better than this, Aunt Sue. You're far too good for him."

"I'll never wear these again." She tossed the earrings into a kitchen drawer. "The nerve of the man! And I suppose he was with his wife."

"Yes." Nara remembered the affection he had shown the woman at the restaurant.

"Well,' she said finally. "I'm glad it happened. Now I don't have to wonder anymore if maybe he did really love me, maybe we could have worked out our relationship. Now it's really over." She started to pull cleaning supplies out of a cabinet. "It's a good day to clean the oven. And you need to go collect your father from the hospital." She turned to Nara, not even trying to hide the tears that still flowed uncontrollably down her cheeks. "Life goes on."

Davis met Terry for breakfast in their hotel and was surprised when Dennis, the annoying little man he had met yesterday, joined them. He tucked heartily into the full English breakfast, while Terry nibbled on toast with her tea. Davis ordered scrambled eggs with toast and a large orange juice. The juice was not as large nor as orange as the juice he was accustomed to in the tropics, but what could one expect? Conversation was strained, the three of them maintaining their separate agendas, but none of them wanting the reveal their hand. Finally Davis played his card.

"Terry, you know I am going to buy, and buy big, but I need to pay a visit to someone today. If things work out, it could benefit all of us." He glanced at Dennis. He wasn't really sure how his relationship with Nara could possibly benefit the man, but might as well keep him in the loop for the moment.

"Oh?" Terry set down her toast and gave Davis the full benefit of her wide blue eyes. "I didn't know you knew anyone in Lincoln."

"Actually she lives in a small town near here. Springfield, I believe."

Dennis stopped chewing and stared at Davis, a forkful of gooey egg halfway to his mouth.

"What a small world," Terry said evenly. "Who would have thought a doctor from St. Clare would have a friend in one of our little Lincolnshire hamlets?"

"She just moved here recently from the island," Davis answered, and was treated to the sight of Dennis's forkful of egg dropping off the fork and onto the front of the man's shirt. Terry closed her eyes and shook her head sadly.

"What's her name?" Dennis asked abruptly.

"Her name is Nara Blake. I doubt you would know her. I was engaged to her at one point."

Dennis dabbed at his shirt with his napkin, which he had dipped in his water glass—and thinking. Lucky he had dropped the egg, it gave him time to think. Should he admit what he knew about Nara, and the house she lived in, or not? Better not, he decided. He didn't want to have to split the takings from the store room, and he felt sure he could remove the goods soon. If only Joe hadn't gone and put himself in the way of a bullet and been dumped in the river. It would be so much easier with two people.

Tonight. He would have to do it tonight. Maybe remove as many boxes as he could of the most valuable stuff. As long as no one noticed, he could come back later for the rest. He put down his wet napkin and took a slurp of tea, earning a scowl from Terry that he ignored. "Can't say as I know her, but I don't go to Springfield often," he replied.

"All right." Terry put down her cup with a clink. "Davis wants to go renew an old love affair this morning. That's his business. I'll even let you take my car." She turned her gaze to Dennis. "You, Mr. M., are going to show me the items you have for sale. If you want to do business with Hadley's, I need to see what you have. I assume you drove here?"

"Of course I came here by car. What do you think I am?"

"Good question," she muttered.

"There's just one problem," Dennis squirmed uncomfortably.

"And that would be what?" Terry answered, her face flushing.

"It's going to be difficult to show you the goods."

"You don't show me something that is worth my time and Hadley's money, and show me today, and we cease doing business." Terry pushed her chair back from the table and prepared to stand up.

"All right. All right. Just give me an hour. I need to get my wife out of the house. That's all."

"One hour," Terry replied, glancing at her watch. "Don't bother calling me, just be back here at the hotel in one hour." She opened her purse. "Davis, here are the keys to my car. Do what you have to do. I'll see you later." She turned to Dennis again, her eyes hard. "One hour."

Dennis left the room without a word, wishing he could do to Terry what he did to Elaine, bring her down, and worse.

Davis tossed the keys to Terry's sports car in the air and caught them. He grinned at Terry. "Get out of here," she said, "before I change my mind about letting you take my car."

"All right. You've made your point. I had hoped to see your beautiful smile before I left."

"You'll see a smile when I get that Dennis Maxwell out of my life once and for all."

"I understand." Davis stood and then impulsively bent and planted a kiss on Terry's cheek before he turned and left the dining room.

"Always has to have the last word," she muttered as she rubbed the spot and watched him as he gallantly held the door open for a couple of white-haired ladies on their way into the room. "He's all show, and I'd give anything to know what the deal is with this girl he's going to see."

Davis slipped comfortably into the red sports car when it came from the hotel garage, and skillfully navigated through Lincoln traffic. He had decided not to call Nara until he reached Springfield; it would give her less time to prepare some independent, Nara-style response—and less time to consult with her father. Davis realized now that he had been wrong not to keep in touch with Nara, at least by e-mail, during the months since she left St. Clare. Now he would have to convince her of his love and string her along until they were married and back in St. Clare.

He wanted Nara's energies channeled where they would most benefit him, without giving her too much authority. She could work at her father's company, as long as she didn't look at the books too closely. He would have to work with Michael to make sure Nara didn't know what really went on at the import company. It would be tricky, because she was nothing if not smart, sensitive, and observant, but he was sure he could pull it off. Maybe get her pregnant and busy with a couple of kids. That would keep her tied down and occupied.

He left Lincoln behind and revved up the car as he hit the open road. The A15 took him through the farmland of what had once been the fens, past several small villages with church spires reaching to the sky. Davis cared little about the drab scenery, with the soil brown as the days headed toward winter. It was a beautiful day today, the sky a brilliant blue, but he paid little attention, and took the car well up past the speed limit, just to experience the sense of power when he handled the car. It felt great, but he immediately slowed as the road neared Sleaford and traffic picked up a bit.

He wasn't sure what he was going to say to Nara; he was sure the words would come to him when he saw her. She was so much in love with him, and he had been with her through the early, frightening days of her father's illness. He could still have a marriage with her; his mother loved her. Maybe she would even come around to his way of thinking, that theirs would be a partnership designed for making a fortune. Love was not a necessary component of such a relationship.

He exited the A15 at Sleaford and drove on to Springfield, which had an amazing amount of traffic for such a small town. The streets were narrow and winding, and seemed to come out in the exact opposite direction of where he expected to come out. When Davis had passed the same stores for the third time, he realized that he would have to stop and either ask directions to the Gate House, or else call and tell Nara that he was in town. He did not have a cell phone that would function in England, and there was no way Terry would have lent her phone along with her car.

He pulled over to the curb to think, narrowly missing a woman with a perambulator built for twins, receiving dirty looks from several bystanders. He could always use the "I'm a stranger in town" excuse for his driving, but the shiny sports car cancelled that out. He ignored them and pretended to look for something in the glove box. What should he do? If he called first, it would give her time to think about what to say to him, which might or might not be a good thing. Anyway it wouldn't give her much time, unless he became lost in this damn town again. If he asked someone on the street for directions, assuming they were correct and just showed up, he was taking the chance that she might not be home, and then what? Wait for her? And make small talk with her dad? Or the aunt he had never even met? Better to call first.

He lowered the car window and looked up and down the street. The post office was a few doors down; they could at least tell him where to find a public phone. The lobby was crowded, but a public phone hung on the wall just inside the door. A pretty blonde girl, no more than sixteen, was just hanging up the phone. She flashed Davis a smile as she headed out the door, flipping her straight hair over her shoulder.

Davis stationed himself at the phone and fished in his pocket for change. He couldn't remember the last time he had used a pay phone anywhere—probably when he was in medical school in the States. He lined up his coins, read the instructions, and dialed the number of the Gate House.

"Good morning. This is the Gate House."

Somehow he hadn't expected her to answer. "Hello, Nara. This is Davis."

There was silence in which he thought he could hear her breathing.

Her voice sounded small when she answered. "Davis. Hello. How are you?"

"I'm just fine. Thank you." That sounded too stiff. "Nara. It happens I'm in England and I would really like to see you."

Again there was the silence. "You're in England? Why didn't you tell me you were coming?"

She always had questions. "I'll explain when I see you. Nara, I'm in Springfield. I just drove down from Lincoln. I just need directions to the Gate House and I can be there in a few minutes and we can talk." There was a pause. "We really need to talk," he added superfluously. He felt as if he was losing his nerve, and she hadn't said more than three sentences.

Her deep breath came out in a sigh. "I'm not sure it's a good idea right now, Davis. You see, Dad is just home from the hospital. I don't want him upset."

So the old man had been in the hospital; he must not be doing well. "Maybe we could meet some place." Davis shifted uncomfortably, aware that an elderly man was standing behind him now, waiting to use the phone.

"All right. I can give you about twenty minutes. Where are you?"

"In the center of town somewhere."

She laughed. "Somewhere?"

"I'm at the post office."

"Okay. It might be easier if you walk. Just go out of the post office and turn right, and walk down to the river. There are some benches there. I'll meet you there."

"All right. I look forward to seeing you."

"Right." She rang off.

Nara hung up the phone and collapsed into one of the kitchen chairs. What was Davis doing in Springfield? Was this supposed to be some sort of romantic surprise? If so, it was too late. She had Alex in her life now and a world and a lifetime of possibilities. In the span of three months since she had been in England, she had received exactly three e-mails from him. He had called once, about a week ago, but she had not been home. She realized now that the call might have been to tell her he was coming to England. But why was he here? He was a medical resident; he didn't have the money for spur-of-the-moment trips. And you couldn't maintain a relationship on three e-mails. Davis was part of her past now; it was over. She had a new life. She made it a policy in her life to always move forward, never backward, because she wasn't the same person she had been in the past. She believed you had a choice in life: grow or be stagnant.

Aware that she had to meet Davis and get it over with, Nara ran upstairs to grab her purse and her jacket. She stuck her head into her dad's bedroom, where Sue was getting him settled with extra pillows and his books on the table where he could reach them. Jack was protesting that he felt fine, while Sue, using her nurse voice, was arguing that the doctor's orders were to take it easy for a few days until his check-up next week.

"I'm going to run out to the grocery store to pick up a few things, Okay? Do either of you need anything?"

"I think we are pretty well set," Sue answered distractedly, as she adjusted the blinds on the window across from Jack's bed. "Oh, we are low on coffee. I forgot about that."

"Sure thing," Nara answered.

"And if you could get some decent orange juice," Jack added.

"I'll try," Nara laughed. It was a standing joke between them that the orange juice from cartons never actually tasted like oranges.

Nara hurried out before she could get involved in any more conversation. She could still see Sue moving around in the room as she backed her car around and headed out into Pinchbeck Road toward the center of Springfield. She parked in a side street a few blocks before the town center. She pulled into a space just as a delivery van had vacated it. She wanted to walk up behind Davis, to see him before he saw her.

Her plan succeeded. As she came around the corner she could see him sitting on a bench just before the bridge, watching two small children throwing bread crumbs to the ducks on the river. Funny, she thought. Although he was training to be a pediatrician, she couldn't remember actually seeing him with children. Even now, he seemed to watch them impassively. You notice so much more about someone when your eyes are no longer clouded by infatuation, and she now firmly believed that had been the basis of her relationship with Davis. What was love anyway?

No time to answer that question now. She walked down to the river path and towards Davis, with what she hoped was a pleasant, but not overjoyed, smile on her face.

He turned his head and saw her. "Nara." He stood with his arms out, ready for her to walk into them. She stopped just outside their reach.

"Hello, Davis." He stepped forward and enveloped her in his arms. She didn't pull away, but she kept her arms stiffly at her sides, and he released her after a moment.

He tilted her chin up toward his face. He did have very sensual hands. "Are you mad at me?" And he had a voice like velvet.

Nara stepped back and sat down on the bench, partly because of her weak knees, and partly so they wouldn't block the foot traffic on the river path. "I don't suppose I have reason to be mad at you, Davis. You obviously had a different idea of where our relationship was headed after I left St. Clare. And I've discovered that you were right. It's been difficult, but I have a life here now and things are going well. My real question is—what are *you* doing here now?"

Davis sat close beside her and took her hand. "Surely you haven't found someone else?" sounding like the betrayed lover.

"And if I have?" She let the question hang in the air. "What are you here for anyway? To take me back to St. Clare?"

"Only when you are ready to go, baby." He stroked her hand, but Nara pulled it away and placed both her hands securely on her purse in her lap. "How's your father doing?" he asked with the utmost concern in his voice.

"As a matter of fact, he is doing very well. The chemo seems to be working, and he is feeling quite well." She looked out at the river as she spoke, watching the ducks swimming across for bread crumbs being offered on the other side now.

"I thought you said he was in hospital."

"He was, just overnight. He had some chest pains that turned out to be nothing serious."

"Then he is thinking about returning to St. Clare soon?" Davis shifted his body so that there knees touched.

"No. Not soon. He hasn't made any plans yet."

"I'd like to see him while I am here."

Nara ignored his statement, but turned to face him while moving away from him on the bench; her eyes blazed. "Which brings us back to my original question, Davis. Why are you here?"

"I'm here on some business, Nara, and to see you." He touched her arm, but she pulled back. "I'm so sorry I didn't call you or write you more often, Nara. That was a very bad mistake on my part. I was busy at the hospital. You knew that. And I thought we had something between us that wouldn't be changed by time and distance. I see now that I was wrong, but I can assure you that I will make it up to you. I love you, Nara."

Nara breathed deeply and stared out at the river, where the ducks floated happily, waiting for more bread crumbs. Just when she thought she knew what she wanted in life, Davis had to show up and complicate things. She thought for a moment of what it would be like if she went back to St. Clare, to her old life there, and married Davis. Although two months ago that was all she wanted, she just couldn't see it now. She had definitely moved on, and she knew what she wanted and it wasn't Davis, not any longer. She turned to face him, fire in her eyes. "I'm sorry, Davis. I'm just not sure I trust you anymore, and the truth is, I think maybe I have found someone else."

Nara watched Davis's face carefully as she spoke the last words. She wondered if she would see hurt or disappointment. She saw neither of those things. His eyes went dark and angry, and his lips narrowed with fury before he spoke again. "You're lying."

"I don't want to see you anymore, Davis. It really doesn't matter why." She immediately wished she had not said the last part. She supposed he had a right to know why.

Davis stood up and stared up river toward the bridge, watching the traffic. When he turned back to her, he was smiling, but she could still see the anger in his eyes, although he was holding it in well. He took a breath and let it out. Nara could smell food cooking at the pub behind them and realized she was hungry. It was crazy that she could think of food along with all this emotional turmoil. Davis sat next to her again. "OK. I'll let you be for now. I'll be in England for a few days. I'll call you tomorrow." Without another word, he stood and strode off toward the town center. Nara stared after him, wondering what he was really here for, and what she really felt about him. In spite of her words, the sight of him, his voice and his touch still brought back memories of their time together. Was that all it was? Memories? How did anyone every really know what they felt? Or what was right?

Nara stood and turned to walk back to where she had parked her car, and noticed a smiling older woman sitting on the next bench. "Fine morning, isn't it? We won't have many more of these. You are Mr. Collier's friend, aren't you? I think I met you last week. I'm Mrs. Westmoreland, from the church." She nodded toward the other side of the river, where the spire of the medieval church rose against the sky.

Nara forced herself to smile. "Yes, I remember you. It's nice to see you."

"I hope that young man you were talking to didn't upset you. It didn't look like a very happy conversation." Mrs. Westmoreland's face showed concern, as she pulled her pink cardigan sweater around her ample midsection.

"No. He's a friend of the family from years ago." Nara hoped her voice sounded casual enough that Mrs. Westmoreland would consider the subject closed.

"Mr. Collier, Alex, now he is a lovely young man. Always good tempered, friendly and patient with us old folks. He's the one you should hold onto."

How do I get out of this? Nara thought. Probably the best thing was to agree with her. "Yes. He is very nice. I'm sure you're right." Nara started walking again. "It was lovely to see you, Mrs. Westmoreland. Enjoy your day."

Mrs. Westmoreland was still nodding and smiling when Nara turned the corner. She could see the woman out of the corner of her eye, although she was trying to walk quickly. Now she would be the topic of gossip in Springfield, on top of all her other troubles.

THIRTY-SIX

Alex Collier sat in the police station with Detective Cushman. His coffee had gone cold and bitter. They still had no solid leads on the break-in at the church, but with the shipment that had turned up at King's Cross, there was enough evidence to search the Gate House. Even if, by some chance, Nara's father was not involved, the residents of the Gate House would have to be questioned about the shipment.

But how was he going to tell Nara that her father might be a thief, or, at best, was receiving stolen goods? There could be some other explanation, but Alex knew that the most obvious conclusion was usually the correct one. It was just too convenient that shipments of stolen goods were going to St. Clare, the very place where the Blakes had lived until a few months ago, and their business on the island was an import company. Alex had a sinking feeling in his stomach, but he sincerely hoped he was wrong.

If Nara had any suspicion that her father was involved in art theft, she would not have mentioned the boxes in the store room or shown him the brooch. She trusted her father and aunt, and he believed she trusted him. He was about to betray that trust, but he had no choice. He had to do his job. He sipped the cold, bitter coffee and shuddered.

A constable stuck his head in the door and called to Cushman. "Excuse me, Alex." Cushman left the room but was back a moment later. "Sorry, old boy. A couple of kids on their bicycles were just attacked by some dogs on one of the paths over near the old tulip farm. I need to go check it out. One of the kids was hurt pretty badly." He took a last sip of his own cold coffee and grimaced. "Are you going to be around? I'll call you when I get back. Shouldn't be more than a couple of hours."

"Right," Alex answered. "I'll be at my house. I need to catch up on some computer work."

Alex followed the detective out of the station. As he unlocked his car, he realized how badly he wanted to see Nara. Would she mind if he just dropped by? Would he give himself away? Maybe he could get some sense of who knew what if he went by for a visit. He found himself heading the car toward the Gate House without having made a conscious decision to do so.

Nara almost forgot she had promised to go to the grocery store, that in fact that had been her reason for going out, and had to turn around just a block before the Gate House. She hurried back to a small market on the corner and picked up the coffee, along with a few impulse purchases, arriving home just ahead of Alex. She was just climbing out of the car with the groceries in her arms when his car pulled in next to hers. He held the kitchen door open for her as they went in, and Nara couldn't help but notice how comfortable she felt with him, a comfort she certainly hadn't felt with Davis this morning. She was making the right decision. She was sure of it.

"You're just in time for lunch, if you would like to stay," she said as she unloaded the groceries and put them away.

"If it's not too much trouble."

"No trouble. We have to eat around here." Nara rummaged in the fridge to see what could be thrown together for four people and found a large container of vegetable soup that Aunt Sue had made the day before. She pulled it out and poured the contents into a pan and set it on the stove to heat. She had bought a baguette at the grocery that would go well with the soup.

She adjusted the fire under the soup and placed her wooden spoon carefully on the spoon rest on the stove. When she turned around, Alex swept her into his arms. She raised her lips to his for a long, lingering kiss. "Is this what you came over here for?" she whispered when the paused for breath.

"Oh, yes. Definitely," he answered as his lips brushed her soft hair on the top of her head. "That and lunch. You know what they say about the way to a man's heart."

Nara rested her head against his chest and felt as if she were finally home. She had been a different person when she had been in love with Davis, or thought she was in love with him. This was real. She and Alex fit together–comfortably. And that was what it was all about. Life wasn't so complicated after all.

They pulled apart when they heard footsteps coming down the stairs. Sue came into the kitchen talking about bringing a tray up for Nara's father. She stopped short when she saw Alex.

"Hello. I didn't know you had come round."

"I asked him to stay for lunch, Aunt Sue. We have plenty of soup, and I bought some good bread."

"Some of that French stuff, I suppose."

Nara sighed. "Yes, Aunt Sue. I bought a baguette."

They were interrupted by Alex's cell phone, and he excused himself and walked into the dining room to talk.

"He seems very nice," Sue said quietly to Nara as she took cutlery out of the drawer. "Looks like the intellectual type."

Nara stifled a smile. "He's very intelligent. But he's a lot of fun, too." Why did she say that? She asked herself as soon as the words were out of her mouth.

Sue grinned knowingly. "I'm sure he is. He must be in great shape. Running and all."

Alex came back into the kitchen just then, saving Nara from further conversation. She looked at him gratefully, only to see a look on his face that told her something was wrong. He looked as if he had just received, or was just about to impart, some particularly bad news.

"Nara. Mrs. Blanchard. I'm sorry." He still stood with his cell phone on his hand, holding it as if he needed something to cling to. "The police are on their way over here. They have a search warrant. I am sure they will want to question all of you, but particularly your father." He looked directly at Nara, his eyes sad.

The atmosphere in the kitchen was thick with tension as no one spoke. Nara felt as if she were sinking into a black hole of disappointment, which then turned quickly into fury.

"You used me." Her eyes blazed as she stared at Alex, locking his eyes with hers. "You used me to get to my father, even knowing how sick he is. We have nothing to hide. The police can search all they want. But I never want to see you again. Please leave now. You've done enough damage." The tears welled in Nara's eyes as she spoke the last words. It hurt. It hurt so much.

Alex said nothing. Nara watched the series of emotions that passed across his face. Regret? Sorrow? What did it matter? She would never forgive him for this betrayal.

He turned to leave, just as the panda car pulled into the car park, and met the two detectives at the door.

"I'll let you to handle it from here," he said quietly as he started out the door.

"No. No, Alex. You come this far with it. Let's see it through. And I need your expertise. No telling what we will find here."

Sue still had said nothing, but had put her arm around her niece's shoulders. Anger and sadness still fought for control of Nara's face.

"Are you Susan Blanchard?" the senior detective, asked.

"Yes, I am." She answered quietly, not taking her arm from Nara's shoulders, as if she were protecting Nara from the evils of the world.

"I have a warrant to search the premises of your house, and would like to ask all of you some questions." He looked around. "I believe your brother, Jack Blake, lives here as well."

Nara snapped out of her shock, fury winning control. "My father is very sick. We just brought him home from hospital this morning. You can't talk to him."

"I'm afraid we make the decisions about who we talk to and who we do not, young lady." He looked at his notes. "You must be Nara Blake. I'll have a few questions for you as well."

Nara clenched her fists at her sides. She wanted to hit someone. She wanted to throw something large and heavy at Alex's head. She wanted to trip this tall, gangly detective and watch him fall flat on his face on the kitchen floor. She knew she would do none of those things. Instead the tears of frustration and shock began to pour down her cheeks, and she made no effort to wipe them away or control them. Let them see what they had done. Let Alex see how he had hurt her and her family. "I need to go be with my dad. I need to prepare him for this." She started to leave the kitchen, wiping her face with her fingers.

"You'll need to stay here, miss," the detective said.

She stopped. "Oh. How foolish of me. To think that being with my father might interfere with police work."

"You need to watch what you say, Miss Blake." It was the other detective who spoke now. His voice was kind, as if his warning was to keep her out of trouble.

"My father is very ill."

"We will take that into consideration when we question him."

"Can I go with you?"

The detectives looked at one another. "You may go in with us to be sure he is awake. Then I will ask you to leave."

Nara nodded and turned to sit at the kitchen table, still littered with recipes that Sue had been sorting earlier. Nara avoided looking in Alex's direction.

A constable walked in the door. Nara and Sue both flinched. Nara felt as if the house were not their own, to have someone, especially a policeman, walk in the door as if he belonged there.

"Constable Jones will stay with you," the senior detective said. "Mr. Collier?" He nodded to Alex to accompany them on the search of the house. Alex followed them without looking at the two women sitting at the kitchen table.

The young constable stood by the door, gazing about the room as if he were exceedingly interested in teapots and framed prints of herbs and edible flowers, Sue's decorating theme in the kitchen. They could all hear the detective moving from room to room on the first floor, opening drawers and closet doors, moving lamps and pieces of furniture for better access. Sue flinched slightly when she heard them in the study where her computer was kept. "I wonder what they are looking for?" she whispered to Nara.

Nara shook her head, rolling her eyes in the direction of the constable, who was still looking everywhere in the room except at them. *He looks very uncomfortable, and barely old enough to be out of high school,* thought Nara. But he had probably been told to listen to anything they might say and was probably more mature than he appeared. People frequently mistook her for a teenager, too.

After twenty minutes, the men returned to the kitchen. "There are two sets of stairs. I assume one leads to guest rooms and one to your private quarters."

"Yes. Yes." Sue said the word twice before her voice was audible.

"Are there any guests in the rooms at present?" The senior detective was doing the talking.

"No one is actually in the rooms. Two of the rooms are occupied, but the guests have gone out for the day."

"Very well. This shouldn't take long. I should like to ask you to be present, Mrs. Blanchard, while we search the guest rooms."

Sue stood and followed them up the guest staircase, leaving Nara sitting alone. The young constable glanced at her once before he went back to studying the room.

Nara was feeling calmer and more in control. She was hurt and angry, but knew she could handle whatever came. She had done it before. "Would you like something to eat or drink? I've just heated up some soup."

The young man looked at her with surprise, as if he didn't know she had a voice. "No, thank you. But thank you for offering."

"I suppose you are not allowed to accept anything when you're on duty."

"Actually, we are. There is no rule against accepting a cup of tea or something like that. But I just didn't think I should, under the circumstances."

"What circumstances?"

His fair complexion reddened. "Well, you are having your house searched and all."

"True." They both fell silent.

Upstairs she could hear the officers, Aunt Sue and Alex moving from room to room, doors opening and closing. *He could at least have warned me,* she thought. And she had voluntarily told him about the boxes in the store room. Did he really think her father had something to do with stolen artifacts?

The sergeant led the group back down the stairs to the kitchen. Nara looked up. "That didn't take long."

"Looking through the guest rooms was only a formality. We really didn't expect to find anything. We would like to question your father now."

Nara swallowed hard. "I'll take you up."

Jack Blake had heard the commotion below, but the footsteps on the guest stairway had convinced him the noise was only guests moving up and down. He was just dozing off, still feeling the effects of the medicines he had been given at the hospital, when there was a gentle knock on his door. The knob turned softly.

"Dad? I'm so sorry to disturb you. There are some policemen here who want to talk to you. They insisted." Nara turned to speak to Alex, but he was gone.

The two men moved into the room. "I'm sorry to have to question you now, sir. I understand you were just released from the hospital."

Jack struggled to sit up. "What do you want to question me about?"

The older officer turned to Nara. "I'm afraid I must ask you to leave."

"No."

"It's all right, Nara. I'm all right, really."

Nara started downstairs to the kitchen but changed her mind. Maybe if she gave them the imp brooch, they would think that was all and leave them alone, and she would have to show them the store room. Alex knew about both anyway. If she didn't mention them, it would only be worse for all of them. She went into her bedroom and took the imp, in its tissue wrapping, out of her purse, the purse she had carried on her date with Alex the night before. What a long time ago that seemed now.

When she returned to the kitchen, the detectives were already there. They hadn't spent much time with her father. They turned to her, from where they had been conferring with a couple of uniformed constables who had been searching the grounds. "There appears to be a store room of some sort, with an outside entrance, underneath the old Gate House structure. Do you have a key?" The question was directed toward Sue.

"I don't know." Sue was decidedly flustered. "I have a lot of keys, keys that were here in the house when I bought it. I haven't tried all of them."

"Have you ever been in the store room?"

"No, how could I if I didn't have a key?"

"It just seems strange that you would buy a house without going into all the rooms."

"I—I wasn't really interested in that part of the house. I assumed it was just full of old junk. I thought I would get around to it sooner or later."

"We need to see inside that store room. Either you find the key or we break down the door."

"Wait." Nara moved to the shelves in the hallway, reached inside the shelf and pushed the latch. The shelves swung outward. She stepped aside. "You can go down this way. But you will need a torch. The steps are treacherous."

The two detectives exchanged a surprised glance at the sight of the hidden staircase. "Jones, get a torch from the car. On the double!" the sergeant called. He glared at Nara, as if she herself had constructed this hidden passageway. Sue's eyes were wide in shock, but she had clamped her hand over her mouth, as if she feared anything she said would only bring more trouble.

When Jones returned with the torch, he once again stayed upstairs while the rest of the group, including Sue, Nara and Alex, who had reappeared, went down the dusty stairs. Dim light shone through the grime covered windows, casting an eerie glow on the interior. The room was empty. There was not a single box in the room, but it was obvious there had been. Tell-tale tracks on the dusty floor indicated where the boxes had been, and where they had been moved across the floor to the outer door.

"They were here." Nara's heart pounded as she realized that she had spoken the words aloud.

"What was here, Nara?" Sue asked.

"Yes, would you mind telling us what was here?" The detective looked as if he were ready to reel in the fish after it put up a good fight.

"There were boxes here."

"What was in the boxes?"

"Old dishes. Some carved pieces. Some jewelry."

The detectives continued to question her, as they explored the scene. Nara answered mechanically but truthfully, looking directly at the detective, whose manner seemed to soften slightly as the questioning continued. She was telling the truth, as she had been taught all her life. "Base your life on the truth and your path will always be clear," her father had told her when she was small and faced with the dilemmas of a child. She had always done so, but now she feared the truth would send her father to jail.

"And I found this," Nara held out her hand, with the imp brooch still wrapped in tissue paper.

The detective took the object from her gingerly and unwrapped it. The jewels caught the dim light streaming in through the dusty windows. "It's the imp." He looked at Alex for verification.

"Yes, it's the imp," Alex's voice was strained. He coughed, as if he had dust in his throat.

"You think it's authentic?"

"I don't know. It could be. The only other one I've seen is in the Usher Gallery in Lincoln, but that doesn't mean others weren't made."

The detective looked at Nara. "You are free to go."

He turned to Sue, who stood just at the bottom of the staircase, her face as pale as the dust motes floating in the air. "I'm afraid I'm going to have to take you in for questioning. And your brother, too."

"No." Nara's voice was firm. "You can't take my dad. He didn't do anything wrong, and he's sick."

"I'm sorry, miss, but the evidence says otherwise. And whether he is sick or not, we shall soon find out."

"You bastards!" Nara was unable to breathe. She pushed past her aunt and raced up the stairs. Her father sat in the kitchen.

"What's happening, Nara?" He looked tired, but his eyes were alert and there was color in his cheeks. But he was sick. The doctors had said so. That was why they had come to England.

"They've all gone crazy. They think you're a criminal." Nara felt dizzy. "I need to get some air." She grabbed her purse off the kitchen counter and ran out the door. She jumped into her car, spraying gravel in the car park as she turned around and headed out on the road towards Lincoln.

Moments later, Alex raced up the stairs, stopping when he saw Jack sitting in the kitchen. "Where did she go?"

"I don't know. But if you had anything to do with this insanity, and if you've hurt my daughter, I will ruin your life."

"I'll find her."

"I'm not sure she wants you to find her."

Alex was out the door, with the thought of Nara suddenly the most precious thought in his life. He should have withdrawn from the case. He should have told the police about his involvement with Nara and withdrawn. But somehow his ego had kept him in — and now look at the mess he had created. He sat in his car, head resting against the steering wheel. Where could she have gone? And what would he say when he found her?

"Alex! We need you in here." The detective called him from the doorway. "The girl will come back, and we don't need her right now anyway. She'll just get in the way."

Alex reluctantly went back into the Gate House to help with his side of the investigation.

THIRTY-SEVEN

Nara sped down the road, tears blurring her vision. She thought vaguely that she might go see Micki and talk to her, or maybe Elaine. But if Elaine's little weasel of a husband was at home, she wouldn't be able to talk to her. She blinked her eyes to clear her vision and passed several slow moving vehicles until the open road was clear ahead.

Soon she was in the Lincoln traffic, heavier than usual on a Saturday. She slowed at a round-about, and spontaneously took the turn-off that took her up the hill to the Cathedral. The imp represented the Cathedral, and somehow it was drawing her there. She pulled out her cell phone. The path was becoming clearer now, although she didn't know for sure where she was going, but that was the way with paths sometimes.

"Hi, Micki. It's Nara. Something awful has happened."

"Shush, love. I'll feed you in a minute." A child cried in the background. "Sorry, Nara. What's wrong? Is it your father?"

I can't go into it all now. Can you meet me at the Cathedral?"

"David's not home yet, and the kids . . ."

"Bring the kids with you," Nara interrupted "I need to talk to someone."

"Come over here, Nara." A child screamed again.

"No. Please. Meet me."

"I'll call you as soon as David gets home," The call disconnected.

Nara put her phone down and concentrated on driving up the hill. She parked next to the ruins of the Old Bishops' Palace and climbed the hill path to the pedestrian tunnel. There were bright purple and yellow chrysanthemums on the hillside. The wind was picking up and bringing in clouds. No umbrella, Nara thought. *Oh well. Micki will have one; she is always so well-prepared.*

Nara walked quickly to the main Cathedral door and pulled it open. The air inside was even colder, but at least she was out of the wind.

Workmen were coming and going in the nave, and someone was testing the sound system. They glanced at her; one said, "Good afternoon."

She walked back toward the Angel Choir along the left transept, stopping for a moment to trace the carvings in the pews in the Angel Choir, as she had the day she had run into Alex here. She thought he cared for her then. Was it all an act? Was he trying to find out what she knew about the Gate House?

The carvings took on a sinister, frightening aspect. As she stared at them, they seemed to be living things. She shook herself and moved on. She hoped Micki would find her here.

She went back to St. Hugh's shrine. She was alone in this part of the building; she could still hear the activity in the nave, but at a distance. She walked around the tomb of the saint who had given so much to create this place. Poor man—his head had been lost thanks to Oliver Cromwell when his men had ridden their horses through the place. Why were human beings so cruel to each other?

Nara moved to the other side of the chapel so she could get of view of the imp, sitting at the top of one of the columns. He was difficult to see in the dim light, so she used her tiny penlight laser on her key chain to find him, as she had seen the tour guides do.

There he was, smirking down at her.

Nara thought she heard a step behind her and turned quickly, her heart pounding, but no one was there. She turned off her light and went into St. Blaise's Chapel. She might as well do what she said she was going to do here. As she entered she stepped on the uneven stones, remembering her encounter with Dennis here and shivered. Maybe this hadn't been such a good idea. Dennis said his father had died here. Nara hurriedly left the Chapel before her imagination completely carried her away. Micki would be here soon. Her practical advice would help put everything into perspective.

She walked over the centuries' old tombs in the floor, stripped of their brass by Cromwell's men, to the tomb of Katherine Swynford, who had lived her life for love of John of Gaunt. She had lived her life for love, and her reward was to lie at rest in this beautiful Cathedral. "I don't seem to have gotten much of a reward for love," Nara whispered. Again she thought she heard a step, but any sound was immediately drowned out by the flourish of an arpeggio on the pipe organ. She checked her cell phone. She still had a signal in here, and Micki had not called back. Surely she was on her way.

As she walked back toward the nave, Nara spied a staircase leading to the next level of the building. She remembered that Elaine said that she sometimes took groups up for tours of the vaulting and the roof area. Maybe if she went up to one of the balconies, she could see Micki when she came in. Carefully she climbed the worn stone stairs, thankful that she was wearing her new running shoes, which gave her a sure grip on the smooth stone.

She reached the first level and looked out down the hill and across the city to the countryside of Lincolnshire beyond. Dark clouds were rolling in. She could see cars winding up the roads that led up to the top of the hill, and hoped one of them was Micki's. "I hope I didn't miss her," she said aloud.

She climbed to the next level, hoping to find a balcony that looked down on the nave of the Cathedral. A balustrade was visible on this side from below, but she had no way of knowing if there was access to it.

The organist had stopped, and she could hear the voices of the workmen below. She must be near the nave, but there was no opening. There was a doorway to her right, but the door was closed and secured with a padlock and chain. She turned the knob anyway and pushed against the door. To her surprise, it opened, allowing a space of a few inches. The voices from the nave were louder, so this must be the balcony she had seen from below. The area was dimly lit, allowing Nara to see what appeared to be cans of paint as well as drop cloths covering some large objects. It was a storage area for the maintenance crew, most likely. She closed the door. She didn't need to get herself into any more trouble by breaking into closed off areas of the Cathedral.

She climbed again, and the voices grew more distant. At the top of the staircase were two doors. The one on the left, she could see, led to another outer balcony that looked down on the Cathedral Close. The wind whistled around the gargoyles, and pigeons took shelter behind the statuary. Nara chose the second opening and found herself on a small ledge looking down at the nave of the Cathedral. The view took her breath away.

The ribs of the vaulted ceiling seemed to reach to heaven, as the architects had intended so many hundreds of years ago. The organist had begun again, and the music reverberated throughout the vastness of the building. From Nara's vantage point, the sound surrounded her, absorbed her. She momentarily lost her balance, and grasped the railing for support. As she looked down, she saw Micki and her two children enter the nave. The little boy turned around and looked up. Nara waved to him, but he didn't seem to see her. She would go back down and meet them.

Nara took a step backward and felt her body being pulled back by rough hands. Then one hand covered her mouth. "I warned you this place was dangerous. People have died here." Nara recognized the voice and the alcoholic breath of Dennis Maxwell.

She tried to kick backward, but he was too strong for her, surprisingly strong. She twisted and stomped down hard on his instep. He momentarily loosened his grip and Nara ran, or ran as well as she could through the twisting corridors of the upper levels of the Cathedral. She knew Dennis was close behind, and the doors were all closed. Which was the one that led downstairs? She had to get down where she could get help. She tried one door and it was locked. She tried another and it opened. She pushed it close behind her and ran for her life along a narrow passageway. She reached the end of the passage and came out, not to a staircase leading down, but to a network of wooden catwalks above the vaulting. She was between the lead roof of the building and the vaulted ceiling. She gripped the railing and took a deep breath to calm her queasy stomach, and as she did so she heard footsteps behind her in the passageway. She had only one way to go–forward across the vaulting to the other end of the Cathedral. There must be another way down at the far end.

Nara ran, again grateful that she was wearing her running shoes. She paused at the center, where another catwalk crisscrossed the first. She could see scaffolding with buckets and tools laid out for work. Of course, maintenance and repair work were constantly in progress in a Cathedral like this. "Oh, please. Let there be workmen up here today." It was the second time today that she had prayed.

She heard footsteps again, faster this time. She was surprised Dennis could run that fast. A quick glance in the gloom told her the footsteps belonged to a much younger man. "Nara! Stop." She knew the voice; it was Davis.

She hesitated for an instant. Was he here to help her? But how did he know—?

She ran again toward the back of the Cathedral, toward the area above St. Hugh's shrine. Davis ran fast and his step was sure. She could have outrun Dennis, but not Davis. She had to reach a passageway down to the main level before he caught her.

"Nara! Stop! We have to talk." He was close behind her.

"No!" As she turned her head to call back to him, she missed a step and slipped under the railing. She reached up and just missed grabbing the bottom of the catwalk before she tumbled down onto the vaulting itself. As she slid she looked for something to hold onto, something to stop her fall. There was nothing. The surface was as smooth as it had been when it was finished 750 years earlier. She had slid about twenty feet when she suddenly stopped. Her foot had hit something solid. She spread out her arms against the vaulting to distribute her weight and regain her balance. Her fall had been stopped by one of the footholds that had been built into the masonry by the original builders, so they could reach the vaulting safely for maintenance and repair. Heart pounding, Nara lay her cheek against the cold surface. "Thank you." But there was no time for prayers now. Davis was right above her leaning over the railing.

He laughed. "Let me help you up, Nara. There must be a rope around here somewhere."

Nara managed to get both her feet onto the narrow foothold. Once again she was grateful that she was small. She was able to maintain her balance without too much difficulty.

"Did you find her?" Dennis's voice echoed across the open space.

"I found her," Davis answered.

THIRTY-EIGHT

For an instant Nara thought that Davis was really here to help her, but then she knew she was wrong. If Dennis and Davis knew each other, and were both looking for her, then Davis was only here to make trouble, and she was in more danger than she thought. If she could just hold out until someone came up here. But how often did anyone come up? She needed a weapon, or at least a distraction. The laser light on her key chain — if she could only reach it. She slid her right arm down along the surface of the vaulting and put her hand in her pocket. She found the light and slowly eased her arm back up the wall and turned on the light just as Davis returned.

"This ought to do." He started to drop the end of the rope over the edge of the catwalk, when the light flashed in his eyes.

"Ouch!" He rubbed his eyes and looked down at Nara. "Drop the light, Nara, and grab hold of the rope."

"No."

"I said drop the light, Nara." Something metallic flashed above her and she saw that he had a gun.

"You wouldn't shoot me, Davis."

"Maybe he wouldn't, but I would." Dennis Maxwell stood beside him. "You've been nothing but trouble since you moved here. Now grab the rope and let's get this over with."

Quickly Nara released the keys from the laser light and let the keys fall down, coming to rest where the vaulting joined the outer wall. She slid the light back into her pocket and took hold of the rope with both hands. While Davis pulled, she easily walked back up the wall, and he helped her onto the catwalk. Before she could stand up she felt a blow to her head and saw stars. She thought she bumped her head on the railing, but just before she lost consciousness, she heard Dennis say, "I know how to not leave a mark."

When Nara came to, she was in total darkness. Before her eyes adjusted to the gloom, her other senses picked up sensations. She smelled mildew, dust, and probably pigeon droppings. She moved her head to avoid such close contact with the cold stone floor, and pain shot through her head. Her ankles and hands were tied, and a gag was over her mouth. It felt like duct tape. She ran her tongue along the inside of it, wondering if she could loosen it with saliva. She might be able to, given a little time.

She thought she heard someone whimpering, managed to sit up, and then closed her eyes until the pain in her head and the queasiness in her stomach subsided. When she opened them she could make out nothing other than dust motes floating in the air, lit only dimly from the light entering the room from above. Had she heard ghosts whimpering, or was it her own voice? What kinds of horrible things had happened in this Cathedral over the years? And now what was going to happen to her?

Nara began kicking on the floor, hoping someone would hear, but the stone was solid. How did they get in here? She didn't see a door, but there seemed to be light from above. She moved around on the floor, hoping to discover something—anything—to make enough noise to attract attention. She kept working at the duct tape on her mouth, trying to rub it against her shoulder. One side of it loosened enough for her to speak, and she tried to scream.

"Damn." The light above expanded, a rope ladder dropped down, and Davis lowered himself into the room. "Shut up, Nara. God damn it; you're only making it worse. Nothing's going to happen to you, at least as long as Dennis doesn't get his hands on you. I have other plans."

He checked the ropes on her ankles and wrists, and then the tape on her mouth. When he found how she had loosened it, he ripped it off and replaced it with another, larger piece that reached back to her ears. As he climbed back up the ladder, the illumination in the room showed that it was piled high with boxes.

Nara was furious. She was sure that the boxes were the same ones that had been in the Gate House. She began scooting across the floor again, toward the boxes, as the light dimmed again. She was about half way there when the seat of her pants caught on something. She inched her fingers down and ran them along the surface. One of the stones in the floor was loose. She scooted some more and followed the line with her fingers. It was rectangular, and definitely loose. She pushed her fingers as far as they could go into the crack. The stone moved. It was a trap door. If only she could open it, or at least loosen it enough that someone would hear her. She kept pushing and could feel the movement. Over and over she pushed back and forth, until her fingers were raw and bleeding. There was no sound from below, and she hadn't heard the organ in a long time either. Her head was pounding. *I'm going to die here,* she thought. She slipped sideways and lay on the cold stone, unable to move, and closed her eyes.

No sooner had she done so than a shot reverberated, echoing in the vast stone building. There were shouts, and the sound of running feet. Someone was pushing against the trap door, and light flooded the room.

"She's here." The light swept around the room. "She's alive."

"There's blood. Has she been shot?"

Someone turned her over. "Get the ropes off her."

"The blood is from her hands. Look."

The duct tape covering her mouth came off more gently than she thought it could, but her face was still raw. She tried to move her hands to her cheeks, but someone was holding them.

"Let's get her out of here."

Strong arms moved her through the trap door and down another ladder. She squeezed her eyes shut to protect them from the bright light; when she reopened them, the first face she saw was that of Alex. His jacket was ripped and there was a cut on his face.

The constable set her on her feet. "Can you stand up?"

"I—I don't know."

She swayed, and Alex caught her with his arm around her waist. "Let's get those hands taken care of." Nara remembered her anger at Alex and tried to pull away, but the sadness in his eyes and concern in his voice stopped her short.

THIRTY-NINE

A couple of hours later, Nara's hands had been tended to in the emergency room, and she and Alex had talked while the doctor examined her, applied antiseptic cream and bandaged her cuts and bruises. She had a lump on her head, but did not have a concussion. But the time she was pronounced ready to go, her budding relationship with Alex was mended as well.

"The evidence was circumstantial," he said. "I'm a better museum curator than I am a detective, I'm afraid. I'll let the police do their work from now on."

"But how did you know I was in the Cathedral?"

"Micki called the Gate House when she couldn't find you here. I've known Dennis Maxwell by sight for some time, but I never would have expected him to be capable of this."

"So where are my father and Aunt Sue?"

"I believe they are out in the waiting room right now."

So they weren't arrested?" She slid down off the examining table and reached for her jacket. Alex gently helped her since her bandaged hands were clumsy, and they hurt. His touch was comforting and right. She was content to allow him to settle the jacket on her shoulders, and then plant a kiss on her forehead. His lips lingered for just a second. "No, they weren't," he whispered. "There will be plenty of time later to explain."

Jack and Sue jumped to their feet when Alex and Nara came out. "I could use some tea," Jack said after hugging his daughter. "Then we can talk all this over."

"Wait!"

They turned to see Elaine Maxwell coming toward them. Her hair was uncombed and her eyes dark, but there was something in her eyes, as if a burden had been lifted. "I'm so sorry, Nara. I'm sorry I couldn't stop him."

Nara looked around. "Dennis. Where is he?"

"He's dead. He died before he reached the hospital."

"I'm so sorry, Elaine." Nara reached out her hand to touch the other woman's arm.

"Thank you." She paused and covered her face with her hands for a moment. "I'm sorry it ended like this, but I'm not sorry it ended. I should have left him long ago."

Nara started to speak again when a doctor came up to them. "Mrs. Maxwell? We have some papers we need you to sign."

"Come visit me. Please. When all this is over." She looked from Nara to Jack.

Jack reached for Elaine's hand and held it a moment. "We're here for you. We will be here whenever you need us to be."

Nara's eyes followed the figure of the older woman, who walked with a straightness and determination Nara had not noticed before.

Later, settled in Jack Blake's favorite tea shop on Steep Hill, Alex told the story, as much as he knew it.

Davis was in custody, as well as a Michael Carrington from St. Clare.

"Michael!?" Nara was shocked to hear the name of the trusted manager of her father's company.

"Yes, Michael," her father confirmed with a sad voice. He sipped his tea, and took a bite of chocolate cake. He chewed a moment. "Apparently he has been smuggling stolen art and antiques into St. Clare for several years, but more so since I've been sick. And then he and Davis started working together." He glanced quickly at Nara.

Alex took Nara's hand. "It doesn't matter now," she said.

Nara looked into Alex's gentle face, admiring the way his lips curved, and his intelligent brow.

Her father cleared his throat. "So anyway. Davis spilled everything he knows, in hopes that the court will go easy on him for implicating people both here and in St. Clare."

"They also arrested antique dealers in both London and Lincoln, including one who had a huge warehouse in Springfield, across the river from the Gate House, though how much they will be able to pin on them, I don't know. They are blaming everything on Michael and Dennis Maxwell, and he's dead."

"How did they find the antique dealers?" Nara asked. She played with her food. She just wasn't hungry, although she couldn't remember when she had last eaten. There were still too many unanswered questions.

"The police received an anonymous tip from someone in London, calling from a pay phone," Alex answered. "Someone's conscience was bothering them, I would guess. And then there were the boxes."

"Right, the boxes." Nara set down her tea without drinking any. "Were they in the room in the Cathedral where you found me?"

“Right. That room has only two entrances. One from above and one from below. It may have been used to hold prisoners in the Middle Ages and other times since, including today.”

“How did they get the boxes up there?”

“Dennis Maxwell worked at the Cathedral, remember? Apparently he had them brought in, acting as if they were supplies of some kind for the Chapter, then he and one of the Cathedral workman moved them up to the hidden room at night. The workman wasn’t involved, by the way. He was just doing as he was told to do by a member of the Cathedral Chapter.”

“So the Gate House was used kind of as storage, where no one would suspect.”

“Yes. And the former owner may have been involved. That may be why he died.”

Nara shivered.

“Let’s go.” Sue spoke suddenly. “I’ve half a mind to sell the place after all this. It’s like it’s cursed.”

“Don’t be silly.” Her brother laughed. “That just adds to the intrigue of an old place like that. It will be more popular than ever. And Nara and I will be here to help you run it.”

Sue was putting her coat on. “You mean you aren’t going back to St. Clare?”

Jack laughed again. “I’m sure Nara isn’t.” He looked fondly at his daughter and Alex, who were holding hands and gazing into each other’s eyes while the other two talked. “And you are my family. I’m ready to sell the business and retire here.”

FORTY

When the tired group arrived back at the Gate House, the light was blinking on the answering machine. "I don't want to listen," Sue said. "It's probably nosy neighbors or reporters."

"It might be important," Nara said as she pushed to button for play.

"Hello. I'm sorry to disturb you." A soft feminine voice came on, with a distinct lilt of a St. Clare accent. "I've talked to the police in London. And before I go home, I wanted to contact you, after all that has happened. My name is Lily Jones. Please call me back at the Sussex Hotel. The number is 51-43-92. I'm in room 236."

"Who is Lily Jones?" Nara looked around the room.

Jack Blake cleared his throat before he answered. "She's your sister."

"My sister ?"

"Come sit, Nara. I have a story to tell you." Jack led her into the den, the same room that had been broken into just a few nights ago. It seemed like ages to Nara. "You two come too," he said to Sue and Alex. "I only want to go through this once."

"Lily is about three years older than you are, Nara. Your mother had her before she and I met. Since the baby was a native, I foolishly insisted that the baby stay with your grandmother, and your mother agreed. But she visited her constantly. That's where she was when she contracted the fever that killed her."

"But why did I never see her? I visited Grandmother."

"Yes, you did." Jack answered. "But I discouraged it. Remember? And she sent Lily out to play with the village children when you visited. Then when you were older, you went away to school, and Lily eventually took a job at the company."

"Wait. I remember! Lily! She was there helping Grandmother with the cooking sometimes. And I thought she was a maid or something. Since we had a maid I thought everyone did." Nara felt sad. She had missed so much when she was growing up.

She looked at her father, at the dark circles under his eyes. His body was healing, but he needed to rest, especially after the stress of the day, but she knew he needed to finish the story for her.

"I resented her, although she was a child. It was because of her that my wife, your mother, died. I wanted you separate from all that, but you always wanted to visit, to know your grandmother. I even gave your grandmother money—for Lily's education, I said it was—so she would keep Lily's identity secret from you."

Nara felt everyone's eyes on her. It must be her turn to say something. She stood and walked to her father's side. "It's all right, Dad. What's done is done. But since Lily is in London, let's call her and invite her here. I want to meet my sister, now that I know she is my sister."

Jack went to bed, after Nara promised she would call Lily back that evening. Sue, also, went to her room to rest, claiming a raging headache, and leaving Alex and Nara alone. Alex was quiet for some minutes, until Nara went over and sat on the arm of his chair. "What are you thinking about?" She touched his cheek.

His arm encircled her waist, and he pulled her down to his lap. "You know. I think I know who made that anonymous phone call."

"Lily."

"Yes. Lily. She is the only one who would know the information that was given about the antique dealers, as well as Michael's and Davis's names."

"This is a pretty crazy family you're getting yourself involved with." Nara smiled as her lips brushed his cheek.

"I love it." He turned his head to face her, their eyes inches apart. "And I love you." The kiss was deep and satisfying, and Nara finally felt that she was home. As they embraced she felt something in her pants pocket, and reached in to pull out the imp. "This belongs to someone," she said seriously.

"Yes, it does." He took it in his hand and studied it. "I would say he's done enough mischief for this century. If we can't find the owner, we'll donate it to a museum."

Alex set the brooch on the table and turned his attention once again to Nara, and she settled comfortably into his arms.

KATHLEEN HEADY'S articles have appeared in a number of publications including *The Tico Times*, the English language newspaper in Costa Rica, where she lived for seven years, and *The Philadelphia Inquirer*. *The Gate House* is Kathleen Heady's first published novel. She is currently completing a novel set in Italy and Costa Rica, as well as planning a sequel to *The Gate House.* Kathleen lives in Pennsylvania with her husband and two cats.

Also in Print from Virtual Tales

Also in Print from Virtual Tales

Visit Us Online
www.VirtualTales.com

COMING SOON FROM VIRTUAL TALES

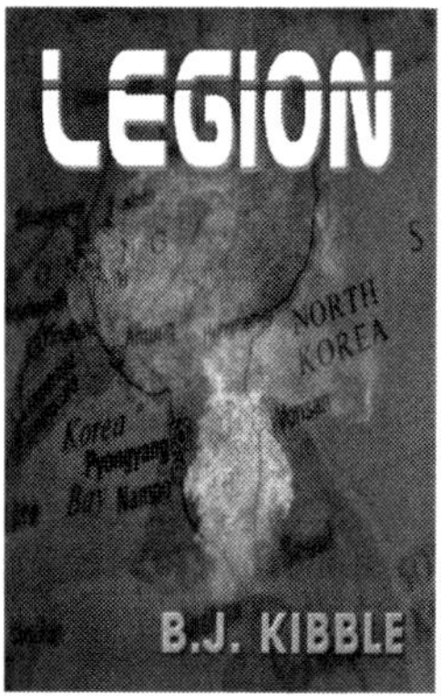

Printed in the United States
221746BV00001B/1/P